RUTH REVEALED

by

KRYS ANTARAKIS

CHIMERA

Ruth Restrained first published in 2002 by
Chimera Publishing Ltd
PO Box 152
Waterlooville
Hants
PO8 9FS

Printed and bound in Great Britain by
Cox & Wyman Ltd, Reading.

RUTH RESTRAINED

Krys Antarakis

This novel is fiction – in real life practice safe sex

He pulled the solitary chair from beneath the room's writing table, and sat down. 'Come here,' he commanded in a quiet voice.

A fierce tremor shot through her body, causing her to shiver in anticipation as she stepped towards him. She knew what to expect, and made no protest as he took her arm and pulled her facedown across his lap. She felt his fingers on the smooth skin of her thighs, and shivered again as his hand slid up beneath her skirt. With a decisive gesture he flipped it back, exposing her bottom, and she bit her lip to contain a moan of excited fear. He caressed her buttocks, smoothing the silk seat of her panties over her soft round orbs. She squirmed.

'And so you might, you little minx,' he whispered.

Chapter One

Ruth checked the fuel gauge as she steered the Beetle skilfully around the continuous bends sweeping down off the high moor. Approaching the grey Yorkshire town, she turned into the little filling station, and smiled as she took it in – a corrugated workshop, two delivery pumps and a wooden chalet that served as cash office and shop. The name board *Keith Thorpe Performance Cars* seemed laughably pretentious.

A young man strolled out from the shop to serve her. He was in his late twenties, attractive, and walked with an air of comfortable self-assurance, like someone at ease with life. Short dark hair neatly framed distinct features and keen blue eyes shining with an inscrutable amusement. His body was firm and well proportioned, powerful but not muscle-bound. He moved with an economy of effort, in command of himself and of the world. 'Yes?' he asked simply.

Ruth unlocked the fuel tank. 'Fill it up, please,' she said, catching his eye and trying not to let his intent stare affect her. His deep, soft voice had started her stomach fluttering, and now she felt her pussy heat up in response to his penetrating regard. She leaned against the car hoping the reflection from the red paintwork would disguise her flushed cheeks.

'Nice car,' he complimented her vehicle. 'You've looked after it well.'

'It's been in my family since it was new,' she said. His approval pleased her so much she had to make an effort to speak calmly. 'It's very reliable.' She thought her response sounded childish.

'So it should be, with its pedigree.' The pump cut out. Withdrawing the nozzle, he held it while the residue dripped into the tank.

Ruth gazed at the phallic metal, and her nipples responded to its overt symbolism by pressing against her bra.

'That'll be twenty-five pounds,' he stated curtly.

She handed him her credit card, and followed him into the cash office, where she watched him process the payment wishing she could prolong the procedure. Her hand trembled slightly as she signed the slip.

'Thank you, Ruth Parrish.'

'My pleasure, Keith Thorpe,' she retorted, regaining a little composure.

'Ah, but I'm not Keith Thorpe.' He tilted his head towards the shop and a mechanic in greasy overalls working on a Porsche's exposed engine. '*He's* Keith, I'm Jack.'

Ruth allowed a fleeting look of censure to cross her face, a visual warning for him to check his conceit. 'Tell me, is there anywhere I can get a decent lunch?'

'Park on the square and you'll have a choice of places.'

She turned for the door, but then paused to look back at him over her shoulder. 'Thank you,' she said.

'My pleasure, Ruth, please call again.'

She hurried back to her car in confusion. It had been years since a man wound her up so suddenly and so intensely, and now she needed a diversion to calm her down.

It was only a short drive into the town centre. She followed a black Ford into a broad, cobbled market square with an ancient town hall looming in one corner. On this

6

Wednesday lunchtime the square was full of parked cars. She found a space, turned off the engine, and stepped out of her Beetle in search of fuel for herself now. A variety of shops and several pubs lay along either side of the square. She glanced curiously towards the Ford she had followed, and saw a thin young woman emerge dressed in a black ankle-length skirt topped by a tight-fitting black jacket over a high-necked white blouse. Her dark hair was combed tightly back from her forehead and gathered into a severe bun at the nape of her neck. Small steel-rimmed spectacles made her features seem austere as she glanced at Ruth, her face registering no reaction as she strode purposefully across the cobbles on flat-heeled black shoes, carrying a black briefcase.

Ruth watched the prim yet authoritative girl vanish across the square. The grim black costume emphasised her slimness to an almost painful degree, and as she locked her car, she thanked nature for her own sensual curves. Crossing the cobbles, she speculated on what impression, if any, she had made on the girl. Had the other female admired the neat profile of an attractive young professional with a good figure and expertly styled hair the colour of polished teak? Had she approved of the trim grey skirt carefully hemmed above the knee, the crisp white blouse and smart black court shoes? Had she seen a young woman in her prime dedicated to her career and full of a passion for life?

Ruth glanced over her shoulder yet again. The girl had sparked off a curious reaction in her, not as potent as the rampant carnal desire stirred up by the enigmatic Jack, but definitely disturbing. Suddenly, she wondered what it was about this town that made her feel so curiously emotional and exposed.

She headed towards a promising looking pub occupying

a prominent corner site, slightly annoyed with herself for permitting her carefully cultured equanimity to fall into disarray. Thus preoccupied, she reached the pub and responded to the notice directing patrons seeking food to use the side entrance. She turned the corner, and walked straight into a woman coming the other way. She stumbled, turned around to apologise as she regained her footing, opened her mouth to speak at the exact moment the other woman did, and they both uttered the same exclamation, 'You!'

For a moment time was suspended, and then both spoke at once again. 'What are *you* doing here?!'

'I'm looking for some lunch,' Ruth was the first to reply. 'What about you?'

'I live here,' Elsa said. 'Well, near enough, and I'll join you, if I may, but not here. There's a much better place further down called *The Fox*. It's where the farmers go on market day.' She immediately took charge, leading the way. 'It's so good to see you again, Ruth. Why didn't you write to me?'

'I did write, but you didn't reply.'

'All my letters to you were returned. I wrote to your digs, and the shop in Exeter.'

'I was headhunted,' Ruth explained. 'The shop closed, but Mrs Shaw promised to send the letters on to me.'

'And I was in the States for six months. Some of my post must have got mislaid. You know how my mother is for losing things.'

'And now we meet again, *here* of all places.' Ruth followed Elsa into a small public house. The bar was compact, opening into a bigger room through an archway. The floor was tiled, the ceiling had dark exposed beams, and the seats looked comfortable. They walked through to the back room, which was empty except for two farmer-types engaged in an earnest discussion. The menu was chalked up on a blackboard, and Ruth eased herself onto a settle bench set against the wall, studying it.

'What'll you have?' Elsa enquired from across the table.

'I'll have the Ploughman's lunch and something inert to drink. I've a long drive ahead of me.'

'A drive where?'

'London. I work for *Greaves*.'

Elsa gave her a respectful look. 'So you'll have been to Broughton Chase? I heard *Greaves* had the Quincy sale.'

'That's right, I've been writing up the picture catalogue.'

'So you *did* specialise.'

'Yes. What about you, Elsa? What have you been up to all this time?'

'I'm in partnership with a gentleman named Morgan. We do restorations and reproductions. We live together near here.'

They ordered food and continued exchanging news, barely interrupting the flow of their conversation to eat.

'What of your mother?' Elsa asked.

'She just left for New Zealand. She has some commissions, and a six-month lecture tour there. Father's gone with her.'

'Impressive. She's still dancing, then?'

'No, she does choreography now.'

'And your sister?'

'Rebecca works in Strasbourg as a translator.'

'And do you have a boyfriend?' Elsa's curiosity was pleasantly relentless.

'Sort of, this guy Stanford. He lives in the city and is part of his family's firm. We go out together every now and then, but it's nothing serious, really. Our careers come first for both of us.'

9

'But you *are* getting your due diet of oats?' Elsa teased.

Ruth blushed. College was a distant memory, and she had been away from Elsa so long that her friend's frankness seemed curiously alien. 'Enough,' she replied, 'though not as often as I used to.'

Elsa laughed, her eyes flashing mischievously. 'Oh yes, I remember the night Rebecca took us to that fetish club. Let me freshen your drink.' Forestalling Ruth's protest, she got up and strode through to the bar, her high-heels clicking efficiently on the tiles.

Ruth watched her with amusement. Elsa had always been assertive, and not much had changed. She had kept her figure, too; the stretch jeans clung tightly to her shapely bottom. She licked her lips, reacting to an unexpected flush of warmth between her thighs. Theirs was a close friendship, but it had never been intimate, and her physical response now disturbed her. Feeling almost guilty, she glanced around the room. A dartboard hung on one wall opposite a board pinned with notices, and as she casually perused them, a phrase caught her eye.

Elsa set their drinks down on the table.

'What's that about a *Slave Auction?*' Ruth asked.

Elsa laughed. 'Oh that. It's one of those passing fads, very popular among the young farmers. They sell their time to each other. You know, "buy me for two hours to muck out your pig parlour", and the money goes to charity. It's just an excuse for a booze up.'

'Oh, is that all?'

Elsa gave her friend a knowing look. 'You thought it was something hot,' she accused. 'It's turned you on, hasn't it?'

'No,' Ruth protested weakly. 'I was just curious. There aren't many farms in London.'

'Don't give me that, you're all hot about it. You are,

10

aren't you? Admit it.'

Ruth blushed as she secretly admitted the truth to herself, and she could swear her old college mate was taking special delight in her discomfort.

'Just *imagine* being a sex slave,' Elsa pursued the subject quietly, holding her eyes. 'Imagine handing your body over to someone and giving them complete power over you, relinquishing all control and allowing them unlimited access to your every secret place. That must be the ultimate sexual kick, don't you think?'

Ruth felt a knot form in her belly and her chest tightened as her heart pounded. A powerful flutter of sensation passed through her pussy, and her nipples tightened against her bra. 'It might be fun as a game,' she replied guardedly.

'Yes, games are fun, but imagine being someone's slave for real, and for always. It would be like a mediaeval marriage, but even more intense.'

Ruth looked deeply into her friend's eyes. 'Games like that are commonplace, but the idea of really being someone's slave is too farfetched, too improbable. It can't really happen these days.'

'Oh, I don't know,' Elsa replied mysteriously.

Ruth swallowed hard, and for the first time in months she felt a sudden, irresistible yearning to masturbate. 'What do you mean?' The question burst forth, denying her rational reticence.

'You're right, you can play games anywhere.'

'Not anywhere, Elsa, not here, for instance.'

'That sounds like a challenge, Ruth.'

'Perhaps it is.'

Elsa smiled, and rummaged in her purse, from which she extracted a crumpled plastic supermarket bag. 'Go to the ladies' room,' she instructed, 'take off your tights, your panties and your bra, put them all in the bag, and

11

bring it back to me.'

'You're joking,' Ruth gasped under her breath.

'And you're not serious about your challenge. *Try* me. If I'm joking, I'll call you back. If you're serious, you'll do it.'

Ruth stared at her old friend, provoked by the light in Elsa's eyes. It was good to meet again and sit over lunch talking about past times and remembering all the fun they had shared. The cocktail of emotions churning inside her contained a sizeable measure of nostalgia; it would be good to rekindle the spirit of their past escapades. After all, it *was* only a game. She drained her glass, took the bag from Elsa with an expression of defiance, and walked self-consciously towards the bar.

The half expected, half hoped for recall came before she had reached the archway. Thankfully, she spun around and slipped back into her seat.

Elsa gripped her wrist. 'One more thing, don't use the loo,' she whispered.

Ruth wrested her hand free, got up again with her heart in her throat, and ignored the two farmers staring at her as she walked to the ladies' room.

When she returned to the table a few minutes later, a fresh drink awaited her. She slid back into her place, and coyly slipped the plastic bag under the table to her friend as she sipped from her replenished glass, futilely trying to hide behind it.

Elsa smiled impishly, placed the bag on the table, and felt inside.

'Not here!' Ruth hissed.

'Hmm, let's see what we have here... a bra, panties, *matching* panties, how nice, and tights, still warm... delicious! Now tell me, how does it feel?'

'I feel very conspicuous,' Ruth admitted.

'What, you don't feel sexy, not even a little bit?' Elsa goaded.

'Well, yes,' Ruth admitted. Although she was burning with shame, the truth was she felt gloriously sexy.

Elsa smiled, and shoved the plastic bundle into her purse. 'You can have these back later. Did you use the loo?'

'No, I didn't.'

'Open your legs, I want to check.'

Ruth clamped her thighs tightly together, only to feel the tip of one of Elsa's high-heels prising at her calves.

'Open up,' she insisted. 'I shan't let you go until I've checked.'

Ruth tried to draw back, but the solid settle prevented any retreat. Elsa's emphatic foot wormed itself purposefully between her knees, and touched her inner thighs. Very slowly, the sharp heel worked its way towards her crotch, wreaking havoc with Ruth's already tattered equilibrium. The hard tip pressed gently against her mound, and she gasped in alarm. 'Cut it out, or you'll have me wetting myself,' she whispered desperately.

Elsa's smile deepened. 'Really? Oh, how delicious.' The tip of her heel carefully peeled her friend's pussy open, parting the swollen labia.

Ruth clung to the table's edge as she tried to contain the pleasure welling up inside her. She sighed loudly and slumped against the bench, pushing her blossoming sex lips forward against the firm intrusion.

'God, you're a hot little bunny,' Elsa murmured, 'and obedient, too, an excellent start.' She removed her teasing, tantalising heel abruptly. 'Now finish your drink.'

Ruth did so in four long draughts, casting an anxious glance at the farmers. 'You bitch, Elsa Fredericks!' she whispered.

'Come on, you enjoyed it, and so did they.'

13

Ruth saw one of the men wink at her, and her face turned scarlet. 'Give me my clothes, Elsa.'

'Not until we get to your car. The game's not over yet.'

Ruth stared at her old friend; the chance to rekindle that vibrant friendship was too good to miss, and secretly she had to admit Elsa was right; so far she *had* enjoyed the game. Behaving outrageously, almost wantonly, was a potent aphrodisiac, and she realised her legs were still parted, as if her pussy was inviting more attention.

'Another drink first?' Elsa asked.

'I'd better not. I've a long drive ahead of me, as I said. Look, we ought to get together soon, and properly. We can have dinner, or something.'

'Of course, give me your number. I'll ring you.'

After the pub's stuffy atmosphere, the air outside felt wonderfully fresh. A little breeze had sprung up that fluttered Ruth's skirt, and the coolness teasing her naked pubes revived her prurience.

Elsa waited while she unlocked the Beetle, and then kissed her on the lips with shameless passion. 'Take care, Ruth,' she purred. 'I'll be in touch.'

'I'd like my things back now, please,' Ruth said, trying to calm herself.

'No, you don't,' Elsa teased, with a mischievous expression. 'I'll keep them until we meet up again. You'll enjoy being bare.'

Ruth held her friend's eyes with a dumbfounded gaze, and then meekly settled into her car, closed the door, started the engine, and drove away.

She joined the motorway and set the Beetle's stubby nose steadily southward. As she drove, the curious lunch hour assumed a dreamlike quality. Its reality was certain, for her skirt was damp beneath her naked pussy, and the seatbelt pressing her shirt tightly against her bosom revealed her nipples were hard as ripe acorns. She was astonished at how meekly and willingly she had followed orders. Elsa had not simply revived her love of doing daring things, she had elevated it to new heights.

As this self-analysis proceeded, the miles slipped by and she became conscious of a pressing discomfort. The drinks she'd consumed at lunch were working through her and very soon she would have to relieve herself. A roadside banner announced the next rest area was twenty miles away. She glanced at the speedometer, which was quivering on seventy, and as she was calculating how long she had to hold out, her mobile phone rang.

'Hi there, baby,' Elsa's voice emerged from the speaker of the hands-free panel. 'I bet you're ready for an orgasm.'

'What I need right now is a good pee,' Ruth retorted. 'It's your fault for buying me all those drinks.'

'Where are you?'

Ruth described her location.

'I know it. In a couple of miles you'll come to an interchange. Leave the motorway and head east. There's a transport café about two miles down. I'll ring you again in, say... five minutes.' There was a clicking sound as the connection was cut.

Ruth drifted obediently into the nearside lane and turned off at the exit. The café was in sight when the phone rang again.

'Hi, you should be there by now,' Elsa's cheerful voice said.

Ruth confirmed she nearly was.

'Good. Pull into the lorry park. Beyond the lorries there's a grassy bank. Park nose-in.'

Ruth followed the instructions and switched off her engine. The pressure in her bladder was intense as she threw off the seatbelt and reached for the door release.

'Get out and face the café,' Elsa's voice continued emerging firmly from the speaker. 'Lift your skirt up around your waist, spread your legs, and give yourself the biggest frig of your life. Now listen for a moment…'

A silence followed, only the crackle of atmospherics indicating the line was still open, and then came a familiar sucking, squelching, slapping sound Ruth recognised instantly – it was the sound of a prick shafting a really juicy fanny. She felt herself heating up, her own vulva ripening between her legs, and any reserve she might have harboured evaporated as she listened to Elsa being fucked. She flung open the car door and stepped out onto the rough ash surface, tugging on her skirt.

Elsa's voice emerged from the car, less controlled, her words broken up by sharp intakes of breath. 'I bet… you can guess… what I'm doing for Morgan. Are you joining in?'

Ruth thrust her fingers into her own wetness, pushing them into her pussy while her thumb stroked her eager clitoris. Figures were emerging from the building, but she paid them no heed. The phone continued to broadcast Elsa's indulgence, but Ruth was elsewhere… seven years in the past, an excited nineteen-year-old perched on a study desk, her hand thrust down the front of her panties, watching, mesmerised, as her half naked friend was shafted by a strapping Nigerian named Ambrose. And she had gone next. She relived the vivid memory of the delicious pain that ended her virginity. Her body had seemed to split open when Ambrose's magnificent cock spread her innocent vagina, driving relentlessly into her unplumbed depths. No penetration since had hurt quite as much or been quite as sweet… the memory swamped her mind as she probed herself, spurring herself on until her pleasure exploded.

The phone was still talking to her as she drifted back to reality. 'Was that good?' Elsa asked.

'Oh yes…' Ruth panted. It had been really good, the best orgasm she could ever remember achieving alone. 'But I'm bursting still. I'll have to go now.'

'Do it on the grass and take the phone with you,' Elsa directed. 'We want to hear.'

Ruth grabbed the instrument, scrambled up the grassy bank heedless of any possible observers, and squatting, surrendered to nature. The relief as she let go was exquisite, and her hand was shaking slightly as she straightened up, holding the phone to her ear.

'Just a little taste of what games can do,' Elsa said, sounding replete. 'We'll be in touch soon.'

Suddenly becoming aware of her exposed position, Ruth ran back to her car. She grabbed a tissue off the dashboard to dry herself, her pussy ultra sensitive and wanting more. Bemused, but feeling deliciously relaxed, she started the engine again and drove away.

It was early evening when Ruth parked in the deserted office garage. She got out and lifted the Beetle's front lid to retrieve her suitcase, but the moment her hand touched the handle she snatched it back as though it was electrified. She had suddenly remembered the security cameras, dozens of them covering every angle leading to the vault. There was no way she was going to offer the security guard titillating scenes of a young woman donning her panties. It would not hurt her to go bare a little while longer.

Grasping her laptop and camera, she slammed the lid closed and hurried towards the lift. All the way down the motorway she had been unable to think clearly about

17

anything except sex, and now the urge to find fulfilment again was almost painfully strong.

The office seemed deserted when she entered and walked through to her desk. Working automatically, she connected the laptop to the network and logged on. It took only a few moments to set the machine to begin downloading its stored text and visuals. She sat in her swivel chair, her legs spread, as the hard drive clicked steadily. Her bare bottom was tingling strangely. 'I'm in heat,' she murmured to herself.

The laptop flickered and displayed its prompt-on screen. She spun the pointer to *shut down* and closed the lid. Alicia could begin transforming the downloaded information into house style prose in the morning, and the graphic's department could begin work on the pictures. She picked up the digital camera next and crossed to the security store that lay along the short corridor. The door on her right was partially open, and as she passed a voice called out, 'Who's there?'

Ruth halted, and peered around the edge of the door into the office. 'Another slave shackled to the treadmill?' she quipped, but the word *slave* sent a delightful chill down her spine and her clit almost vibrated in response.

Lewis Stone looked up from his work. 'Oh, it's you.' He looked and sounded pleased to see her. 'What news from the frozen north?'

Ruth slipped into the room. 'Excellent. There are over two hundred paintings in the collection. Most have cast iron provenance, and about ten of those are significant works by mainstream artists. There are even two possible Josiah Parry's.'

Lewis was looking at her but not meeting her eyes, apparently unmoved by the news. Ruth could feel him staring at a point halfway between her throat and her navel,

18

and suddenly she knew why. Her nipples were standing out like hat pegs, creating large dark peaks through her crisp white cotton blouse. When he finally replied his voice sounded detached and distracted, as though he wasn't really hearing her. 'Good. What's your estimate?'

'Three quarters to a million, without the Parry's,' she told him. 'I've put my report into the system. We can talk it over now, if you like.'

This offer, combined with the generous figure, seemed to break Lewis's trance. Raising his eyes, he met her smiling gaze. 'That *is* excellent,' he enthused. 'That's quite a haul for a minor collection. I expect you've done your usual thorough job. There was no need to come back at this hour, though.'

She laughed lightly, shrugging off the compliment. 'Thank you, but I had to bring the camera back. By the way, is your ID handy? I've left mine on my desk.'

'I'll bring it.' They stepped across the corridor to the door of the secure room. He fed his card into the slot and entered his pin number. The door clicked and hummed open.

Ruth reached up to place the camera in its marked spot on the top shelf, and it was no real surprise when she felt his hands reach round and close over her breasts. She said nothing, just held her position, savouring the contact. She ought to have turned and slapped his face, issued dire warnings about sexual harassment, and clung to her dignity as a female professional. With any of the other principals she would not have hesitated to do so, but Lewis was different. Until now she had trusted him implicitly, and from the moment his eyes had fixed on her nipples, she had been turned on.

She replaced the camera carefully, closed the door, and turned into his embrace. His face was red, whether with passion or shame she did not know, or care. She flung her arms around his neck and kissed him. Their lips parted and their tongues explored each other. He held her tightly against him, and then pushing her away slightly, he began fumbling with her buttons, tugged her blouse open and she dropped her arms so he could slip it off her shoulders without interrupting their passionate kiss. His hands groped her hungrily, stroking her back, cupping her breasts and pinching her nipples.

She pulled away. 'Not here,' she whispered, and grasping his hand led him across the corridor.

He kicked his office door closed behind them and they began tearing impatiently at each other's clothing, and he groaned in astonished delight when her skirt slid down and revealed her naked sex.

'It was very hot in the car,' she explained, 'but now I'm cold, so stoke my fire.' She jutted her pelvis towards him with a teasing smile.

He came to her, almost vulnerable in his naked excitement, and bent her back across his desk. There was nothing vulnerable about the big erection that parted her labia, however. Moaning, she raked her pussy over his glistening knob, and taking the throbbing stem in her hands, guided him in. He was hard and thick, and his girth made her gasp as it spread her open. She sighed with pleasure and gave herself to him freely, moving and twisting beneath to keep her clitoris in contact with his firm body as he pounded into her. He did not lack stamina, but within moments his conclusion burst upon him. The swelling and pulsing of his thick shaft inside her was heaven, and she cried for joy when his thumb found her clit and brought her to orgasm while he spurted inside her. Then he slumped heavily against her, and it was a few moments before he raised his head and studied her face closely.

The hum of a vacuum cleaner carried up from a lower floor. 'I have to go,' she said, gently pushing him off her. He straightened up slowly, and his still semi-rigid penis slid out of her with a gentle plopping sound that made her want to giggle, but she controlled herself. Regaining her feet, she slipped her skirt back on and reached for her blouse.

'I'll see you home, Ruth,' he offered politely.

'That's okay, it's not far,' she coolly declined his chivalrous offer. 'And I have my car.'

'All right… you'll be here tomorrow morning?'

'Naturally.' She stood up on tiptoe and kissed him lightly on the cheek. 'Thank you, goodnight.' There was a light in his eyes she had never seen before, and which she deliberately ignored as she turned away.

Ruth let herself into her flat, and its familiar surroundings seemed slightly alien after being locked up and unventilated for a few days in the summer heat. She turned on the air conditioner then went directly through to the bedroom, where she kicked off her shoes and stripped away her skirt and blouse. She was still simmering with excitement as she unpacked her small suitcase thinking about the day's events. In a curious and indefinable way, she had changed since the morning. The day's encounters had opened a door inside her and illuminated aspects of her character she had never suspected were there. In truth, she had behaved outrageously, yet she had no regrets, and apart from the interlude with Lewis, she had retained her anonymity.

Turning towards her full-length mirror, she studied her reflection. She would have to learn to control this new self who had been born today. Tomorrow, Lewis would see her as the normal, predictable, professional Ruth, and their carnal interlude would never be repeated. Her hand strayed to her pussy, and palmed the still moist flesh. She sniffed her fingers, savouring the lingering aroma of her juices mingled with a man's semen, and wondered why her resolution not to repeat what had happened in the office lacked conviction.

But it was time to put the day's events behind her and get ready for her date with Stanford. Hopefully a dose of normality would calm her down. She took a last appreciative look at her reflection; and decided she was in excellent shape. She had a neat but curvaceous figure, a flat belly, long and shapely legs, and well-formed breasts with plump, upturned nipples. 'Impudent tits' an early boyfriend had christened them.

Elated by her youth and beauty, Ruth reached for her robe and headed for the shower.

The rattle of the taxi's engine faded down the drive. The morning breeze sweeping off the moor was gentle and cool on Ruth's skin. She moved to lift the iron knocker and hesitated, her hand poised over it trembling slightly with trepidation, for this was the biggest decision of her life. She was naked except for the collar around her neck, the silver cuffs on her wrists and ankles, and the chains linking them, secured by padlocks she had fitted herself. She was a captive, a willing captive but a captive nonetheless. Only weeks ago she had been a free spirit, then a chance encounter had changed everything. The keys to her chains, and the shape of her future lay beyond this door, and to knock would be to commit herself forever… Her mind scrolling through exciting memories at the speed of light, Ruth resolutely grasped the knocker…

Chapter Two

Ruth stepped out of the shower and slipped on her robe, anxious to reach the telephone. As she hurried across the bedroom her heart was racing. An urgent longing for it to be Elsa on the line had boiled up inside her the moment she heard the ringing sound, and the desire to be ordered to perform another shameless act gripped her.

But it was only Margaret, to suggest they meet for a workout in the fitness suite. Margaret, the stylist at Ruth's favourite salon, lived three floors up. They met regularly to keep trim, but tonight it was difficult to crave sobriety when the alternative was so diverting, and she was getting ready for a date, so she turned down the invitation.

As she dressed for her night out with Stanford, she felt her emotions fizzing like champagne, which amazed her. She was all fired up and ready for more naughtiness. Therefore, from her wardrobe she selected a crimson jacquard dress with a full skirt and a mandarin neck. It was a wonderful garment, specially made at great cost, but one she hardly ever wore because she thought it made her look too mature. It was just what she needed tonight to contain herself.

Casting a thoughtful glance at Stanford, Ruth nestled into the soft leather seat as the thoroughbred Bristol purred towards the West End. The great car symbolised the comfortable, high-rolling lifestyle to which she had grown accustomed.

In the wine bar the crowd was as lively as ever, but

tonight the banter sounded hollow and the shoptalk about classic cars failed to incite any response in her. Afterwards in the restaurant even the food tasted strangely bland, and it was only during the drive home that Ruth's spirits started lifting in anticipation of more sex.

Back in her flat, she hurried Stanford through to the bedroom, hastening the proceedings by stripping naked as she went.

He watched her askance, but made no comment as seizing the opportunity, he threw off his own clothes, grabbed her around the waist, and lowered her onto the bed. Rapidly, more quickly than usual, he spread her legs and thrust his rigid penis into her welcoming pussy. Despite her wetness the rough action dragged at her sex lips, causing her to cry out softly in discomfort, and lying beneath him, pinned down by his weight and his prick, she felt used and strangely violated... whereas Lewis had given her real pleasure...

She wriggled, settling herself more comfortably around Stanford's cock, squeezing it tightly with her inner muscles and urging it to greater fullness. She was rewarded by the sensation of his erection swelling within her, and she closed her eyes to savour the sensation of being completely filled.

Driving deeply into her, he shafted her as though his life depended on reaching a climax in record time, and almost at once he achieved his goal, his cock jerking wildly as he pumped her full of his semen. Then he slumped across her, panting. But when he tried to pull out she hooked her legs over his back to keep him inside her. 'Let go,' he protested. 'I want to lie down.'

'No,' she said, and giggled playfully as she held him more tightly against her.

'Don't be childish,' he responded sourly, forcing his

24

body upward to break her hold on him.

Feeling hurt, Ruth let him go.

He rolled inelegantly onto his back next to her and turned away, pulling the duvet up over him.

Ruth lay still and gazed up at the ceiling, anger and disappointment simmering inside her. Her craving for another orgasm had intensified all evening only to remain unfulfilled. She fingered herself surreptitiously, slipping a finger into her pussy, which was still oozing his warm semen, and the action soothed her somewhat. Determined not to capitulate to a destructive mood, she turned towards him, pressing her breasts into his broad back. She reached over his body, groping for his prick, and felt him stir as her fingers enclosed his soft length.

'Oh dear,' she murmured, 'you've gone all floppy. Now that's not right. You should be strong and straight, stiff and hard, a really big spear to shaft me with.' As she spoke she eased the foreskin back to expose his glans, and nipped it firmly between her thumb and finger.

Stanford responded with a yell. 'Hell's teeth!' he cursed. 'Have you taken leave of your senses? That bloody well hurt! Now go to sleep and leave me alone.'

'No,' she retorted. 'I want another fuck, and a proper one this time, one where I come first.'

'Not now, I'm tired,' he grumbled. 'In the morning, all right?'

'Please,' she begged as she continued to manipulate his penis, and despite his reluctance, his erection was returning.

'God, haven't you had enough?' he complained, and then grudgingly relented. 'Okay, but you'll have to go on top this time.'

Ruth straddled him eagerly, and slowly eased herself down over his growing weapon. It did not spear her, but she had the satisfaction of his girth swelling to fill her as she slowly worked her hips and bottom against him. He cradled her breasts, gently pinching her nipples as she began easing her pussy up and down over his stiffening length. Gradually the orgasm she craved bloomed inside her, filling her whole body even as it focused itself in her pelvis. In her ecstasy she ground her pubis into the root of his cock until the dam of joy burst and her mind went misty with pleasure.

Slowly, she surfaced from her climax, still feeling its beautiful heat as she fell forward and kissed him passionately all over his face and chest. Then she pulled herself off him, and slid down to take his tumescence in her mouth, licking and sucking him fervently until he stiffened again, and burst against her tongue, flooding her throat with his salty seed. She swallowed it eagerly, and then sat up, licking her lips and smiling. 'Thank you,' she said fervently.

'Are you satisfied now?'

'For the moment.'

'Bloody hell,' he grumbled again, then turned over and slipped off to sleep.

Ruth lay quietly beside him drifting through her memories of what had been a most remarkable day. When sleep finally came to her, it was disturbed by dreams in which Elsa figured prominently.

Ruth woke suddenly, her mind racing and her mouth dry. Automatically she fingered her clitoris, stroking it and savouring the pleasure before she inserted a finger into her pussy and began gently finger-fucking herself.

With a mutter and a few unattractive snorts Stanford surfaced from his slumber. 'Wha... what are you doing?' he mumbled.

'What do you think?' she whispered dreamily.

'I… I wish you'd have the decency to do it in the bathroom and let a guy get some sleep.' He buried his head beneath the duvet.

Anger welled up inside her, destroying her relaxed sensual mood. She abandoned her pastime, got out of bed and seized her robe. Shrugging it on, she went to the kitchen and turned on the kettle. As she indulged in an internal grouse waiting for the water to boil, the phone rang.

'Tell me what you've been doing since yesterday,' demanded Elsa's disembodied voice.

'Not now,' she whispered. 'It's late and Stanford's only in the next room.'

'So what? Tell me, and speak up.'

'I'll ring you back later.' Ruth knew her voice lacked conviction; despite her resistance she needed to talk.

'Later won't do. I can't wait that long.'

So Ruth told her everything she had done since they last spoke, all the while casting anxious glances towards the bedroom wishing she had closed the door.

'And how do you feel now?'

'Really randy, actually,' she admitted. 'I keep wanting to fuck. I'm never satisfied.'

'I can satisfy you,' Elsa promised softly.

'How?'

'Learn a little patience,' the voice teased. 'I'll be in touch.'

As the early morning light crept through the narrow gap between the closed curtains, Stanford woke reluctantly beneath her urgent shaking. He rubbed his sleep-filled eyes, and stared uncomprehendingly at the breakfast tray being offered to him by a naked girl. 'What in fuck's name is going on?' He hauled himself up into a sitting position.

'My thanks to you,' Ruth said, positioning the breakfast tray beside him. Then peeling back the duvet, she knelt beside his legs on the bed.

'What's got into you?' he demanded, reaching for the coffee.

'Just a gorgeous prick.' She reached beneath the duvet and took his flaccid member between her fingers. 'And I want it again.'

'Bugger off, woman, and let me eat in peace.'

'No, I want you to eat in love.' She began to play with him, urging his penis erect with one hand while feeding him with the other.

Stanford squirmed, but there was no way to escape her attentions. Despite his protests, his cock grew hard.

Straddling him, Ruth eased herself over his erection, squeezing it with her pelvic muscles while she continued feeding him with her fingers. Instinct guided her and enabled her to exercise total control until he had eaten his entire breakfast, and not until after he had finished his coffee did she encourage him to begin thrusting, her libido boiling. Relentlessly she ground herself down over him, rubbing her clit against the root of his throbbing shaft. He leaned forward and his teeth closed over one of her taut nipples, nipping it sharply. She cried out, but the pain was delicious and inspired her to give herself to him completely. On a wave of euphoria she rode him to a full conclusion, grinding her vulva down against his pubic bone. Heaven revealed its glory and she plunged into a vortex of total sensual indulgence.

Lazily, Ruth released Stanford's softening cock from her clinging pussy, and then sent him to shower and dress. Afterwards, he joined her in the kitchen, where she stood naked.

'You should cover yourself up,' he commented, indicating her discarded robe.

'I'll dress when you're gone.'

'It's Maidenhead this evening,' he went on, changing the subject to one of normality. 'Pick you up at seven?'

'All right.' She saw him to the door, and stood in the hallway watching the lift's flickering light track his descent as his sperm trickled from her pussy. She felt deliciously daring and yet slightly apprehensive that one of the other tenants would appear suddenly and see her naked. She stayed out in the corridor another nerve-racking minute, and then turned back inside to dress for her ten-thirty meeting with Lewis.

She chose white panties and a matching seamless bra to wear beneath a white blouse and a short grey skirt. The neatly pressed collar of the blouse called for a necklace, and she sifted through her jewellery box for her gold cross and chain. As she searched for it, her fingers encountered an ankle bracelet given to her by an aunt for her twenty-first birthday. She had been in university then, going about with Elsa, and an ankle bracelet had seemed appropriately decadent. Elsa had one too, and they wore them like badges, as visible testimonies to their rebelliousness. Ruth decided to start wearing it again; it would mean going around bare legged, but that was no problem in the summer. She slipped it on, and when she walked the slight caress of the chain made her feel deliciously promiscuous, which matched her present mood perfectly.

The large open office was already full when Ruth arrived at nine-thirty. She checked with her typist, Alicia, and made sure the survey she had downloaded last night was being processed before she began the task of tidying her notes for the meeting. Then she booted up her terminal and checked her e-mail. When she saw the message from Elsa her mouth went dry and a curious tension, part excitement, part apprehension, tightened her belly. She glanced guiltily around the room as she keyed-in the print command, and tried her best to look nonchalant while the printer hummed. As the page flipped clear, she grabbed it and read the message again, still doubting her own eyes.

Slave required, training provided. Come this weekend, if you dare. Elsa.

She darted a glance around the office, certain everyone must be staring at her. Her heart was pounding, and she felt so hot she imagined her face was the colour of a beetroot. Then her phone rang, and with a trembling hand she lifted the receiver. 'Hello?' she asked shakily.

'Ruth? Hello, how are you? This is Robert.'

'Oh hi, I'm fine,' she stammered. 'How are you?' Robert managed an exclusive retail dealership in the West End *Greaves* sometimes used to sell special items. Ruth strove to regain her composure as Robert conveyed the details of a sale, then afterwards, when she hung up, she stared at the crumpled paper in her other hand. Even now it seemed to be burning into her palm. She smoothed the paper back out, and slipped it in her briefcase. No sooner had she done so than the phone rang again.

'Have you had time to consider?' Elsa enquired.

'No,' she snapped tensely. 'I only picked up your message five minutes ago.'

'More than long enough, especially since you know perfectly well you want to, Ruth.'

'Elsa, you know nothing,' she lied desperately.

'Oh, but I do, I know exactly what you want. I can read you like a book. I'm sending you a parcel. Look out for it.'

The phone went dead and Ruth glared at the receiver. Elsa could be so boorish at times, so self-assured, expecting everyone to fall in with her plans. Well, once upon a time Ruth might have, but not now. She sat at her desk, and although she tried to look like she was working, her imagination was whirling like leaves in an autumn gale fantasising about what the parcel might contain. She could not concentrate, and the more she tried to focus on her forthcoming meeting, the more she found herself examining her actions of the previous evening. It was going to be truly difficult to project calm while she talked with Lewis. The incident between them should never have happened. In four years there had not been the slightest hint of any impropriety between them despite his reputation around the office. He had been the perfect mentor to her; he had been kind and supportive and totally professional, earning her respect and trust. There was no question that had changed; she still regarded him as the fountain of all knowledge, but now she would have to face him trying not to remember how very nice it had felt to have his long stiff cock inside her.

Growing hotter and wetter by the second, she decided to seek respite in the ladies' room, where she locked herself in one of the stalls and sat down for a pee. The relief was good, and calmed her while adding to her general feeling of sexiness.

The outer door of the toilet opened, and the voice of Lewis's secretary called, 'Ruth, are you in here? Mr Stone is ready for you.'

'Thank you, Janet,' she answered, 'I'll be there in a minute.'

'Okay, I'll tell him.' The door closed again as Janet left.

He was waiting for her, but gave no sign of being

impatient. 'Good morning, Ruth,' he said. 'I've got your report on screen. Sit here and take me through it.' He indicated a second swivel chair that had been positioned for her behind his desk.

Ruth sat on the comfortable seat, and sat with her knees together. She could not shake off the memory of the previous evening, when she had lain across this same desk as he fucked her, and glancing down at her blouse, she saw her traitorous nipples again visibly pressing against the soft material.

Lewis was coolly in control of himself. He smiled and encouraged her to begin.

In a shaky voice, she began checking off the long list of pictures and their descriptions. As she got into her stride she lost some of her nervousness and her voice grew steady, even as her nipples insisted on betraying her. By the time she reached the major items she was feeling much more like her usual self.

'Abraham Quincy saw himself as a patron of the arts,' she began winding down her report, 'in a naïve, provincial way. Apparently he used to visit exhibitions all over northern England and bought any pictures that took his fancy, whether they were actually worth anything or not.'

'Some of them are pretty awful,' Lewis agreed, 'but not all of them.'

'Every lottery has some winners. A few of his artists became well known and successful. At least half are now considered collectable, and some are esteemed at a parochial level. You'll see I've noted ten works that should attract the attention of municipal collections and raise their price.'

'And the two Parry's… it's strange the probate inventory made no mention of them.'

'I think the executors haven't realised what they have.

32

The recent rise in prices for Parry's work isn't common knowledge yet. Someone is obviously collecting Parry, but as yet the identity of this buyer remains unknown.'

'But he's clearly pushing up the value, and if these two are genuine they'll certainly attract attention, which is why we have to give them maximum publicity. Let's print a cautious but tempting description and get the catalogue circulating. Then we should authenticate them beyond a shadow of a doubt. I don't question your judgement, Ruth, but it's advisable for me to view them myself at once.' He reached for his diary. 'If I free up Monday and Tuesday we can go and see the pictures together. How does that sound?'

She caught her breath; Fate seemed to be conspiring to trap her. 'I was planning to spend the weekend with an old friend who lives quite near Broughton,' she said. 'I could easily meet you at the house on Monday afternoon, then we could do the whole thing in one day.'

Lewis studied her face for a moment, and then buzzed the intercom. 'Janet, I have a meeting with *Frobisher* on Tuesday morning. Will you contact them and try to reschedule it for Wednesday? Thank you.' He switched off. 'One of the perks of this profession is that you're expected to make close, unhurried inspections. It will do you no harm to have an extra night away at the company's expense. I take it you have no other pressing plans for Monday evening?'

'Nothing that can't be postponed.'

'Good,' he said, smiling. 'I can promise you an excellent hotel and gourmet food.'

Ruth experienced a tightening in her tummy and her throat went dry. The prospect of being seduced by Lewis was more than appealing. Her pussy warmed up as she recalled the feel of him inside her, remembering the wanton way she had invited him to stoke her fire. 'I'm looking forward to it already,' she said quietly.

He tilted his head to one side. 'With as much pleasure as you displayed last night?'

She blushed. 'Mr Stone!' she exclaimed, feigning shock. 'I think we should draw a line under last night. We were both… carried away.' The platitude came spontaneously, as a concession to convention, because they both knew she didn't mean it; her body language kept giving her away.

'Please call me Lewis,' was all he said.

She blushed more deeply, and commonsense told her this was the time to leave. 'Is our meeting concluded?' she asked. 'Or is there anything else we should be doing?' She mentally kicked herself for the unintentional tease.

Lewis's eyes were riveted on her creamy thighs. 'I can suggest a number of things,' he said. 'No work is ever so pressing that it cannot be set aside for a few moments of pleasure.'

She rose from her seat, intent on escape, yet instead she fell willingly into his embrace. His lips pressed to hers and his hands clutched her buttocks, pressing her to him and crushing her breasts against his chest. She took his head in her hands, denying him the freedom to break away from their kiss, as his hands slid lower, lifting her skirt and seeking the cool, soft skin beneath. His moan of delight filled her mouth as he cupped her panties, and in moments her skirt was around her waist and his hand was inside them as he excitedly exploring her labia, probing for her opening as his hardness pressed into her thigh.

'Ruth, you are delightful,' he whispered. 'Can I hope you will favour me again?'

She wriggled out of his grasp. 'I want you now,' she breathed huskily. 'Make me feel really good again.' She turned and leaned over his desk, lifting her skirt and spreading her legs to offer him access to her from behind.

'You're gorgeous,' he gasped, frantically opening his trousers. Then he lunged for her, gripping her hips as his thick cock brushed aside the gusset of her panties.

She gasped in delight as his thickness speared her, and pushed her hips back to gain maximum penetration. 'Oh yes!' she whispered as his pendulous balls slapped against her wet vulva. 'Oh bliss,' she breathed as he withdrew and then rammed into her again. He thrust with long strokes, letting his bulbous tip pull almost clear of her pussy before penetrating it again, and she rode the ecstasy, absorbing his power and vigour as she soared inside her own personal wonderland. His every penetration drove the breath out of her, but she was oblivious to any discomfort, all pain being pleasure. The more she took the more she wanted, and her capacity felt boundless. When she reached her peak she jerked and twisted beneath him without shame, gasping her triumph.

Her pinnacle past, she slipped dreamily down to a more normal state of mind while Lewis's crisis loomed. Finally she felt him coming, his cock pulsing deliciously inside her, and she ground her clitoris back hard against him. His first jet of sperm spurted hotly into her, and a fresh wave of pleasure engulfed her as the sensation plunged her into a second, truly satisfying orgasm.

Then, at that untimely moment the office door opened. 'Mr Stone, what are you doing?' a woman's voice cried.

Ruth felt Lewis pull out of her, and looked up to see Janet Dobson framed in the doorway, blushing scarlet as she babbled, 'Oh, I'm so sorry, Mr Stone, I'm so sorry! Please forgive me. How rude of me to come in without knocking! Oh dear…'

Ruth straightened up, clasping her skirt around her

waist, while Lewis attempted to hide behind his desk as he pulled up his trousers.

'Oh dear!' Janet exclaimed once more, and slammed the door closed as she retreated.

'Don't worry,' Lewis said breathlessly. 'Janet is very discreet. I'll talk to her. You're not the first.' He cleared his throat. 'Um, you don't mind not being the first, do you?'

'I'd be surprised if I was,' Ruth answered him truthfully.

He nodded towards her skirt, which was still bunched up around her hips. 'You'll need to tidy up.'

'Perhaps I could take an early lunch?' she asked sweetly.

'Of course, my dear, and take your time.'

Ruth drove the short distance to her flat and enjoyed a leisurely shower, letting the warm water cascade over her skin while she reviewed the morning's events. An enormous change had taken place inside her. Meeting Elsa had revived the fun loving, adventurous side of her nature, but it had also unleashed an aspect of her sexuality that was bewildering. She had never been a shrinking violet, but overall her sex life had been fairly conventional. Now suddenly her sexual appetite was hovering on the insatiable, and twice within twenty-four hours she had abandoned conventions that had helped her sustain a productive professional relationship with her boss and mentor.

Then there was the way she had behaved with Stanford. Thinking about it, she could hardly believe the extent of her lasciviousness.

Stepping out of the shower she reached for a towel and thoughtfully dried herself off. She was bewildered but not alarmed. She had enjoyed herself too much lately to regret anything she had done, and the prospect of more daring episodes excited her. Even now, after a calming interlude, her heart was pounding and the lovely tingling sensation between her thighs seemed to be spreading through her whole body. As she dried her leg she fingered the ankle bracelet. Its symbolism was strong, arousing her all the more, and as a concession to her mood she decided not to dress until she had eaten. Roaming the flat naked was just the sort of stimulus she craved right now.

Neat and tidy in fresh clothes, Ruth returned to work. Taking the bull by the horns she went straight to Janet's office, and the woman looked up at her with an almost pleased expression. Ruth liked Janet. She was approximately her mother's age, and pretty open-minded about most things. She was easy to talk to, and she had been a good source of advice over the years. But this afternoon Ruth felt uneasy in the older woman's presence. But it was more than conventional embarrassment at being discovered *in flagrante delicto*; being watched had actually proved to be a potent turn-on.

'About this morning,' Ruth began hesitantly. 'If what you saw shocked you, I apologise. The truth is—'

'Say no more.' Janet held up a hand. 'I was at fault. I should have knocked. I *was* surprised, however. It was the last thing I expected to see. Mr Stone has had his moments over the years, but he's never been so careless before. Yet I wasn't offended. After all, you were only behaving naturally. I enjoy sex too, you know. As I said, it was the unexpectedness of it that shook me.'

'You don't think it's wrong then for Lewis and I to have sex?'

'It would only be wrong if he coerced you into it, and I assume he didn't since you were so obviously enjoying yourself.'

'Actually, I think I encouraged *him*,' Ruth confessed.

'Well, no harm done, in fact, it's probably a good thing. Mr Stone has been quite lonely since Juliette went to New York. He needs someone young and active in his life. Good luck to you, Ruth.'

'Is he in now?'

Janet smiled knowingly. 'I'm sorry to say he's out visiting a client all afternoon. I can give you his home number if you want to try him this evening.'

'No, I've got a date for this evening, but thank you.'

The evening proved to be a sterile disappointment. Ruth was highly aroused and eager for sex, but Stanford was preoccupied and distant. The reception at the country club was boringly predictable, and on the way home Stanford asked her to accompany him to a vintage car show on Sunday. When she declined he became peevish, and in her flat, while they were making tepid love, he noticed her anklet and grew oddly agitated.

'Take it off,' he ordered, 'it makes you look cheap.'

'No, I won't take it off, and I might get a tattoo next week, too.' She had no such intention, but the effect of the mock threat on Stanford was enlightening. He became hostile, called her names, and stormed out of the flat.

She went to bed feeling increasingly confused. She liked Stanford, but what he represented was frighteningly conventional and superficial when she compared it to her wild craving for exciting and challenging sex.

Chapter Three

Ruth spent Friday morning in a state of nervous arousal. Stanford's angry departure had left her frustrated, so her expectations of the coming weekend were high. But with no further message from Elsa, and the non-appearance of the promised parcel, she was experiencing severe sexual starvation in the interim. In an effort to stem her yearnings she tried constructing fantasies, but they only served to stoke her libido even more painfully. Her body was in turmoil, throbbing with a need she could not relieve.

A further trial was Lewis's absence from the office. He was visiting a distant client, and her only contact with him was an e-mail he sent her confirming their meeting on Monday.

By midday Ruth was near to bursting with frustration, and she treated her co-worker, Gavin, to a torrent of well-deserved scorn when he made some fatuous remark about PMT. Her tirade was interrupted by reception ringing to announce the arrival of a parcel. She hurried down to the foyer, where she found a well-wrapped package with a transparent pouch glued to the outside. She tore the pouch open, and extracted a handwritten note along with a sealed envelope. She quickly read the note.

Looking forward to a really wicked weekend. Use this ticket, and we will meet you at York. Wear only these clothes, nothing else, and bring only your purse, we will supply everything else you will need. But only come if you are prepared for anything – and we mean anything.

Ruth's heart seemed to skip a beat, her mouth went dry, and she tore open the envelope with trembling fingers. Inside was a rail ticket for the teatime departure from King's Cross. She examined the parcel. Curiosity battled with caution and she was desperate to look inside, but she decided not to open it until she was in the privacy of her flat. Carrying it as though it might explode in her hands, she returned to her desk.

Gavin, unabashed, leered across the aisle at her. 'Present from an admirer?' he said.

'Just a new bra – get your own if you're jealous,' she retorted, and hurriedly cleared her desk. She had booked a half-day's leave for an appointment at Margaret's salon, including a manicure, a pedicure and a leg waxing, in anticipation of what promised to be a very special weekend.

Time was running short when Ruth reached her flat after her relaxing afternoon in the salon. In unseemly haste she tore open the mysterious package. Inside a cardboard box she found a pair of black high-heeled shoes and some folded black leather. She quickly shook it open and discovered two items – a zip-fronted jerkin and a tiny skirt. At the bottom of the box lay a minuscule black lace thong. Uncertain whether to laugh or cry, she held the skirt against her body. It was outrageously brief, and her excitement vied with embarrassment as she glanced at the clock. Time was not her ally. She had to decide right now.

Reaching for the phone she booked a taxi. Then she scooped up the box and its contents and hurried into the bedroom.

After a quick shower she slipped on the thong. It felt deliciously naughty, and she liked the way the string pressed against the sensitive ring of her anus. The skirt was indecently short, barely covering her bottom, and the zip on the jerkin exposed most of her deep cleavage. She squeezed her feet into the extremely high-heeled shoes, observing in the mirror how they accentuated her calves, bottom, and the thrust of her breasts.

Stanford might well call her cheap now, because she certainly looked it, but a potent thrill made her shudder and hug herself as she glanced down at her ankle bracelet. Elsa's conditions told her she should remove it, but she was reluctant to do so. It was symbolic, and served to bolster her decision to accept this terribly naughty challenge, so she left it on.

At the station Ruth felt some of her self-consciousness slipping away. People intent on reaching home had only half an eye for a girl flaunting herself in tight leather. She received a few hostile glances from women, and some appreciative stares from men, but not as many as she had feared and expected. She blended into the rushing crowds, stepping carefully in her heels, feeling vulnerable and yet curiously serene and secure. The brevity of her costume gave her a buzz, and the fresh air flowing around her buttocks gave her the impression of walking naked. The jerkin was loose fitting, and her breasts swayed provocatively inside it.

Once on the train it was a different matter. No matter how she sat, whether with her knees held tightly together or with her legs crossed she could not avoid exposing her thighs, and if she relaxed for just a moment she would also expose her crotch. Occupying an aisle seat as she was, everyone seemed to be staring at her. She wanted to curl up and slip under the seat, yet all the time a quiet internal voice kept repeating, *they're looking at a really pretty, sexy young lady. You're beautiful and desirable. They all want to shag you.*

The train rolled into the soaring hall of York station just a few minutes late. Ruth stepped down onto the crowded platform, and joined the throng as it hurried towards the exit. There was no sign of Elsa.

Reaching the footbridge she slowed down and started down the steps knowing her modesty depended on a fringe of leather, a string, and the cleverness of nature's own design. She breathed a sigh of relief when she stepped off the far side, but beneath her outward calm she was feeling increasingly anxious.

'Don't look around,' a familiar voice said from just behind her. 'Keep walking and turn right when you reach the street.'

Ruth's heart leapt, but she obeyed. Beyond the exit she turned as directed, conscious of being closely followed.

'Stop when you reach the litter bin,' the voice instructed.

Breathless with excitement, Ruth stopped and turned around. Elsa, wearing a pretty cotton shift, was right behind her, accompanied by a man with black wavy hair and deep dark eyes, whom she assumed was Morgan.

'Take off your knickers and put them in the bin,' Elsa ordered. 'You'll not be needing them again.'

Ruth stared at her friend in mildly amused confusion. 'Okay, stand in front of me, then.'

Elsa laughed and looked at Morgan. 'Just listen to her. I had such high hopes for her, too.' She turned her attention back to Ruth. 'Now, let's get things straight. That wasn't a suggestion. You came, so you agreed to follow the rules.'

An icy shock clasped at Ruth's heart. There was a harsh tone in Elsa's voice that was new and unexpected. For a moment it frightened her, but her fermenting desires

42

swamped her natural inclination to refuse the cold command. Feeling extremely vulnerable and exposed, she groped beneath the leather skirt and hooked her thumbs over the thin elastic of the thong's flimsy concession to modesty. And on a public street, in full view of passing traffic, she pulled the thong off, letting it fall round her ankles so she could step out of it. A crowded bus drew to a stop, and faces stared through the windows at her. In the bright summer evening there was nothing she could do to conceal her actions. Her face felt cherry-red as, burning with embarrassment, she bent over, picked up the scrap of black leather, and tossed it casually into the litterbin.

'Excellent,' Morgan said. His voice was deep and richly resonant. 'Now turn around and place your hands behind your back.'

In a sort of trance, with her heart beating hard, Ruth did turn around and she did put her hands behind her back. Then she immediately felt him take hold of her wrists, and cross them. Then she heard the tearing sound of Velcro, and felt a strong, flexible band enclose her wrists. Within seconds she was firmly bound.

Morgan spun her around again and raised an arm towards the street. In response an elderly black cab with darkened windows came sliding through the traffic, and he opened one of the doors.

Elsa climbed in, signalling for Ruth to follow her. 'Kneel on the floor and rest your chest on the seat,' she instructed as Morgan joined them inside and the cab moved off while Ruth struggled to comply. 'Push your bottom up and spread your legs,' Elsa elaborated, pulling up her friend's miniscule skirt. 'Well, Morgan, is she as pretty as I said? See how sweetly her inner lips peep out between her thighs, just like a ripe bud.'

'She is beautiful,' he agreed. 'What do *you* think, Cooper?'

'Looks bloody wonderful from here,' the driver responded.

'What a shame we tied her hands,' Elsa mused. 'It would be so nice to have her pull her cheeks open to expose her little rear entrance for us.'

'Well, we'll just have to do it for her,' Morgan said.

Ruth felt hands groping her buttocks. She clenched, resisting, but a sharp slap across one of her bottom cheeks changed her mind. A firm finger, Elsa's judging by the prominent nail, stroked the tender entrance to her anus.

'What do you think of *that*, Cooper?' Elsa prompted.

'Magnificent,' came the gruff response. 'I'm ready to bugger it right now.'

'I don't remember Ruth ever being buggered, but things can change,' Elsa mused. 'Have you ever been penetrated here before, Ruth?' she asked, lightly tapping the kneeling girl's little rose with the tip of a finger.

'No, never,' Ruth gasped.

'How wonderful, a virgin bottom,' Elsa declared. 'We shall have to give the matter great consideration.'

'In the meantime, there are plenty of other areas to explore,' Morgan commented, and as he spoke Ruth felt strong fingers parting her labia and teasing her inner lips before they slid up into her pussy. She could hardly contain herself then, and was sure the mere brush of his thumb against her clitoris would plunge her into a cataclysmic orgasm. Nothing she had ever experienced had brought her so close to the brink so rapidly.

'Please,' she whispered, 'I need to come. Make me come, *please*.' Her voice, muffled against the seat, nevertheless sounded strangely loud to her in the confines of the cab, and her disgraceful plea incredibly sluttish.

'All in good time, little pet,' Morgan said in his deep, soothing voice. 'She has very little self-control,' he observed.

'She'll learn control in time.' Elsa stroked her friend's hair. 'But for now, enjoy being played with,' she urged.

Ruth felt her face burning with shame. Her pussy was throbbing with need, and she squirmed as Morgan's fingers probed her innermost secrets while another finger, Elsa's, pressed more insistently against her anus.

'Push back on me, my pet,' Morgan said quietly, 'and make it easy for her.'

Ruth pushed back against the probing digit, and felt it slip a little into her tight bottom. There was a moment of delicious discomfort, and then the lovely sensation of being filled as Elsa's finger thrust through her ring, and slid all the way up into her rear passage. She twisted her hips from side-to-side and kept pushing back, drinking deeply from the pleasure of this most intimate intrusion as she felt the cab make a sharp turn, and proceed down a stony path before suddenly coming to a halt. The engine died away, all the fingers slipped disappointingly out of her, and she felt abandoned, discarded. Suddenly she just wanted to cry.

'Get out,' Morgan commanded.

Ruth scrambled out of the cab, her dignity discarded along with the thong.

An ancient stone farmhouse occupied one side of the cobbled courtyard, a barn the other.

'Time to pay Mr Cooper his fare,' Elsa told her.

Ruth looked at her blankly while Morgan released her bonds, and then she took stock of Cooper as she flexed her wrists. The driver's appearance did not match his voice; he was younger than she had imagined and tall, with a muscular frame accustomed to manual labour. He had large hands and powerful arms, and his narrow features were made quite attractive by a pleasant smile.

'Lets see the colour of her,' he said, reaching for her jerkin. The zip came down and he peeled it off her, handing it to Elsa. His eyes lingered briefly on Ruth's firm nipples, and then he reached for her skirt, his stout fingers surprisingly nimble on the delicate fastening. The strip of leather fell around her ankles.

'Part your legs and make him welcome,' Elsa prompted.

Ruth stepped out of the crumpled leather, distancing herself from him, her heart racing, and she was filled with apprehension as she opened her legs a little. None of her fantasies had been as stark as this cold, casual reality.

Cooper's smile deepened sardonically as he cupped her pussy in one large hand, stroking her vulva before he probed into her labia, pressing his thumb against her clitoris as he thrust a demanding finger inside her.

Ruth fought to control her response, knowing she ought not to climax so quickly, but the battle was a hard one as his finger moved in and out of her like a cock. She cruised dangerously close to an orgasm as his skilled digit worked her while his other hand reached for her breast and his thumb strummed her nipple, sending waves of barely containable pleasure surging through her body. She gasped with joy and stress, struggling against her lascivious inclinations.

'This is the one I told you about, Cooper,' Elsa said, 'the one who peed for a crowd of men outside a transport café.'

His face lit up. 'So, you're an exhibitionist as well, huh?'

'Y-yes,' Ruth stammered quietly, feeling ashamed to admit it, to him or to herself.

'Would you like to take her here, in the barn, or indoors?' Elsa asked, matter-of-factly.

Cooper continued with his concentrated stimulation, studying Ruth closely as he rubbed her clitoris. 'Neither, I'm going to bank this one.' He pulled his finger out of her pussy. 'I want time to appreciate her. She'll be better when she's matured and I'm truly keyed up. Be good and learn well.' He flicked Ruth's nipple sharply and turned back to his cab.

She watched him go feeling empty and not at all sure whether she was relieved or disappointed. He frightened her a little; judging from the proportions of his body his prick would be huge, and the thought of taking anything so large inside her made her feel weak with trepidation… and desire.

'No shoes in the house for you,' Elsa snapped, interrupting her thoughts. 'Slip them off and pick up your clothes. Did you enjoy that?'

'I suppose… in a way…' Ruth replied quietly.

'The bathroom is upstairs,' Elsa went on. 'Clean up, and *don't* be naughty and touch yourself.'

When Ruth emerged from her bath, pink and naked, Elsa led her down into a big farmhouse kitchen. Feeling exposed and vulnerable, she nevertheless followed her compliantly.

'Have you eaten anything?' Elsa asked her.

'Not since breakfast.'

'Have this for now.' She indicated the crackers and cheese on the table.

Ruth perched humbly on a stool, and picked at the food. Then Morgan offered her a drink and she gratefully accepted. It was a delicate cordial tasting of elderberry, cool and refreshing. She drank it down quickly, and was rewarded with another glass. She surveyed her surroundings curiously while reflecting on recent events. Nudity made her feel conspicuous, but the condition was not actually unpleasant. Each time she glanced down she was riveted by the size of her nipples, red and succulent as ripe raspberries. She touched one cautiously, and instantly sparked a warm reaction in her pussy. Yet if her capacity for wantonness amazed her, more astonishing still was her insatiability. Instead of calming her desires, each experience only served to augment her ardour.

Elsa was studying her closely. 'Do you need to come?' she asked candidly.

'You can't *know* how much I need to come!' Ruth enthused.

'Oh, I do, believe me.' Elsa looked at Morgan. 'Shall we take pity on her?'

'Eventually,' he decided. 'Bring her over to the doorway.'

Ruth allowed herself to be led across the kitchen, her pulse racing as she speculated on what the couple had planned for her.

Elsa steered her charge into position. 'Feet astride and hard against the frame,' she ordered.

Ruth obeyed as Morgan crouched down and brought his face level with her crotch. He pushed her foot firmly against the woodwork, passing a restraint around her ankle to snap it closed with a sharp click. The sound made her stomach churn, and instinctively she pulled at the loop to test its strength. It was firm, unbreakable, and a shiver of desire made her knees feel weak. The second clicking sound made her gasp softly in anticipation, and before she knew it, Morgan had also attached her wrists to straps hanging from the top corners of the doorway. She was securely tied and vulnerable to intrusion – utterly helpless.

He stood before her and looked her directly in the eye as his hand stroked her labia, parting her inner lips to allow his finger to play on the moist threshold of her pussy before moving up to her erect clit. Ruth thought she would faint with pleasure as he pinched her little bud, making her cry out from the exquisite pain. He did it again, this time while he sucked both her nipples in turn.

Meanwhile, Elsa pulled off her dress, exposing her full breasts with their proud aureoles. Then she eased off Morgan's shirt and tossed it away. And while he continued to pleasure their new slave, she rubbed her breasts against his back and began unfastening his trousers. He had to step aside to get them off and she took his place, carefully touching her nipples to Ruth's while planting a light kiss on her lips. 'I've always regretted we didn't explore this side of ourselves all those years ago, Ruth,' she purred. 'If only we'd been more informed. I've spent the last four years pining away for you. We've so much lost time to make up for.' She sank to her knees and kissed her friend directly on her clit.

Ruth moaned, tugging at her bonds as Elsa's tongue salved her aching pussy.

Morgan, completely naked now, put his hands under Elsa's breasts, pulled her up, and slipped off her panties.

When fully naked herself Elsa moved away and casually began preparing a simple supper of bread and cheese and pickles, while Morgan helped her. They played with each other as they laid the table, and each time they passed Ruth they played with her too, probing her pussy, flicking her nipples or kissing her belly. Then they took their meal feeding each other, Morgan sitting on a chair with Elsa astride his lap impaled on his erection. She ground herself against him as she ate, smiling impishly at Ruth. Then he spread butter over her nipples and proceeded to suck her clean very slowly, after which the meal became secondary, and was soon forgotten.

Restrained, immobilised and ignored, Ruth's desire became unbearable as she watched the couple consuming each other. She yanked impotently at her bonds, longing for someone to lick her clit, or better yet, for a big cock to thrust into her hungry pussy.

Morgan lifted Elsa bodily onto the table's edge without slipping out of her. He then rutted frenziedly as she cried out and clung to him, hooking her legs around his and absorbing his onslaught.

Ruth continued to struggle desperately against her bonds, longing to relieve her deepening tension as she watched Elsa's lithe body flush pink with mounting excitement. Suddenly she fell back across the table, dragging Morgan down with her, and abandoned herself to ecstasy. He uttered a wild grunt of triumph, and his body convulsed as he shot his seed into her.

They remained lying on the table, embracing and caressing each other, ignoring the pinioned Ruth as she sobbed with frustration. When Elsa finally turned her head and smiled at her contentedly, Ruth hated her.

Elsa studied her friend's face intently. 'Our little pet looks in need of attention,' she said to Morgan, who was clearing the table.

'I concur with that,' he said.

Elsa padded silently away, moving beyond Ruth's vision, and moments later her warm body pressed against Ruth's back and her hands came up and around to cup her breasts, lifting the upward-pointing nipples to increase their prominence. Morgan, moving to stand in front of the bound girl, took both peaks between thumb and forefinger and twisted and squeezed them until she cried out in exquisite agony.

'Did you enjoy my finger in here?' Elsa asked, pressing firmly on the tight entrance to her bottom.

'Oh yes, it was really nice,' Ruth admitted, willingly to

say anything she felt they wanted to hear, 'much nicer than I had imagined it would be.'

'But you were glad it wasn't Cooper's big cock?'

'I think I'd like to feel a cock in there…'

'Ah, you will, Ruth, I promise, very soon,' Elsa cooed. 'But first you must be educated.'

She had no time to ponder this enigmatic statement because Morgan's finger suddenly joined Elsa's in an invasion of her sex. She moaned and squirmed as two fingers roamed freely around her lips' sensitive folds, probing the hidden areas of her most sensitive self. Then through the haze of delicious sensation she heard Morgan ask her, 'If I release your legs, do you think you could take me now?'

'Oh yes,' she breathed. 'Yes, I know I could.'

Ruth felt the straps fall from her ankles. With her wrists still confined, she shuffled forward and spread herself open, conscious of the unfamiliar fullness in her bottom in the form of Elsa's finger. She thrust her pelvis forward, inviting Morgan's cock. He stood firm and solid, with his erection jutting straight up and out from his hairy groin. She felt his heat touch the moist flesh of her inner lips, and the wonderful sensation of his throbbing tip against her vaginal ring told her he was ready. She thrust her hips forward again, and he slid in smoothly.

Elsa withdrew her finger from Ruth's anus and both her hands closed over her friend's swollen teats.

Resting her head on Elsa's shoulder, and pulling against her wrist straps for leverage, Ruth surrendered to the living flesh embedded in her cleft, a great peace filling her as all the waiting and anticipating reached a swift culmination. His thick hard cock rode in and out of her, making her pussy seem to glow with joy as Elsa played an arpeggio of pleasure on her nipples. Her pulse was racing, her breathing fast and shallow, and soon reality drifted away as she surrendered to an orgasm of such intensity she felt her mortal flesh touching infinity…

'Mm, that was good,' Elsa murmured.

The words seemed far away, and then Ruth realised she was leaning heavily against her friend as Morgan reached up to snap open her wrist bands, his cock still semi-hard and gleaming with their mingled juices.

'Time for you to attend to your duties,' Elsa whispered, still sensuously stroking Ruth's skin. 'See how wet you've made Morgan? You must clean him up now.'

'What shall I use?' she asked naively.

'Why, your tongue, of course.'

She fell to her knees and took hold of the warm penis that only moments before had been buried deep inside her. The taste and texture of their combined fluids was deliciously obscene, and the feel of his turgid flesh delightfully carnal. She felt outrageously lewd, and she loved it. Her tongue lapped him greedily while her lips sucked him in, savouring his taste and texture as he gripped her hair and forced himself deeper into her obliging mouth. His cock was stirring into renewed action and she could feel his restraint as he fought the urge to fuck her mouth.

Then he stepped back and Elsa presented her pussy to Ruth's eager tongue. She caught hold of the other woman, feeling her soft plump buttocks beneath her outspread fingers as she buried her nose in her springy pubic bush. Elsa's labia was still full and distended, a sure sign of her continued arousal as her warm wetness was stroked and cleaned of her abundant juices, as well as of the sperm still trickling out of her. She moaned long and passionately as Ruth worked on her with a vengeance, probing every fissure while sneaking frequent visits to the exciting firmness of Elsa's swollen bud.

Then Ruth's contentment increased exponentially when she felt the touch of hands on her buttocks. Without pausing in her oral task, she lifted her hips to offer better access to her bottom. Strong fingers were teasing her anus as a cool fluid was spread around her sphincter and worked inside it. The thick firmness that followed made her gasp with trepidation and desire, and she moaned as it pushed into her, contesting her natural resistance. The hurt was blissful as her sphincter tightly gripped the hard, insistent intruder. Then she felt it burst through her ring, stretching her and filling her as she had never been filled before, and happiness overwhelmed her as she embraced her perverse submission.

Ruth was called to assist Elsa and Morgan in the shower. She took delight in soaping their gorgeous bodies, as moving around with a plug in her bottom offered a new spectrum of sensations she eagerly absorbed. Then Elsa showed her to a small bedroom under the eaves, simply furnished with bright chintz fabrics and a double bed that looked invitingly comfortable.

'You've made a good start,' Elsa said, giving her a big hug. 'Tomorrow will be a busy day, so you need to have a good undisturbed night's rest. Otherwise we would have you in our bed to play. But just so you don't feel neglected, this can stay.' She tapped the base of the butt-plug. 'And a nice companion for it as well.'

Morgan entered the room holding a black dildo, and Ruth bit her lip as she considered its impressive dimensions. A little teasing of her labia notched up her mood, however, and she pushed willingly at the rubber head when it was presented to her threshold. It slid in, lubricated by her juices, and made her feel deliciously full again.

'Just so they don't slip out, you shall have a little restraint.' Elsa produced two chiffon scarves. One she passed around Ruth's waist, knotting it firmly, and the other she rolled into a tight sausage, fastening one end to the middle of the first. The main part was then passed between Ruth's legs and tugged deep into her cleft. It was snug against her clitoris and pulled tight to force the dildo and the plug firmly into her before the ends were secured behind her back. Ruth then climbed carefully onto the bed and snuggled beneath the light duvet Elsa laid over her.

'Goodnight, little pet, sleep well,' she whispered.

The light went out and the door closed.

Starlight floated through the window, and in its soft glow Ruth dwelt on how excited it made her feel to be restrained, very conscious of the objects plugging her body. She felt marvellous, highly aroused by her mild discomfort, an arousal that was spiced by a tinge of apprehension. She lay motionless as her mind raced, reliving the day's events over and over until exhaustion intervened and she fell into a fitful sleep.

Chapter Four

Ruth awoke after a night of vivid dreams. She rolled onto her back, acutely conscious of the fullness in her bladder and the unrelenting tightness of the scarves. The chiffon over her crotch was drenched with her juices, and she was desperate to relieve herself. She debated whether she should go to the bathroom and whether, having reached it, she should dare to unfasten the scarves.

But before she had decided what to do, the door opened to admit a smiling Morgan. He approached the bed and gently peeled back the duvet. 'God, the way that scarf is buried in your pussy is fantastic,' he said emphatically. 'It's slicing right into you.'

Ruth spread her legs in an instinctive response to his lustful compliment.

He sucked air between his teeth and lunged at her, tearing at the knots to drag the chiffon away. He pulled the dildo out of her and knelt on the bed, positioning himself between her legs. She lifted her hips invitingly and he lowered himself as she guided him in, relishing the feel of his cock opening her up. He sank deep, and she worked him with her pelvic muscles while rubbing her clit against him as he thrust into her. His even rhythm brought her swiftly to the brink of ecstasy and held her there until the moment of his conclusion, when his erection jerked inside her as he ground against her.

Afterwards he moved up and straddled her chest so she could obediently suck him clean. 'You have the makings of a perfect pet,' he said breathlessly. He studied her face as he groped for her butt-plug, and extracted it with a single tug. Then he got up to leave, only pausing in the doorway to indicate the dildo and the plug he had left lying on the bed. 'Wash them in the bathroom,' he said, 'they'll be needed again soon.'

As she handled the objects, Ruth reflected on the intimacies she had permitted the relative stranger. All through her life she had taken great care to preserve her modesty. The thought of anyone viewing her sex or her bottom had been unthinkable, until now. In the last few days she had shown her pussy to Elsa, Morgan and Cooper, not to mention Lewis and a dozen anonymous lorry drivers. And when she thought about it rationally, as she did now, her brazen behaviour alarmed her, but at the time any shame she'd felt had been veiled by a profound excitement.

In the kitchen Morgan had laid out breakfast. There were only two chairs, and Ruth wondered where she would sit, or stand. At one side of the kitchen she noticed a low pine table with a plate of food sitting at one end.

'This is your place,' Elsa announced, indicating that low table. 'You squat on this end of the bench facing us. We've decided you shouldn't conceal your sex unless for natural reasons, such as walking. Sit there, and tuck your heels against your bottom, toes pointed, feet apart. Lower your knees as far as you can… you see, in that position both your breasts and your pussy are visible to us. Even your cute bum-hole is discernable when you lean back. Now you can eat and we can enjoy looking at you while you do so.'

Ruth was so hungry it helped prevent her from dwelling on the extent of her exposure. She was growing accustomed to being naked in Morgan's presence, and despite a nagging modesty, the experience of blatantly exposing herself fed her excitement.

After breakfast Elsa produced a thin cotton shift with spaghetti straps for Ruth to wear. The plain cream fabric was virtually transparent. The hem barely covered her bottom, and the bodice only seemed to enhance her nipples beneath it. She was offered no shoes.

Morgan joined them again, and Ruth was given a tour. The old house was a warren of stairs, passages and small rooms. All the furniture was antique pine, simple but appealing, and Elsa and Morgan shared the largest bedroom, which boasted a king-size bed, three wardrobes and a large antique chest.

Outside, the original farm buildings had been converted for work and storage while retaining their outward integrity. The warehouse was stacked full of pine furniture, some old, some new. One barn was empty, spotlessly clean, with straw bales lining two walls. The workshop smelled of freshly sawn wood and varnish, and various partially finished pieces stood around.

Ruth's eyes lit on one that resembled a large rocking horse. The cylindrical body was covered in sheepskin and four stout legs splayed from the corners, but no rockers were fitted. A suspended bar did duty for stirrups, and where the head and neck should have been was an arrangement not unlike a set of handlebars.

'Interesting, isn't it?' Morgan caught her eyeing the structure. 'Tell me, what purpose do you suppose it serves?'

'You're making a rocking horse?' Ruth guessed naively.

He chuckled. 'Nearly correct. We call it a *shaggy horse*. See here?' He pointed to the centre of the body where the rider would sit. Ruth peered in and saw a hollow space containing a shiny metal cup. 'For these,' he explained; a piece of knotted rope hung like a tail. He tugged on it and a narrow drawer slid out displaying dildos standing in a neat row like rigid soldiers. 'The horse is one of our specialities; it sells very well. Would you care to test it?'

'Do I have a choice?' she asked carefully.

'No, not really.' He chuckled again. Let's call it a pre-delivery quality control test.' He took a dildo from the rack and placed it in the metal cup. 'It fits in here, we twist the ring, just so, and it locks tight. It pivots to suit the angle of the pussy. You do that once you're mounted.' He smiled at her and pushed the drawer closed.

'You must be naked to get the full effect,' Elsa added, so Ruth pulled her shift off obediently, and without its minimal covering she felt very vulnerable again, and a thrill of trepidation shot through her.

She swung herself up on the horse and stood astride it, her feet on the stirrup bars. Around the socket the sheepskin had been reinforced by leather and extended to form a contoured seat. More leather patches formed kneepads, and she looked down at the pink dildo aimed at her cleft with a mixture of apprehension and hunger.

Gripping the handlebar with one hand, she altered the dildo's angle. The movement was smooth and firm. Satisfied with its position, she lowered herself gingerly onto the plastic shaft. She was already naturally lubricated and the rounded tip slid into her easily. The latex organ was wide in girth and filled her nicely as she pushed down on it, stretching her tender sheath wide, yet the discomfort was perversely pleasant. Being so full was wonderful, but she was so extended she was afraid she would hurt herself when she began moving. The artificial stiffness was an unaccustomed presence inside her, and she did not feel quite ready. But then she tentatively squeezed her vagina around it, and instantly her clitoris throbbed and she pulled back to increase the pressure against it.

Elsa reached for some twine from the workbench, and deftly tied Ruth's wrists to the handles. Another length of twine was fastened around her ankles, and now she was well and truly trussed to the horse.

Excited by the restraints she lifted herself, and the perpetually rigid penis sliding out of her induced tremors of delight inside her. Her clit pulsed and popped from its hood as she pushed down again, eager to feel the thickness filling her again. Her need grew urgent as she moved rhythmically, riding the full extent of the great hard shaft. The presence of an audience spurred her on at first, yet it was soon forgotten as her concentration turned inwards and she rode frantically to her conclusion. The delicious tightness grew in her tummy, and she was moaning and gasping as she forced herself swiftly towards fulfilment.

Her climax came as a divine blessing. She tilted forward, pulling the dildo out so its tip was against her clit, and rubbed and rubbed against it to prolong the joy. It was some time before she was fully replete and ready to dismount.

'Did you enjoy that?' Elsa sounded amused as she untied her.

Ruth inhaled deeply and sat up straight. 'It was wonderful!' she beamed.

They resumed the tour of the house and grounds, including a walk around the paddocks.

'One day we intend to hold an erotic Olympics here,' Elsa informed her. 'There are lots of couples who share our penchants. In fact, we are taking you to visit one such couple this very afternoon.'

Back at the house Ruth was stripped again, and for the following hour was left alone in her bedroom. Being denied the framework of control she was growing accustomed to, she felt strangely lost and cast around for something to focus her attention on.

Investigation of the wardrobe revealed four dresses on hangers. One by one she held them against her body, longing for a mirror. A bedside cabinet disclosed a small collection of books. She selected one containing photographs, and reclined on the bed to browse through it. Every picture was erotic, and she pored over them avidly. One particular photograph, of a girl trussed in leather straps, seriously stirred her imagination.

She set the book aside restlessly and closed her eyes, sighing deeply. She had yearned to be here, now it was real and most of her reservations had dissolved. So far her experiences had exceeded her wildest fantasies, and there was much more to come. Like an explorer she had reached successive pinnacles only to discover new conquests awaiting her.

'Lunchtime,' Elsa announced, entering the room carrying a broad leather belt, which she buckled very tightly around Ruth's slender waist. It emphasised the fullness of her hips and bosom, and cuffs dangling from short chains were strapped around her wrists. With her arm movement limited to a few inches, Ruth felt provocatively trussed and her libido instantly notched itself up. Identifying with the girl in the photograph, and proudly self-conscious, she followed Elsa down to the kitchen.

A cold luncheon buffet had been laid out. 'You are to serve us this time, Ruth,' Elsa told her. 'Try to memorise the layout of the various dishes.'

She was allowed to practice picking up plates, which she could only do by bending stiffly at the waist with her bottom thrust out, and then Morgan slipped a blindfold over her eyes. 'Listen closely, and bring the food we ask for,' he said.

Ruth nodded. Although testing, the task seemed straightforward enough, and she heard the sound of chairs being occupied.

'I'll start with an egg mayonnaise,' Elsa declared.

Ruth rapidly scanned her memory and bent in the direction she thought was correct. As her fingers spread out to feel for the food she felt another finger probing for her anus. She straightened up with a startled cry, shying away from the intrusion.

'Silly girl,' came Morgan's voice from close by. 'Now you've lost your point of reference. Really, little pet, you must cultivate more self-discipline.'

'I'm sorry,' she murmured, 'it won't happen again.' She was at a loss to explain why apologising should turn her on as much as it did. Admitting her own failure was like receiving the most intimate of caresses.

'Where is my egg mayonnaise?' came Elsa's impatient voice.

'Coming…' She resumed her search for the food, full of expectation, but Morgan did not touch her again. Slightly disappointed, she carried the dish across to the table slowly, and her thigh bumped into it.

'Clumsy,' Elsa chided her. 'I'm over here.'

Ruth edged around until she could feel her friend's warmth, and put the dish down where she imagined the place setting to be. Her fingers clattered against the cutlery as she leaned forward, and at that crucial moment a finger insinuated itself into her anus. 'Oh!' she cried in surprise, and her lack of attention was rewarded by a vicious pinch to one of her nipples.

Morgan asked for some pâté, and slipped his finger out of her bottom so she could go fetch it.

Moving gingerly across the room, Ruth was very conscious of the lingering sensation in her bottom, and as she returned and bent to serve Morgan she felt another intrusion. Learning from the previous experience she pushed against it, receiving the insistent presence of the butt-plug again. She accepted it steadily, feeling the delightful give as its widest section passed inside the ring of firm muscle resisting it. She gripped it tightly, loving the sensation of being filled and having the flange pressing against her rosebud.

'Let's see how long you can retain it,' Morgan said.

The lunch proceeded with Ruth shuffling awkwardly across the kitchen and groping around the table. Every dish she delivered was accompanied by some intimate attention, and her enjoyment was enhanced by not knowing where they would touch her next. By the time she was released and given her own meal, she was simmering with lust.

As at breakfast she ate squatting on the low bench. Her nipples throbbed, her exposed pussy was begging for attention, and the black plug peeped lewdly from her bottom. She felt gloriously wanton.

In the late afternoon Elsa spent a very happy hour tending to Ruth's hair and make-up before dressing her. The dress she produced was pale yellow with long, close-fitting sleeves. It was made from a nearly transparent material printed with a shadowy motif designed to resemble lace, which afforded her only a slight measure of modesty. Apart from matching high heels, Ruth wore nothing else, which did not greatly concern her. She was discovering that being exposed was a potent turn on. The dress was extremely short, and she hoped the proposed journey would not include many stairs. Being exposed in public was one thing, but being exposed in public *and* flaunting a butt-plug was quite another.

They travelled in Morgan's jeep, and when they drew to a halt Ruth shrugged off her anxiety. The town was busy and hot, and her minimal dress would pass relatively unnoticed amongst the scantily clad crowds.

A light breeze wafted the skirt around her thighs, stirring up her excitement, an effect accelerated when Elsa adjusted the dress. Its sleeves had concealed hooks, which met with loops sewn into the hem, and when they were brought together her arms were effectively pinioned at her sides. There seemed no purpose for this restraint beyond Elsa's whim, but as before, being bound exerted a profound effect on Ruth. Chords long dormant deep in her subconscious began resonating, and liberating a wild urge to venture into uncharted territory, to throw aside inhibition and seek out all kinds of forbidden pleasures.

She was made to walk ahead of Elsa and Morgan, and stepping confidently through the crowds, she imagined her swaying buttocks were deliciously obvious beneath the taut and transparent fabric. She was attracting lots of attention from passers-by, and she wondered whether the butt-plug might also be visible. Its presence in her bottom was uncomfortable yet perversely agreeable. The combination of restraint and exhibitionism with stimulation and embarrassment fuelled her sexual response at a fantastic rate. If she was ordered to publicly masturbate, she would hesitate before doing it, but she would do it.

Beyond the town centre they passed through the gates of a formal park and walked between immaculate lawns and lush flowerbeds. People were stretched out in the sun, and heads turned to gaze up at the skimpily clad girl strolling by.

They emerged from the park beside a road. On the opposite side of the street another pair of gates guarded a footpath winding into mature woodland. They entered its cool privacy and away from the public gaze, and Ruth's anticipation began projecting itself onto the coming encounter.

They turned off the main path through a rustic gate, and after a few yards entered a clearing in which stood a house built in a style common in the late nineteenth century when landed gentry became besotted with all things Swiss. It sat, quaintly charming, beside a matching coach house on the bank of a small lake.

Their arrival was greeted by a couple stepping off the front porch, and Ruth was shepherded forward. The man before her was tall and distinguished, greying at the temples but still possessed of a fine athletic body that projected authority. The woman was well endowed and her alert brown eyes shimmered attractively. Her dark hair was long and held back by a colourful band that matched her caftan. She looked beautifully mature.

'Oh, Elsa, she's beautiful,' their hostess declared.

'She certainly exceeds your description,' a man concurred, his tone clipped but polite.

Elsa released the sleeve hooks. 'Ruth, please meet Nick and Judy,' she prompted.

'Hello,' she said, not really knowing what to say. 'It's a pleasure… um, I was at college with Elsa.'

Judy stepped forward, and kissed her on the cheek. 'Delighted to meet you, Ruth. We hope you will enjoy your stay.'

Before Ruth could reply, Elsa whispered, 'Undress.'

Ruth instantly slipped into her submissive role and grasped the hem of her dress.

'She responds very quickly,' Judy observed as Ruth handed over the dress. 'Keep the shoes on, please,' she added, checking Ruth's next action. 'I think a naked girl looks so nice in high heels.' She subjected her to an intense visual examination, followed by a tactile assessment. She placed her hands firmly on Ruth's shoulders and slid her soft palms down her arms to take her hands. 'You are quite beautiful, Ruth,' she concluded. 'And you're also highly aroused. You need to come, don't you?'

'Oh yes…' She glanced at Elsa. 'Sorry, am I allowed to say that?'

He friend shrugged. 'Why not? But whether you will be allowed to come is another story.'

'She's encountered your horse?' Judy asked.

'Yes, this morning.'

'Go with Nick, Ruth, and help him carry our horse onto the lawn.'

Ruth followed obediently as Nick led the way to the coach house. He opened a wicket door and she stepped into the spacious building. It had been cleared and the walls painted white. A number of large articles were scattered about, and a plain carpet covered the entire floor. The horse was heavy but had handholds cut into the underside. Walking backwards, Nick took the head, leaving her to support the rear.

'You have quite remarkable breasts,' he observed.

'I'm glad they please you, sir,' she said meekly, blushing at the overt compliment.

'They do indeed please me. Will you allow me to feed off them?'

She blushed even more. 'Certainly, sir, I'll look forward to it.' It was a bizarre conversation, but Nick had an air of authority about him that induced her to respond respectfully. She was certain sex with him would be an experience to remember, and the prospect was making her exposed pussy hot and wet.

The lawn was behind the house and partly shaded by the surrounding trees. Beneath two large umbrellas were four chairs and a table laid out with drinks and snacks. Nick set the horse down close by.

Judy studied Ruth, who was perspiring from her efforts. 'You know, there is something decidedly sexy about a girl when she has been exerting herself. You look quite delicious, Ruth. Now select the dildo that suits you best and mount up. I want you to enjoy yourself. After all, your pleasure is our pleasure.'

'She likes to be restrained,' Elsa pointed out. 'So we brought these along just in case.' She produced some leather straps.

Ruth's heart skipped in her breast and she turned obediently to select a dildo from the rack. Judy owned a black latex shaft, wickedly curved like a thick scimitar with a ribbed surface. She fixed it into the holder, closed the drawer, and mounted the horse. After a quick adjustment of the angle she lowered herself over the inhuman phallus, but her aim was faulty so she lifted herself up and tried again. She gasped with amazement as the thickness opened her up; it felt incredibly good. She wriggled around to ensure the best fit while her wrists and ankles were strapped down.

Judy smiled and reached up to pat one of Ruth's perky breasts. 'Have a lovely time,' she said.

Ruth concentrated on the satisfying feel of the great dildo filling her. She sat motionless for a moment, savouring it, squeezing it tentatively. If she moved one way the massive penis pressed against the butt-plug, and if she moved another way the fullness was almost too much for her. She glanced across at her audience. Elsa was reclining in a chair, and Nick had pulled down her dress to fondle her voluptuous breasts. Judy and Morgan were seated side-by-side on a lounge chair, and she was casually handling his very stiff cock. Ruth experienced a pang of jealousy. She felt a proprietary claim on Morgan, and viewed him with intense affection now. Then Judy caught her eye and smiled and her jealousy evaporated.

It was peaceful in the clearing. The sun shone, the air was soft and the water in the lake sparkled – all this and a full pussy, too. She was in paradise.

After Ruth had ridden to a swift orgasm, her cries filling the clearing as she came on the wooden horse and the curved black latex shaft, Judy announced, 'I think a swim would do us all good.' She pulled off her caftan and Elsa followed suit, discarding her own clothes.

Ruth, her bonds released and feeling she was included in this invitation, lifted herself off the horse and followed the two couples into the cool and limpid lake. After her exertion, the swim was a luxury. The cold water was fresh, cleansing and invigorating.

A few minutes later she was lying on the grass, her eyes closed, soaking up the sun and listening to the laughter of the others still playing in the lake. This place was idyllic. There were no hang-ups. Here nudity was accepted without question, sex was as natural as holding hands, and all desires were freely expressed and indulged. She was so glad she had accepted Elsa's invitation.

Chapter Five

Judy spread herself down on the ground beside Ruth, spraying her with cool water droplets that felt wonderful against her warm skin. 'Are you enjoying yourself?' she asked.

'I am, it's wonderful,' Ruth beamed in response. 'This is the best time I've had in years. Elsa and I had some great times together in college, and I'd forgotten how good they were, but they were never as good as this.'

'It can be even better,' Judy promised.

'I find that hard to believe.'

'The things you've done with Elsa and Morgan, and now with us, do they turn you on?'

'Oh yes,' Ruth admitted openly. 'I'd never have guessed how sexy these things could make me feel. When Morgan first fitted me with cuffs, I almost climaxed.'

'That's because you're a natural submissive, Ruth,' the woman told her seriously. 'You have a rare gift, and you should explore it. You'll discover a profoundly deep satisfaction in surrendering to your natural desire to please and to serve. Look, there's a group of us who share your inclinations. We throw parties occasionally, informal affairs. Nick and I are holding one next Saturday night. Elsa and Morgan are coming. Why not join us?'

'What would I have to do?' Ruth asked cautiously.

'Whatever you like. You don't have to take part if you don't want to – just come and watch.'

'She's truly an anal virgin?' Nick asked Morgan as the two men emerged from the lake.

'Yes, she's never taken a living cock up the ass.'

'Then her induction should be quite something. At our party next Saturday, do you think?'

'Most appropriate,' Morgan agreed.

'Have you chastised her yet?'

'Not yet. We thought to start her off with a spanking.'

'Good idea.' Nick sank to his knees before Ruth, and eased her legs apart. 'May I?' He smiled, and before she could respond his cool erection sank into her warm pussy with breathtaking precision, filling her up as her back arched from the sudden joy. She flexed her vaginal muscles, gripping his rigid member and milking its firmness.

'Your reward,' he whispered in her ear as he began to thrust, a vigorous action that made her breathless with pleasure. This was direct physical sex – pure, raw carnality, and she gloried in it. Moaning and perspiring beneath him she felt him reaching his peak, and her inner muscles clung to his pulsing cock as he pumped her with his seed.

'Time for dinner,' Judy announced, retrieving her discarded caftan and heading towards the house.

In the dining room five places had been set at the table. Ruth was placed between Nick and Morgan, facing the other women. She tried to sit demurely, but they did not permit it. At every opportunity the two men fondled her, making it impossible for her to concentrate on the meal. She sat with her thighs parted and her pussy inched forward on the seat, torn between two very different kinds of hunger.

After the meal they repaired to the lounge, where Judy served coffee. Ruth drank hers sitting astride Morgan's lap while he teased her nipples and her clitoris, a gentle, almost playful attention that had her feel like purring with contentment.

'Ruth is thinking she'll join our party next Saturday,' Judy announced. 'Will you stay with Elsa, or would you like to come to us, Ruth?'

'She'll stay with us,' Elsa interjected. 'You'll enjoy that, won't you, Ruth?'

She mentally detached herself from Morgan's attentions just long enough to say, 'Yes, Elsa, I will enjoy that... thank you.'

'Would you like a taste of what's to come?' Judy enquired.

'Oh yes, please,' Ruth sighed, trying to concentrate on what was being said, despite Morgan.

Judy took her hand, eased her off his lap, and they all led her out to the coach house. It was growing dark so lighting was necessary as Nick and Morgan pulled out a piece of equipment resembling a high stool. The narrow top was padded, and attachments dangled from the splayed legs. Ruth was told to lie facedown across it with her feet on the floor so her ankles could be fastened to one pair of legs and her wrists to the other. The top was contoured to support her hips and shoulders, but cut away to let her breasts hang free. With her legs widely spread, her sex was fully exposed. She tugged experimentally on her bonds, and felt desire flooding her body yet again when she realised how helpless and vulnerable she was.

'This is a whipping stool,' Elsa explained. 'But we're not going to whip you just yet. Tonight is for milder pleasures.'

The mention of whipping made Ruth's skin crawl and her stomach knotted with a mixture of antipathy and craving. 'Will, um, will I be whipped next weekend?' she asked anxiously.

'Perhaps. Think about it. Imagine how it might feel. Imagine a lash cutting across your pussy or curling around your pert breasts.'

A hand she could not see began stroking her bottom, moving smoothly over the curves of her buttocks towards the valley between them. It was not Nick's hands because he was on his knees beside her, reaching for one of her nipples with pursed lips. He took it firmly in his mouth, and sucked her deep and hard while on her other side Morgan did the same. Then the hand on her bottom became two hands reaching into her cleft and down into her vulva, teasing her anus and probing her pussy simultaneously. Ruth began to writhe and moan, expressing her delight in all this attention.

The gentle, loving caresses and fervent sucking continued for some time, until Nick and Morgan stood up and passed beyond her field of vision.

There was a pause in the stroking, then it began again, and it was stronger now, delivered by stronger hands. Nick appeared before her, his erection huge, his foreskin drawn back, his helmet glistening purple. She instinctively lifted her head and opened her mouth to accept his gift, and he eased himself in between her lips, pushing deep into her mouth until he was touching her throat. She nearly gagged on him, but he pushed harder, and with immense effort she regained control and began sucking him, feeling his girth grow against her tongue. Then from behind came another invasion as her pussy opened to Morgan's dick, which pushed vigorously into her wet passage, and his balls touched her sex at the same instant that lips closed over her nipples again. Nick gripped her head, Morgan grasped her hips, and Judy and Elsa suckled her breasts while stroking her thighs and her clit, nearly drowning

71

her in stimulation.

The men shafted her with long, purposeful, powerful strokes; no quarter was given. The rubbing of her clitoris was relentless, and Ruth writhed against the bench as she rose swiftly to her peak. She sensed the tension in Nick's erection first and used all the skill she possessed to delay his climax until Morgan's thrusts gained the same familiar urgency, and then she abandoned herself to total pleasure, plunging into an orgasm that reverberated through her body as she drank deeply from both ends of their combined pleasure.

She was not released. Even as her climax ebbed away she was presented with a bush of soft hair, and eagerly she pushed her face into Elsa's pussy and began licking it, combing the labia with the tip of her tongue, dipping into the sweet wetness while unseen fingers built another climax in her throbbing clitoris. Again she pitched into a luscious maelstrom as the woman riding her tongue danced and twisted in her own triumph.

Breathless and hot, Ruth cruised somewhere on the verge of paradise, but an uplifted skirt offered her yet more pleasures, and probing fingers stirred her honey pot yet again. She took it all, pushing her tongue into the rich wet sex before her, working assiduously to grant its owner release.

Yet even after that she was not finished. Two erections were offered to her for attention and she took each one into her mouth readily, darting from one to the other, pulling at the still rigid shafts with her lips while fingers teased her to yet another blinding epiphany.

Sunday was a leisurely day. Ruth was given many small opportunities to please her two hosts, and at midday she was dressed in her black leather outfit and driven to the market traders' pub. No one could see that, once she was seated, she was shackled to the table leg, or that without panties she was open to intrusion. She ate her meal while trying to appear placid, a difficult task with fingers touching and teasing her beneath the table. She was discovering that there existed two levels of stimulation – the intense, relentless assault on her senses that brought her to mind-shattering orgasms, and this gentler, steady teasing that, combined with self-control, induced a continuous, steady, almost hypnotic pleasure.

'This is a very pleasant accompaniment to a meal,' Morgan commented over lunch. 'When we were doing this at Judy's last night, I was thinking how the chair restricts access. What we need is a chair that allows Ruth's skirt, such as it is, to hang clear, and a seat that supports her but exposes her sex and her bottom-hole completely. If we added restraints, and something to part her legs, she could sit at the table and offer full access to anyone. I've thought out a basic design, and even if there isn't a market we could have one for ourselves and for the group to use.'

'It's a fabulous idea,' Elsa enthused. 'And Ruth should be the first to test it. What do you think, Ruth?'

She could not reply. A mouth full of salad and a fanny full of fingers was inhibiting her powers of speech. She managed to nod her approval, however.

Back at the house she was dressed in the transparent shift again and the three of them sat out on the patio with ample supplies of cool lager to discuss the weekend. Elsa and Morgan probed closely into her feelings, wanting to know what she had enjoyed most and what, if anything, had put her off.

Ruth recounted her impressions. 'Really, it's been far more exciting than I could ever have imagined. In the past few years sex has taken second place to my career. I've been bonking fairly regularly, but all very ordinary stuff. Meeting Elsa again was like opening a shuttered window. I knew there was real sex out there, but I'd forgotten how varied and wonderful it could be. Thank you for having me, and thank you for making me do all these things and opening my eyes to them.'

'You could make a regular arrangement with us,' Morgan suggested.

'I still have to consider my career,' she replied guardedly.

'We run our business and have a full and exciting life,' Elsa pointed out. 'So can you.'

The conversation shifted to sorting the problem created by meeting up with Lewis, namely travel and clothing. The first matter was easily settled; Elsa would drive her to Broughton Chase. The second required some agreement. Ruth vehemently resisted the idea of wearing the leather outfit again. 'I can't take dinner in a four star hotel dressed like that!' she protested.

'You could if we made you,' Morgan pointed out agreeably.

'I'd refuse.'

'In that case, we couldn't invite you to the party. You'd not be sufficiently obedient, you see.'

'You can borrow the yellow dress for the evening,' Elsa conceded, 'but you must go to work in the leather.'

'I can't wear transparent yellow with black panties!'

'True, you need something that will blend and yet be obvious. Anyone wearing a see-through dress must demonstrate the fact. I shall lend you another pair of panties. I've got some in wild peach.'

'Wild peach?'

'They were a present; I didn't choose the colour. Just trust me, it will show, and they're real silk.'

The solicitor acting for the Quincy estate seemed disturbed by the sight of Ruth's long legs as she climbed out of Elsa's utility. Lewis, on the other hand, exercised commendable self-restraint. As the solicitor ushered them fussily along the corridors, he whispered, 'I think I'm dreaming. You look fantastic. If it's to please me, then I'm duly flattered.'

Further comments were forestalled by their arrival at the two Parry paintings. 'They depict the valley as seen from contrasting viewpoints a hundred years ago,' the solicitor explained. 'Of course, they were an immense piece of conceit. See how the Quincy mill has been made to dominate the scene.'

Lewis snorted. Ruth knew he detested being lectured about the obvious. He climbed the portable stepladder and gave his full attention to the pictures while the solicitor made small talk and ogled Ruth, an entirely different piece of work.

At last Lewis delivered his verdict. 'I agree with you, Ruth. These are certainly Parry's.' He rounded on the solicitor. 'Parry was dismissed by his contemporaries. Criticism almost destroyed him and he only survived by taking these commercial commissions, but his genius breaks through. These are masterpieces in their own right, rediscovered thanks to Ruth's expertise. What we need from you is evidence. Why are there no receipts for these?'

The solicitor became defensively pompous. 'I would suggest the artist's charges were paid directly by the mill, therefore, there would be no corresponding entry in the domestic private accounts the family kept.'

'Then search the mill accounts, if they exist. Find an invoice, or a ledger entry. Establish provenance and the price will rocket.' Lewis scanned the room, and pointed to a glass cabinet. 'Are these ceramics to be sold as well?'

'A local dealer has offered a fair price,' the solicitor confirmed. 'They are of little value.'

Lewis snorted. 'Balderdash! There's a small fortune in there. The vase alone is worth three thousand pounds. If you feel the matter to be of interest, I can arrange for a formal valuation.'

The solicitor looked a little flustered. 'I think we must reconsider our decision,' he said.

'Good. Arrange it with Ruth, and also set up a time for her to come and prepare the lots for display. I'll wait in the car.'

Ignoring the solicitor's lustful stares from his window, Ruth settled into the passenger's seat and pulled the door closed. Lewis reached over and slid his hand beneath the leather jerkin to cup her breast, sighing as he encountered naked flesh. 'Ruth, you're incredibly lovely. I must be the luckiest man alive.'

'I can take it off for you, if you like,' she offered cheekily.

'Teasing can be dangerous to middle-aged men,' he warned.

'You're not middle-aged, are you?' she flattered.

'I'm in my forties, but only my closest friends know that.'

'Then you're still a young man, and sex keeps you young, so shall I take it off?'

'If I said yes I'd be unable to concentrate on the road.'

'I'll just have to be patient, then,' she sighed.

He gave her breast one last longing squeeze, started the engine, and the silver Mercedes was soon rolling effortlessly across the moors and swooping down the dale. As they shot past Thorpe's garage, Jack looked up and Ruth, tingling all over suddenly, wondered if he had recognised her.

Lewis, sensing her reaction, studied her curiously between concentrating on the road.

'Just thinking nice thoughts,' she explained.

On the motorway she lay back and daydreamed while the miles sped by. By mid-afternoon they were rolling into the forecourt of a country house hotel nestled in the folds of the Dukeries.

The liveried porter scanned Ruth's costume disapprovingly, and Lewis said quietly, 'I advise you to register under your own name, Ruth. You can have a separate room should you prefer.'

She studied his face, amused by his quaint courtesy. 'Thank you, but a double will be fine.'

So he marched up to reception, announcing in a loud, challenging voice, 'Mr Lewis Stone and Miss Ruth Parish. We have a reservation for a double suite.'

The woman at the desk scanned Ruth from head to toe as if trying to decide whether she was trash living it up, or quality dressing down. Ruth smiled at the woman's prudish indecision.

'To save you further pointless speculation,' Lewis interrupted the desk clerk's private debate, 'we are very much in love and we intend to make full and appropriate use of our bedroom, so please ensure we are given a large one.'

The woman recovered from her discomfiture with astonishing aplomb. 'I assure you, sir, that the hotel's only concern is for your comfort and pleasure. We wish you a pleasant stay.'

Another porter showed them up to their suite – two rooms and a bathroom overlooking the rolling parkland. He departed with a handsome tip, and a longing glance at Ruth.

'*Now* I can take it off,' she said, setting down the small overnight case she had borrowed from Elsa.

'I shall wake up soon,' Lewis mused as he watched her arrange the leather outfit on hangers. He came over and put his arms around her, caressing her naked belly. She could feel his hardness pressing against her bottom. 'You're gorgeous,' he breathed in her ear, kissing her lightly on the neck.

Ruth, luxuriating in his embrace, surrendered to his tenderness. He clasped her breasts, smothering her neck and shoulders in kisses, and she felt a warm glow spreading to all those special, sensitive places. Her desire for sex was strong, but the quality of her need was different with Lewis. This was neither simple lust nor the complex arousal stimulated by restraint. This was deep affection of a rich and sensual kind. She pushed the black thong over her hips and stepped out of it. Then turning and holding his head firmly in both her hands, she kissed him with more passion than she had ever felt before.

'I want you, Lewis Stone,' she whispered. 'I want you to fuck me, over and over again. I want you to fuck me because… because I *love* you…' She then took his hand and led him over to the bed.

They made love continuously until early evening. Afterwards they lay beside each other staring contentedly up at the ceiling. The complex patterns in the plaster merged hazily, mixing and separating like the thoughts drifting through her mind. She wallowed in happiness, feeling totally relaxed. Her fingers reached down and absently fingered her pussy, still slick with Lewis's seed, warm, comfortable feelings flowing through her.

'Lewis,' she finally broke their cosy silence, 'would you enjoy making love to me if I was tied up?'

'What a curious question,' he replied lazily.

'Seriously, would you?' she persisted.

'I don't see you that way, Ruth,' he decided. 'I want to be with you, not control you.'

She turned onto her side, and rested a hand on his stomach. 'You're a very kind and considerate lover, Lewis Stone,' she told him, and her fingertips began tracing random patterns across his chest. 'But there are many ways to satisfy a girl. Let's suppose I get lots of feelings from being tied up – feelings I really enjoy. If that were the case, would you enjoy it too?'

He stared up at her. 'Is that how you really feel?'

'Actually, yes, I like being restrained, sometimes.' She heard his sharp intake of breath. 'Now you're shocked,' she said, suddenly feeling very stupid and ashamed. 'I'll go and get dressed.'

He grasped her wrist. 'Stay, please. Ruth, I'm truly fond of you. I want you to feel really good, I want to please you—'

She placed a finger to his lips and shushed him. 'One more please, lover, then we must get dressed for dinner.' She could feel his penis hardening against her thigh as she cuddled him closer.

Ruth pulled on her borrowed panties, and the silk was soft as gossamer against her skin. The yellow dress elicited admiration from Lewis and she turned slowly around for him while at the same time critically assessing herself in the mirror. Elsa had been correct; the peach colouring was just the right shade to be discreetly visible through the sheer fabric.

'You poor thing, so enveloped,' she commiserated, stroking his tuxedo.

'A discomfort I suffer gladly in the cause of chivalry,

and it provides the contrast essential to enhance and dignify your naughtiness.'

They attracted immense attention as they entered the restaurant, and during dinner their conversation wandered over a range of topics, including work.

'Your assessment of the two Parry pictures was excellent,' Lewis praised her again. 'Your analysis of his style and techniques was informed and thorough. With that level of expertise, you should be thinking of applying it to your own advantage. You should publish and gain recognition.'

'Publish a book?' Ruth gasped. 'Not in your wildest dreams! I haven't the talent to write an authoritative work.'

'You certainly have the knowledge,' he insisted.

'If you say so, but I'd have to track down all the paintings, and they're mostly in private hands, which creates special difficulties.'

He shrugged and sipped his soup from the ornate silver spoon. 'Promise me you'll think about it, Ruth.'

She took his hand across the table. 'I promise,' she assured him, 'but right now I'd rather think about other things.'

After the second course she excused herself and went to the toilet by way of the foyer. In the hotel shop she bought some specific items and had the package sent up to the suite. Smiling happily, she then returned to Lewis.

'Shall we take drinks in the lounge, or have something sent up?' he enquired at the end of the meal.

'Sent up, so we can enjoy every second of our time together. Do you agree?'

He did.

Inside the suite, she went and stood in front of the window, gazing out across the open countryside even though it was primarily invisible in the darkness. 'This was where Lady Chatterley is set, isn't it?' she asked.

'Lawrence was born in Nottinghamshire. You've read the book?'

'Naturally. I think every teenager dips into it out of curiosity. It didn't do much for me. I thought it a rather depressing tale, in fact.'

'But it didn't dull your appetite, did it?' he teased.

She giggled. 'Certainly not.'

He eased the dress off her shoulders and ran his hands down her naked body. Still framed in the window, she let him remove her silk panties and then her heels. He set them aside, and walked over to the bar. 'What will you... hello, what's this?'

She turned around. He had the package in his hands and was trying to guess at the contents by feeling it. 'Something to play with,' she replied suggestively. 'Why don't you open it?'

He tore carefully at the wrapping, and shaking out some chiffon scarves, shot her a quizzical look.

'I'll have a vodka and tonic, please,' she said, 'and when I've drunk it, you can use those to tie me to the bed.'

His eyebrows lifted. 'You don't waste time, do you?'

'"Why put off till tomorrow something you can enjoy today?"' she quoted mischievously.

So, with a little improvisation Lewis managed to tie her to the bed using the scarves as bindings for her wrists and ankles. Her feet were spread to the lower corners and her wrists were fastened to a belt looped around the headboard fittings.

She lay still, exposed and vulnerable, her heart thumping as she gazed up at his naked body. 'Blindfold me, please,' she whispered. 'Use the spare scarf.'

'Are you sure you want me to?'

'Don't ask, please, it destroys the atmosphere. Just use me.'

Lewis obliged, quite inventively. She had expected him to leap on the bed and take her, but instead he began teasing her, touching her here and there. He played her body expertly, revealing his long and varied experience with women by bringing her to the verge of orgasm time and time again, until she was silently screaming for release.

'Oh, for mercy's sake just let me come,' she cried in frustration.

'No,' he said firmly, and slapped her sharply on her wet pussy.

She went rigid, and then plunged into a whirling kaleidoscope of mingled pain and pleasure. She tried to protect herself by clamping her thighs closed, only to be frustrated by the restraints. Her scream as he slapped her pussy again was part agony and part ecstasy. She tugged wildly at her bonds and drove herself deeper into the vortex of conflicting sensations.

He did not touch her again until she had calmed down, and then it was with his cock. Kneeling astride her, he lowered himself and touched her navel with his helmet. Her flesh seemed to ripple with delight, her throat crooning softly as he stroked her with his hot satin tip. He moved up, touching first one nipple and then the other. Then he crouched over her face, brushing her lips and hovering over her while her tongue searched for him. He allowed her to lick his helmet, and then moved back down to her nipples and from there to her navel. When the tip of his erection touched her clitoris, she thought she would explode with joy. Again and again he touched her there until she could bear it no longer, and then finally his rigid length spread her sex lips open and drove deep and hard into her body. He took all his weight on his arms even as he lowered his lips to hers and silenced her cries with a violent kiss.

Chapter Six

'So, did you have a nice weekend?' Janet asked eagerly.

'Wonderful!' Ruth exclaimed. 'It was really two weekends rolled up into one, first with my friends and then a second one with Lewis.'

'And judging by the sparkle in your eyes, he was very attentive.'

She blushed. 'Actually, I feel a bit awkward, Janet. I mean, he knows I've not been celibate, but will he expect me to be faithful to him and him alone?'

'Well, fidelity *is* the expected norm.'

Janet's almost sanctimonious tone struck a chord in Ruth that sent her into turmoil. The mere concept of fidelity challenged the ultra-powerful instincts driving her to discard all conventions.

Janet, reading her perplexed expression, quickly apologised. 'Sorry, Ruth, I was only teasing.'

'Oh, that was horrid, Janet, you made me feel so guilty,' Ruth playfully admonished the woman, relief making her feel more relaxed. 'You see, recently I've been so sexually charged that I can't refuse any offer that turns me on. I think perhaps I'm becoming a nymphomaniac, or something.'

'You look perfectly healthy to me. That sparkle in your eye denotes a girl at the peak of her sexuality who is being fully provided for.'

'But I've been experimenting widely, Janet. Do you think that's wrong?'

'Everyone has fantasies, so why should it be wrong to

indulge them?'

'Lewis has asked me to go with him to a charity dinner on Thursday.'

'I know the one, you lucky girl,' Janet said enviously. 'That's one of the biggest events of the year. Now, details about your weekend, please, and don't leave any juicy ones out.'

'It was a ploy,' Lewis confessed when Ruth entered his office in response to his summons. 'I just wanted to see you again. You look gorgeous.'

She smiled happily.

'Everything you wear looks perfect on you, even formal business clothes,' he added. 'Which brings me to another point. I'd like to buy you something special for Thursday night.' He cut short her protest. 'I'm not trying to buy your affections, Ruth, just let me indulge myself by pleasing you. Go shopping, buy whatever you want, and send me the bill. Choose something that really does it for you.'

'Please, Lewis, this is not how I want things to be between us,' Ruth did manage to protest, albeit with little conviction. 'Just let me buy myself a dress. I shall love you all the more if you do.'

'Did I hear a certain word again?' he asked soberly.

'You did, and I mean it,' she confirmed. 'I'll buy something very special, but let me pay for it myself, please.'

'As you wish,' he conceded, 'but let me buy you lunch today, at least.'

'I'm sorry, I can't,' she declined. 'I have to meet a client in Bromley.'

'Dinner this evening, then?'

'I've another engagement, I'm afraid.'

85

'Oh dear.' He sighed dramatically. 'Will you come and stay with me this weekend?'

She slipped her arms around his neck. 'I really do enjoy being with you, Lewis.'

'But…'

'But I need to visit my friends again in Yorkshire. There are some critical issues I must sort out if we are to take this relationship forward. And I've arranged to prepare the Quincy collection next Monday and Tuesday so I can save on a journey.'

'How would it be if I joined you up there on Monday?'

'It would be lovely.' She kissed him affectionately on the lips.

It was six o'clock when Ruth reached her flat. She went straight to her bedroom and hung her precious new outfit in the wardrobe before opening the post. There was a brief note from Elsa.

Your first try was very good. Since you are coming again, we think you will benefit from being under partial control all of the time. Therefore, from now on you must not wear trousers, shorts or tights without our express permission. Occasionally we might decide you should not wear panties, either. We'll let you know when. Be good. Be obedient. Elsa.

Ruth swallowed hard and a tremor of excitement sprang up from her pussy that made her whole body glow.

The bedside phone rang, and she picked it up.

'Hello?'

'Tomorrow is a no panties day.' Elsa's voice travelled down the line. 'Take them off now, and expect a parcel later in the week.'

Wednesday was long and tedious. Lewis was out all day and Ruth could barely concentrate on her work, pining for him on the one hand and longing after the exciting prospect of the weekend on the other.

In this charged atmosphere of inaction, Stanford's invitation to an evening in Maidenhead was a welcome diversion, offering activity plus a bed companion to wile away a lonely night. Stanford was rather stuffy when he discovered she wasn't wearing panties, and her explanation that she was trying to turn him on only partially appeased him. Their lovemaking was energetic, but something was lacking again, or so Ruth felt as she lay beside him in the half-light afterwards.

'Stanford,' she said softly, 'will you tie me to the bed and fuck me again?'

The words took a moment to penetrate his torpor, then he sat bolt upright. 'What the hell, Ruth?'

'I just want to try it out and see what it does for me. Some men find it quite a turn on to tie a girl up.'

'Well, not *this* man,' he huffed. 'What comes next, photographs leaked to some sleazy magazine unless I pay up?'

It was her turn to sit up abruptly. 'How dare you make such a suggestion, even in jest? I think you'd better leave.'

'I will, right now,' he sulked. 'What's infected you, Ruth? What are these friends of yours feeding you?'

'Just go, Stanford!'

'You bet!'

She turned away on her side and pulled the covers up over her head. She heard the front door slam closed, and sniffed to hold back her tears – tears of anger.

Thursday was a better day. The promised parcel arrived – a small oblong package. She cautiously slit the outer wrapping open while Gavin was in the loo. Inside, there was a sealed cardboard box bearing the legend, *To be opened on Saturday. Be obedient.*

Ruth gazed at the box with bubbling curiosity. What were its contents? What humiliations and excitements did it contain? The temptation to peep was very strong, but she resisted. Resolutely she consigned the box to her case, her libido simmering vigorously. Her pussy was hot and the familiar hollowness in the pit of her stomach betrayed her prurient desires.

Lewis took her to lunch, and afterwards they made love in his office. Then he sent her home to prepare for the evening.

He arrived promptly at eight, as arranged. She released the lobby door to let him up, and when she admitted him to the flat his eyes practically burst from their sockets.

'Oh Ruth, you are exquisite!' he gushed.

Her hair was immaculate, and her outfit was stunning. It consisted of a clinging ankle-length skirt of sheer silk dyed a delicate shade of viridian green, and worn over a tiny pair of slightly darker panties. Above it she wore a long-sleeved shirt of the finest tulle the colour of mint, and four closely spaced buttons fastened it across her cleavage. Below, the edges flared away to expose her navel, into which she had cemented a tiny brilliant. Gold pendants swung from her ears, and on her feet she wore the lightest of high-heeled sandals, three tenuous golden straps framing her delicate feet.

Lewis took her in his arms and kissed her carefully, so as not to smudge her lipstick, and she could feel his manhood, hard and eager where he pressed himself against her. The warmth of his hands on her skin through the diaphanous material seemed to brand her, and immediately moistened her tiny panties.

She felt totally gorgeous as her boss, looking very handsome and distinguished himself in a formal tuxedo, escorted her to the car. The light evening breeze caused the delicate material of her skirt to alternately float around and cling to her thighs, and the reception was everything she had imagined it would be. Mixing with so many famous people was exciting, especially when she sensed from the attention she received that she was physically on a par with the best of them.

Afterwards, as they waited in the foyer for their taxi to pull up, she felt intoxicated by the experience of being so gloriously exposed even while her ankle bracelet never ceased reminding of her new chosen destiny.

'You carried that off to perfection,' Lewis whispered in her ear. 'You were magnificent. Did you notice how everyone's eyes followed you all evening? The paparazzi were giving you plenty of attention, too. Expect calls from the society glossies tomorrow.'

'I don't care about that.' She snuggled against him as he slipped a protective arm around her shoulders. 'I just enjoyed being with you.'

The taxi bore them to Lewis's suburban home – a discreetly detached house nestled in a modest garden. Ruth was bubbling with curiosity to see how he lived, and she was not disappointed. The house was comfortably furnished with a studied economy refined by excellent taste. She settled down in the elegant sitting room while he went to make coffee in the kitchen, but then she got up restlessly and followed him in. The brightly lit space was ultra modern.

She slid up behind him and eased off his dinner jacket, dropping it over a chair. Then she put her arms around him and rubbed his nipples through his shirt while at the same time pressing her breasts against him. 'I feel distinctly overdressed,' she whispered, kissing the back of his neck.

'Easily remedied.' He turned, undid her four buttons, and the filmy tulle slipped from her body like mist. His hands supported her pert breasts while his thumbs stroked her jutting nipples. 'You are incredibly beautiful,' he murmured.

She closed her eyes and held her breath, trying to extend the moment. Never in her life had she felt so secure and peaceful as she did now; it was as if she had been created to feel like this. The gentle passage of his thumbs across the sensitive tips of her nipples was heavenly. She tilted her head back, parted her lips, and ran her tongue seductively over her white teeth. His mouth promptly closed over hers, inviting her tongue in, and when he closed his teeth over it gently she thought she would faint with pleasure. They kissed long and deeply as with one hand she stroked the firm contours of his back and with the other sought his manhood, cupping him through the material of his trousers.

His fingers closed over the waist fastening of her skirt, but she checked him. 'In a little while,' she said. 'What I'd like us to do now is take coffee into the living room just as we are. I feel deliciously decadent, and I want to savour it. Then afterwards you can take me to bed.'

He smiled, a generous, understanding smile, and turned on the percolator.

They took their coffee with him sitting in an armchair and her kneeling and leaning against his leg, gazing up at him adoringly. From time to time he reached down and caressed her breasts, making the light in her eyes sparkle.

'I'd like to make you truly happy, Ruth,' Lewis said quietly.

'You are, believe me. Am I pleasing you?'

90

'More than I deserve, but that doesn't mean I can't crave more. I'd like to spend more time with you, Ruth. Must you go away this weekend?'

'I must,' she said firmly. 'There are things I have to be certain about, Lewis.'

'What sort of things, if I may ask?'

'Aspects of myself,' she said cryptically. 'What makes me tick, how I'm put together, and so on.'

'It sounds seriously profound. And these friends of yours, they'll help you in this quest for self-understanding?'

She nodded.

'I'd like to meet these people who exercise such an influence over you, Ruth.'

'Why not? I'm sure something could be arranged this weekend.'

'I have no desire to intrude, but I shall be privileged to share every aspect of your life.'

She knelt facing him, and taking his hands placed them beneath her breasts. 'Like you share my bed? I think it's time.'

He undressed her tenderly, an act of worship, and laid her across the large mattress. She reclined luxuriously against the pillows, watching him undress. He came to her, kneeling manfully between her thighs, his cock large and virile and pointing straight at her sex. She breathed deeply, coveting its magnificence, but he bent and kissed her labia, teasing her lips apart with his tongue. Then he licked up to her belly and the glittering stud in her navel as his fingers caressed her pussy, causing her to writhe in pleasure. He reached forward, gripping her wrists, and pinioned her arms against the pillows. She felt his power capturing her and twisted to escape it, but he was too strong and she happily capitulated, lifting her hips to meet his. Finally, the tip of his erection locked into her eager, moist opening. She sighed. He pushed. She parted. His thickness plunged deep, spreading her open with its power and heat, and she was gloriously filled. A great wave of well being surged through her, and she made a token struggle against his hold on her as he buried himself to the hilt inside her.

Chapter Seven

Over breakfast on Saturday morning, Ruth opened the mysterious parcel. There was a note inside instructing her to wear only her brief black leather skirt, and the matching tiny bikini bra that lay at the bottom of the box.

Her mouth was dry with excitement as she zipped up the skirt, its touch bringing back vivid recollections of the previous weekend. The bra had a halter string and fastened behind her back. The minuscule triangles barely covered her nipples; she was all but naked above the waist and hardly more modest below.

She dipped into the box again and from beneath a layer of tissue paper fished out a silver ring that fastened to a matching bracelet, the two joined by a tapering silver chain. She slipped it on and gazed at it, feeling its weight, and guessed it was a symbol of her slavery.

The box contained one more object – a sinister black plug. Staring at it, she experienced the familiar cocktail of feelings swamping her reason.

She lubricated herself, and touched the entrance to her bottom with the plug's hard tip. It made her tense, and a desire to be humiliated possessed her. The smoothness slid easily into her tightness, and again she experienced the strangely wonderful sensation of her sphincter being stretched. The plug drove in, forcing her open as her inner muscles resisted its thicker base. Then suddenly she felt it pop into place, and she was comfortably full. She wiggled her bottom experimentally, and scarcely dared anticipate the greater pleasures to come.

The drive was uneventful and rather monotonous even as every bump in the road kept Ruth mindful of the plug in her bottom. It was continuously feeding sensations to her nerve-endings that kept her desires boiling. As she entered Nottinghamshire, the direction signs triggered pleasant memories, and those further north caused Ruth to blush with shameful excitement as she recalled her naughtiness.

The moment she drove through the gate she was greeted by Elsa and Morgan. The couple had been awaiting her arrival sitting on their front porch.

Elsa looked her over dispassionately. It was only their close kinship that enabled Ruth to detect the glimmer of pride in her friend's eyes.

Morgan circled, examining her critically before stepping close to smooth a palm over her bottom and to probe the valley between her buttocks, pressing on the black plastic still tightly sheathed in her anus. 'Excellent,' he said. 'All perfect and aching for attention.'

'I think we should allow her a light lunch,' Elsa suggested, 'and then you should give her a thorough shafting to tune her up. A little time under restraint would be good for her as well.'

Lunch was cold chicken and salad served at the large kitchen table. As before, Ruth was made to wait on her hosts before taking her own meal squatting on the low trestle table. As she ate she examined her emotions, noting how different she felt being here than she felt when with Lewis. She was turned on, as intensely turned on as she had been in Lewis's sumptuous house, but there was a different quality to her excitement. Here her arousal had a sharpness to it that fed a different side of her character. She had come here to discover more about herself, and already she understood that she needed both kinds of outlets for her sexuality, the more conventional as well as the more daring, because apparently each one satisfied a different aspect of her sexuality.

As the meal progressed she was repeatedly called to the table to attend the needs of the couple she was here to serve. Each visit was accompanied by intimate touches and caresses, and as a result, she was the last to finish eating. Then Morgan stripped naked and moved over to her, his large erection swaying before him. Exhilaration gripped her, and her gaze locked onto his rigid cock's hypnotic swinging. It was about to plunge into her sex, filling her and stretching her subservient flesh…

He pressed her facedown across the table, flattening her breasts against the hard wooden surface. With his foot he spread her ankles apart, and then he gripped her hips and sank into her pussy from behind. His groin pressed against her bottom, driving the plug deeper and forcing the air from her lungs.

A hand gripped her wrist and she looked up to watch Elsa looping a rope around it. It was pulled tight and threaded under the table, where it was wound around the leg, and the procedure was repeated with her other wrist.

Morgan shifted his stance, exquisitely reminding her that his cock impaled her, as more rope was wrapped around her ankles, securing her to the table legs. She tested her bonds, seeking freedom of movement, and discovered she had none. Roped tight and pinned down by the erection thrusting into her, she was completely helpless, and a wave of emotion engulfed her as she teetered on the knife-edge of anxiety and anticipation. He rested his hands on her buttocks, caressing her and crooning softly as he eased himself outwards, retracting his cock until the rim of his swollen plum was lodged tight in her threshold. She tugged at her bindings, striving to twist her hips and draw every morsel of sensation from him. She flexed, squeezing him, and heard him moan. Still caressing her buttocks, he began inserting himself again. She felt his veined surface rippling into her, and gasped in profound delight when his knob nudged her cervix. She squeezed him again, using her inner muscles to milk him. He withdrew, but returned in one long sweeping motion that made her cry out with pleasure, and then gripping her hips even more firmly he began building a rhythm of measured strokes that made her wild with desire. Every thrust made the plug in her bottom add its unique note to the sensual music in her flesh, and she began cruising on a symphony of sensations. She would orgasm soon, and it would be wonderful, but at the moment what she most longed for was the protracted arousal of a big dick steadily reaming her. She hoped Elsa had thoroughly milked him that morning to guarantee him a sustained performance, and it looked as though she was not going to be disappointed.

Long, hard and vigorously, Morgan drove into her, bringing her to a climax long before he reached his own peak. As his turgid member thrust mercilessly in and out of her pussy, Ruth began a cascading orgasm that went on, and on, and on. It seemed like an age before he finally came, and through the mists of her ongoing climax she felt his sperm erupting into her body, filling her with its sweet warmth.

He stayed embedded inside her for a few moments, stroking her back and her buttocks, allowing his erection to slowly subside while she continued working him, hungry for yet another blinding release. Finally she lay slumped in her bonds, perspiring and exhausted, but perfectly at peace. It had been a magnificent fuck, and she was content.

Ruth was left tied to the table for some time. She lay

there, nearly oblivious to her surroundings, like a discarded rag doll amid the detritus of lunch. She felt wanton, sluttish, and totally feminine.

She was startled awake by the sound of a voice in her ear.

'Time to prepare you for your debut,' Elsa was saying. 'No, lie still, let's take this out first.' She parted Ruth's bottom cheeks, her fingers groping around her sensitive ring to pull out the butt-plug.

Ruth bit her lip as she felt it move, savouring the pleasant discomfort as the bulbous nose stretched her during its slow exit. A moment of uncomfortable heat, and then it was gone, replaced by an empty longing that almost made her cry with its intensity.

'Don't fret, little pet,' Elsa said soothingly. 'There will be something much nicer filling you soon. Now clear the tables and load the dishwasher, then go to your room and rest for while. I'll come and make you ready later.'

Ruth spent a quiet time browsing through the books in the guestroom, too excited to sleep, and it was well into the evening when Elsa arrived and took her to her own room to make her up and dress her.

Ruth was fastened into a corset made of supple leather that pinched her waist almost to nothing when it was laced closed, emphasising her round hips and bottom and making her breasts jut out above it. A very short wrap-around skirt fastened by a Velcro strip completed the outfit. The back of the corset was fitted with loops into which her arms were strapped, and then she was sent to wait in the kitchen. Walking down the stairs, she was acutely conscious of her appearance. There was a cheap quality to the outfit that felt boldly erotic. The skirt was incredibly short, which meant that when she sat down she would be totally exposed. The shoes – black suede with tall, thin heels – emphasised her bottom, and the corset made her nipples feel as hard as pebbles. They were tingling and so was her clitoris, all three buds aching to be stimulated. Being restrained added to her sensual urgency, notching up her sensitivity, and whilst standing submissively in the kitchen she clamped her thighs together in a vain attempt to placate the ravenous needs possessing her.

Elsa appeared a few minutes later looking ravishing in a golden cocktail dress. 'Almost time to go,' she announced, unfastening Ruth's arms. 'Now, when you sit down, lift the skirt clear so your skin is on the seat. Do it now and show me.'

Ruth lowered herself onto a chair, having to bend forward to lift the skirt. Once seated she instinctively parted her legs, and Elsa clucked approvingly.

The sound of a vehicle drawing into the yard coincided with Morgan's appearance, and they all stepped outside.

Ruth saw the shape of Cooper's taxi in the twilight. Cooper himself was holding the rear door open, leering at her, and she averted her eyes. A conventional trepidation made her skin crawl, but the awful fascination of the man wound up her desires even more. The thought of his huge penis driving into her made her shudder inwardly even as between her thighs a curious longing began smouldering.

Elsa released Ruth's arms and ordered her to enter the taxi after Morgan, who indicated the strange fitting placed against the partition. 'Kneel there,' he said.

Two padded troughs placed on the floor were fronted by a short pedestal with a padded top, and near the base sprouted a bar with handgrips. Ruth lowered herself gingerly, sliding her knees to the front of the troughs, which were set well apart. There were sockets for her feet, and the padded top was contoured to support her shoulders, with an indentation for her chin that relieved any strain on her neck. Her hands fell naturally onto the grips, which she discovered were twistable.

As soon as she was settled, Elsa flicked a switch on the pedestal. A soft humming started up, accompanied by a gentle hissing sound. Next she drew out a little rubber cup attached to flexible tubing, and pulled it towards Ruth's left breast. As it came close, Ruth felt herself go cold all over as air rushed over her skin. Then with a plopping sound her nipple was sucked into the cup and a wonderful sensation bloomed from her sensitive bud all through her bosom, making her whole chest pulse with delight. A second swift suction captured her other nipple, treating her to double the joy. The suction was not steady but came in regular pulses that dragged delightfully on her teats.

'The design is adapted from dairy equipment,' Morgan whispered in her ear. 'If we put you on this often enough, you'd start lactating. Twist the handles.'

Ruth tentatively turned the grips. At once the sucking pulses quickened. The farther she turned the handles the faster the cups sucked on her nipples, and at maximum speed it was like having a vibrator clamped on her teats. She fought the temptation to go for orgasm and eased back, losing herself in the soft, easy delight of gentle and continuous stimulation.

So diverted was she by the attachments on her nipples that she gave no thought to the way her posture left her exposed until Elsa folded her skirt up over her waist. With her shoulders dipped, her naked bottom was thrust high, pushing her sex out, which was made even more accessible by her parted thighs. Her vulnerability was further demonstrated by the sudden insertion of a finger deep into her vagina. She gasped and reflexively twisted the handgrips. Assaulted at both ends she cried out. A sharp smack on her thigh evoked a second cry, and a second smack. Her smarting skin began to burn, and as the warmth spread she felt it infuse the tender membranes encircling the probing finger. Instinctively she clamped it firmly with her vaginal muscles, and it felt so good she nearly climaxed.

Her pleasure escalated throughout the journey as Elsa and Morgan probed and teased every fold of her body while the machine sucked relentlessly at her breasts. She was only dimly aware of the taxi's motion, and hardly noticed when it stopped. Then Elsa leaned forward and killed the switch. The suction cups dropped away from her breasts, and she felt oddly naked now that all contact was withdrawn from her body.

Morgan slapped her lightly on the rump. 'Out you get now,' he instructed. 'That delectable fanny will see plenty of action later, and Cooper wants his fare.'

Ruth disentangled herself from the wonderful machine and stumbled out of the taxi. The pavement hit her heels and she recognised the Alpine profile of Judy's home. There were lots of people there already, judging by the number of parked cars on the drive, and the cool night air made her shiver.

'Shall we settle the account now?' Elsa asked Cooper.

He shook his head. 'I'll wait for later,' he declined. 'You'll want me for the return journey as well, I take it?'

Morgan answered in the affirmative, and fastened Ruth's arms to her corset as she trembled in anticipation.

Chapter Eight

Judy and Nick emerged from the house to welcome them. 'Do you understand your position here?' Ruth's male host enquired, and she nodded.

'While you are wearing the ringed bracelet you cannot decline to participate in any activity,' he elaborated. 'If you change your mind about your role as a slave, you must find one of us and ask to be released. The release word is *Houdini*.'

Ruth nodded again.

'Excellent,' he said, smiling indulgently. 'Listen carefully to every instruction, and always be obedient. Now go and mingle, and enjoy yourself.'

Elsa took charge, ushering Ruth to the rear of the house.

She glanced around her excitedly. There were perhaps twenty-five people outside in the grounds. Some were dancing, others were relaxing on loungers, and a few were cavorting noisily in the lake. Then they reached the coach house where she saw a cold buffet and an impressive selection of wine and liquor set out on tables.

'You may help yourself at any time,' Elsa explained. 'But don't get drunk, and commands take precedence over everything.' She released Ruth's arms.

Just then something was happening, arresting the attention of the crowd, and both women turned towards the source of the disturbance.

Walking across the lawn was a man dressed entirely in black. He was an imposing figure, mature and yet possessed of a youthful aura. He was tall and powerfully built, and his clothes clung tightly to his firm body. In his hand was a silver chain, the other end of which was clipped to a clit ring adorning the vulva of an incredibly beautiful woman. Slender and curvaceous, the slave walked with cat-like elegance, her head held proudly high but her eyes downcast, and she was totally naked. Apart from the genital piercing and her slave bracelet, she was devoid of any covering, including hair. Even her head was shaved clean.

Ruth's mouth went dry. She held her breath, staring in fascination, and then asked Elsa in an eager whisper, 'Who are they?'

'Conrad and his principle slave, Zelda,' her friend replied, a note of respect in her voice.

'*Principle* slave?' Ruth gasped. 'What do you mean?'

'Conrad collects slaves the way some men collect paintings. Zelda was his first slave, and she is his most perfect. She is totally devoted to him. But I'll explain more later.'

Ruth returned her attention to Conrad, staring at him, mesmerised by his presence. He radiated a charisma that invaded her soul. Then she considered Zelda, pondering enviously at the bonds linking this beautiful master with his gorgeous slave. Everything about her physical appearance was superb, and her demeanour was at once placid and secure.

Elsa handed Ruth a drink, which she sipped gratefully. Then she felt a hand on her arm, and fingers playing suggestively with the silver chain at her wrist. Turning, she found an elegant woman standing beside her.

'You're Ruth, I believe,' the woman said. 'Tell me, Ruth, do you lick pussy?'

Taken aback by the forthright question, she hesitated to respond. The woman had a handsome face and a fine figure clad in an expensive black cocktail dress, and her ruby necklace sparkled with inner fire where it caught the light. 'Um, of course,' she eventually stammered, Nick's warning that she had to obey all commands echoing in her brain.

'How lovely.' The woman smiled. 'Then you shall. Come with me.'

Ruth set down her unfinished drink and allowed herself to be led away. They walked across the lawn to a little arbour cut into the edge of the woodland.

'I'm Olivia,' the woman introduced herself. 'And that is my husband, John.' She indicated a couple fucking furiously on a bench. 'He'll join us shortly.' She settled down on another bench. 'What I want you to do is make me feel nice until John arrives. Then I shall want you to bring me off with your tongue while he screws you from behind. And I want us all to come together. Can you do that for me, Ruth?'

'I, um, I'll try my very best, mistress.' The appellation came naturally, and made her feel strangely secure as she knelt between Olivia's feet.

The woman lifted her skirt, revealing a pair of creamy thighs and a delightfully neat sex crowned by a thick dark bush. 'Panties are a superfluous affectation at parties such as this,' she remarked.

Ruth leaned towards the altar of sex, and a wave of delicate perfume wafted into her nostrils, the subtle fragrance overwhelmed by the more potent odour of femininity as she came closer to the rich dark junction. Olivia had a plump labia, quite charming to look at and delightful to touch, as Ruth soon discovered. She ran the tip of her tongue delicately up the tempting groove, and was rewarded by a profound shiver of excitement passing through Olivia's body. Ruth repeated the action, pressing more firmly, parting the thick lips and feeling the heat beneath the smoothness. Three more long caresses from her tongue, and she drew back to stroke the plumpness with her fingertips. She was intrigued by the vision of the woman's outer labia slowly peeling back to permit a narrow pink crest to peep through that looked smooth as satin, an impression Ruth's probing tongue confirmed as Olivia crooned quietly. There was no rush, and although her own pussy was heated and craving for attention, she was able to contain herself and hold her mistress at a constant level of pleasure.

It came as a surprise to feel a hand clamp firmly over her vulva, and the thrill transmitted itself through her active tongue into Olivia's responsive sex.

'A little higher and a little wider will grant Olivia the kicks she covets,' said a man's cultured voice.

Ruth paused in her pleasurable task, and would have turned to look at the source of the voice but for Olivia grabbing her hair. 'Oh no you don't,' she groaned. 'Keep at it, Ruth. Don't you dare leave me now.'

Her mouth was forced back into the hot and silky folds, and she responded to their moist softness instantly, her tongue vigorously probing this most inviting place.

Olivia squirmed, moaning in pleasure at the lithe intrusion.

The hand cupping Ruth's crotch, a broad hand, lifted her bodily into the desired position, and the pressure upon her highly charged tissue made her juices flood. She clutched Olivia's thighs as two fingers inserted themselves into her pussy, and her legs were eased wide apart. The intrusion caused her to buck and twist her hips, but she kept her tongue working desperately, and felt the tension rising within Olivia in response. There was a moment of emptiness when the fingers withdrew, and then a sensation of being deliciously pulled apart as something hot and throbbing filled her void. She pushed back on what she thought must be the biggest cock in the world. It filled her until she thought she would scream, and she tried to accommodate it by stretching her abdominal muscles. Wedged between a man and a woman, she felt herself drowning helplessly in sex. She gladly surrendered to the inevitable, sinking into a sea of pleasure as she worked at the lovely pussy pressed against her face and rode the huge erection ploughing her from behind. Time lost all meaning as she surged up and down on a violent, saturating ocean of pleasure, and her orgasm broke seconds before the others' did. She pitched into its frenzy, rolling from one ecstatic peak to another, oblivious to the intensity of her partners' conclusions.

As the silent sensual echoes faded Ruth collapsed into a heap on the floor, sliding off John's rampant shaft. The corset clamping her ribs caused her breathing to be heavy and laboured, and her breasts heaved as she gulped down air.

'Are you all right?' Olivia asked solicitously, her voice cracking slightly with lingering emotion.

'Yes,' she gasped. 'I just need to catch my breath…'

'Here, drink this.'

Ruth looked up at the figure towering above her. He was handsome and naked, his impressive cock still jutting rigidly from his crotch. He held a glass of clear liquid to her lips and she sipped it, recognising the bittersweet taste of a gin and tonic. 'Did I please you, mistress?' she asked woozily.

'Certainly,' Olivia replied. 'And I think we may require your services again later this evening,'

Once Ruth had recovered she was escorted back to the coach house, where Elsa joined her. 'Have you just taken big John?' she asked mischievously.

'Yes,' Ruth confirmed, still somewhat breathlessly, 'and Olivia, too.'

'Hmm, knowing John, I expect you're feeling a bit sore now, but you'll soon recover,' she said, with a knowing twinkle in her eye. 'Have something to eat. There's a show in a couple of minutes which will give you a little respite.'

'A show?' Ruth asked.

'You'll see.'

Ruth edged up to the buffet. Quite a number of the guests were naked, some still wet from the lake, but no one seemed in the least bit self-conscious. Most of the women were topless, and Ruth began to feel overdressed. Then she saw another girl wearing a linked bracelet like hers and moved towards her.

At that moment the music issuing from the sound system changed, the mainstream rock-n-roll giving way to an elemental rhythm played at a slightly lower volume. Then a collective sigh of admiration focused attention towards the makeshift arena, where Conrad was leading his acolyte forward. Zelda followed him, still tethered and proudly subservient, carrying a coil of rope. No words were spoken. He seemed to be controlling the young woman by thought alone as she stopped precisely where a double rope hung from a roof beam. She bent to place her burden on the floor, her supple body gleaming beneath a battery of lights trained on the central spot where she stood. Then she straightened up again and extended her arms.

Conrad snapped handcuffs on her wrist, and with a rapid movement hooked the dangling ropes to the cuffs. From above came a humming sound as the ropes hauled

Zelda's arms high above her head, the action lifting her breasts and emphasising the large, dark nipples. He then bent down, drawing her legs apart, and secured her ankles with loops of chain fixed to rings set in the floor.

Ruth imagined the touch of steel and the sense of helplessness imposed by restraint, and felt her stomach churn with that intoxicating blend of desire and fear. She sensed someone close behind her, and turned to see Morgan. He was naked, and his arms slipped around her, his hands gripping her exposed breasts. He drew her backwards, lowering himself into a chair and pulling her down onto his lap. She straddled him as he tore away her tiny skirt, and she instinctively reached between her thighs for him. His erection sprang naturally into her hand, hard and warm, his skin tight and silky. She began to caress him while he played with her nipples, but she could not take her eyes off the trussed girl.

Conrad was continuing to bind his slave. One end of a length of rope had been looped twice around her waist, drawn tight and secured with an efficient knot over her belly. Then the end was passed between her legs and worked deep into her cleft before continuing up her back to be secured under the waist loop. Conrad then pulled sharply on it and Ruth saw Zelda's body go rigid as the slender rope bisected her vulva, parting her labia and digging into her pussy. Not one flicker of emotion crossed the placid face of the slave, however, though her discomfort must have been intense. So deeply buried was the rope that it seemed to vanish, as if it was threaded straight through her body.

Conrad continued to truss the helpless girl. The rope was passed around her chest just under her breasts and fastened behind her. Then a second loop passed just above her nipples, compressing her breasts and forcing her teats into prominence. Then her arms were lowered and the handcuffs removed. The suspension rope was divided and hooked onto her waist rope, front and back, and held clear of her face by a spreader bar positioned above her head. Her arms were pulled back and bound tightly from elbow to wrist, and finally the overhead cables were raised until her feet were barely in contact with the floor.

A hypnotic trance held Ruth captive as she realised that the greater part of Zelda's weight was being carried on the rope buried in her pussy, slicing into her delicate inner lips and crushing her clitoris. The thought ignited a flame in her own crotch, and she seeped eager juice onto Morgan's hand as he slipped it down between her thighs to probe her moistness. A tension gripped the whole room and time seemed to stand still.

Ruth tore her eyes away from the spectacle for a moment. Elsa and Judy were playing with Nick, and near them was a man she recognised. She lingered on his face, puzzling over why it was so familiar, and then suddenly she recognised Jack Thorpe, the arrogant man from the gas station. He had a girl in his grasp, a pretty dark-haired thing. She was naked except for an elaborate harness of leather straps and the silver bracelet and ring on her right hand. Ruth's heart seemed to miss a beat, and what she had experienced on that fateful morning suddenly made sense as a passionate longing sprouted inside her.

Movement caught her attention and she returned her gaze to Zelda and her master. Conrad held a whip, a short, vicious-looking black whip that trailed at his feet. His position left no doubt about his intentions, or his target, and Ruth's mouth went dry. She gripped the rock-hard penis in her hand more tightly and Morgan grunted, pressing his thumb into her clitoris. The wave of pleasure was almost painful, but she hardly noticed it as she watched Conrad raise the whip. It curled back and lashed down, and the crack of leather on flesh filled the room. Zelda's body bent like a bow beneath the impact, and she screamed as the whole gathering gasped in awe. A vivid white welt was cut across the slave's perfect bottom, that suffused with blood as everyone watched.

'Ah…' The collective gasp was one of approval.

Zelda was biting her lip, her head thrown back and her eyes closed, and Ruth tried to imagine the shock and pain as the thin leather cut into her lovely, flawless skin. Conrad raised the whip again and Ruth closed her eyes to blot out the sight, but prurient curiosity forced them open again as she heard the weapon's sinister whistle. The lash was too fast to be seen, but she could predict its course and she saw the impact curling around the helpless girl, followed a fraction of a second later by the deadly cracking sound and Zelda's cry of pain. The evil black tongue seemed to lick the slave as it slid from her body, and a white welt formed across the earlier one, which was now blazing vividly.

Conrad traced her marks with his fingertips as Zelda trembled. Then again the whip was raised, and a third blow delivered, followed by a fourth. More followed that, and Ruth abandoned sympathy; the emotion that gripped her now was much more like envy as she watched the beautiful slave being whipped by her master.

Conrad shifted his position, and the next two strokes landed across the front of Zelda's thighs, so precisely placed that she seemed to have red bands tattooed across her legs. Her face was contorted with agony, but the underlying serenity of her expression remained. As her master repositioned himself her eyes followed him, alive and shining with love. She seemed to be imploring him not for clemency but for greater affliction. The whip rose high, slicing through the air as it sped down to lay its harsh caress on her lovely body. The crack was hardly audible, but her scream rent the room, and Ruth stared in awe as the white band just above Zelda's nipples began to turn red. Her hand was jerking at Morgan's erection as she ground herself against his thumb. Her need for an orgasm was extreme, and she could feel Morgan's pleasure building as she pumped him feverishly. He pulled back, pushing her up away from him, and tears of frustration welled in her eyes. But then he pulled her back down, and she whimpered in triumph as he drove it into her with such force that her orgasm immediately broke around him.

When she could focus again, Zelda was being taken down. Conrad was unwinding the ropes with amazing speed and tenderness, and as soon as her hands were free his slave took his head in her hands and kissed him passionately. When the last rope fell clear she took his hand and led him across the room to a whipping stool. She lay back across it, spreading her legs and lifting her arms in welcome as he began removing his clothing.

Ruth, still bemused by the intensity of her own experience, viewed the girl with respect, wonder, curiosity and empathy. She gazed in admiration at the angry red welts marring those lovely thighs and breasts. Then Conrad closed in on his slave, and his impressive erection sank into her striped lusciousness. The room was full, but they were in a world of their own.

Ruth's thoughts were tumbling in disarray. Whereas she was a mere amateur playing with forbidden fruit, Zelda possessed total commitment. She looked around her, and saw Judy being possessed by two men at once. One man was lying beneath her while the other man fucked her mouth. Then she watched Elsa giving a blowjob for a moment, before Morgan released her and another couple intent on a threesome seized her. Then she was made to take one of the male guests in a number of different positions.

There was a short respite while a pretty slave demonstrated her skill at picking up objects with her vagina, and then Ruth was engaged yet again. This time she had to fuck a man while his wife rode the shaggy horse, and afterwards she tottered back towards the buffet, desperate for nourishment. She was perspiring, her hair was dishevelled and she had a raging thirst. She helped herself to a glass of lime and lemon juice, and as she drank deeply, a vision of loveliness appeared before her.

Ruth surveyed the girl with envy. She was naked and had a perfect body covered by amazingly flawless skin. Her eyes were brown, deep dark pools devoid of empathy as they regarded Ruth with disdain.

'Kneel down and suck my tits,' the girl commanded, and Ruth found herself obediently sinking to her knees. The posture brought her face to just below the girl's breasts, and instinct took control. She reached up a little and took a firm nipple in her mouth, and sucked it avidly. It was succulent, smooth and firm, and desire began to churn in her tummy.

'Now this one,' the girl snapped, pulling free and presenting her other breast. 'And put two fingers inside me while you do it.'

Ruth invaded the silky labia, probing the plumpness at its peak. It was so soft and warm and moist…

The girl sighed and squirmed as Ruth explored her secret depths, and then she said sharply, 'That's enough for now. Come with me, my brother wants to screw you. I think you'll satisfy him.' Without waiting for a response she seized Ruth's hand and pulled her towards the whipping stool.

Ruth looked around, wondering who was brother to this dominant creature, and standing beside the stool, watching her closely, she saw Jack Thorpe. The girl pulled her roughly over the stool and began fastening her wrists to the uprights.

'So, we meet again, Miss Parrish,' Jack said, smiling. 'You're a deep one, for sure. Is Karly treating you respectfully?'

'Yes, sir,' Ruth replied cautiously.

He laughed. 'Then it will be the first time she has. Karly does not respect slaves. Do you, princess?'

'No,' the beauty snorted. 'They're only toys, after all.' She was bending to secure Ruth's legs, and she jerked viciously at the strap as if to emphasise her contempt.

Ruth felt inexplicably aroused by the humiliation.

Karly straightened up. 'Now listen, slave, I want your tongue in my cunt, and I want to feel it. If I don't it will be the worse for you. Ignore what he's doing to your back end and give me something to remember.' With that she spun around and bent over, clasping her ankles. Her pussy was every bit as beautiful as Ruth had imagined it would be. Her pubic hair was short and curly, and above it, centred in the lovely space between her bottom cheeks, a tight little anus winked out at her. Karly backed up, and Ruth poked her tongue into the gorgeous vulva, parting the outer lips to comb the delicate innermost folds of flesh as she drank greedily of the abundant juices. Karly was keen, pushing back and twisting herself to provoke deeper and longer contact. And as Ruth tried desperately to please the girl, she was pierced by a demanding penis that drove into her from behind, stretching and filling her.

'Oh, *yes*,' Ruth cried, her vagina hungrily gripping the

beautiful intruder.

'You stopped!' Karly accused, so Ruth applied herself to the girl's pussy with greater effort, but it was difficult to ignore the marvellous sensations being coaxed from her own stuffed sex. Trussed as she was, she could not use her body to respond to the pleasurable assault, so she tried to compensate by giving everything to the girl before her. Soon her tongue was aching from the effort.

Suddenly Karly stepped away, straightened up and spun around in one movement. 'It's no good, the slut's just not trying,' she snapped. 'She's too busy thinking about what's happening in her cunt to give me any pleasure. She needs a proper lesson to teach her some manners.'

Ruth felt tears welling in her eyes. 'That's not true,' she blurted, 'I was doing my best!'

'Enough!' Karly pushed Ruth's head down. 'No one asked you to speak.'

Ruth coughed and spluttered as Jack drove himself deep inside her, pushing his groin against her bottom and holding himself there. 'A spanking, do you think?' he asked.

'Yes, a really hard one,' his sister agreed.

Ruth's stomach turned. She had spent hours fantasising over this moment, imagining all sorts of light-hearted, almost romantic scenarios in which Elsa and Morgan initiated her into the mysteries of corporal punishment. But this was quite different; this pair meant to hurt her. Already humiliated, she was to be degraded as well. The urge to abdicate her role as a slave was strong, and then she caught sight of Elsa in the front line of the audience gathering around them. The thought that this might be a set-up flashed across her mind, and helped calm her turmoil somewhat. This was not the time to have an attack of the nerves.

Jack pulled out of her, leaving her feeling er

exposed. She heard the buzz of speculation surrounding her without listening to it, trying to close her mind to everything except her determination not to capitulate. But it was impossible to concentrate when Jack touched her, caressing her buttocks. His finger raked her cleft, and then prodded her anus, not very gently. She jerked and stiffened, tightening the ropes around her as she struggled futilely against them.

'Wonderful,' he murmured.

An impact exploded against her taut skin, and she cried out as a searing pain burned through her flesh. The smacking blow had landed on the fleshiest part of her right buttock. The biting sting turned to heat, penetrating the deeper layers of her muscle as it spread downward and outward. But before she could fully adjust to this new sensation there came a second shock equal to the first, this time on her left cheek, and again she cried out.

There was no respite. Jack landed one blow after another across her cheeks with his open palm, spreading the heat over the whole of her tender hemispheres. Yet after the first few smacks the shock lessened, and as the heat burned deeper the hurt began to dull, replaced by a pure yet beguiling pain that made her pussy feel warm in a totally new way.

'Four more!' Karly's command echoed eerily through Ruth's trance-veiled mind. 'Give her four hard ones right on her cunt.'

Before Ruth could think what this meant the first of the four blows had landed, and the shock was beyond description. She thought she must surely die as pain ripped through her most sensitive place. Then suddenly her torment turned to lust and, amazingly enough, she was craving more of the terrible torture. Three more explosive smacks landed squarely on her labia, provoking her clitoris into a frenzy of feeling. A moment of total silence enveloped her as the fire in her crotch blazed, consuming her whole being. Then, as though she was surfacing from a deep dive, noise enveloped her again and she opened her eyes. Karly was offering up her pussy again, and she extended her tongue to meet the sweet gift of the other girl's moist labia.

'Now make me come,' Karly ordered, 'or you'll get more of the same.'

Ruth's tongue probed the succulent folds as she felt a cockhead brush over the searing surface of her bottom. She almost screamed beneath its touch, but steeling herself, she licked and sucked at Karly's juicy delights. The cock was exploring, moving purposefully up, and anticipation fed her imagination as the smooth tip traced its way up her valley to hover over her anus. She struggled against her bindings, grimly seeking to thrust herself up in welcome. She flexed and stretched as the hot tip pushed against her, pressing hard. She felt the reflex resistance building in her sphincter, and then her inner muscles relaxed as the bulbous tip drove in through her ring. She thought she was splitting as the pain of the penetration merged with the echoing agony of her freshly spanked bottom, and in that moment she was transported to another dimension of ecstasy as the cock sank deep and she was filled to the brim.

Ruth drove her tongue deep into the luscious young vulva against her face as she felt a fingertip touch her clitoris. The orgasm that instantly burst through her was immense, plunging her into a maze of joy. She had crossed the threshold to this paradise just once before and ever since then had ached to rediscover the entrance, and now, at last, it was found. And on the tip of her tongue, another climax was vigorously echoing her own spiralling joy.

Chapter Nine

It was in the early hours of the morning that the party finally broke up, leaving Ruth dishevelled and weary, and mentally shocked by her own lascivious behaviour even as a strange peace filled her soul. She had been penetrated in every conceivable manner, and as to how often, she had lost count.

In the taxi she was thankful to be put back in a kneeling position, which was preferable to sitting on her smarting bottom, and she gladly submitted to the suction cups' seductive pleasures while Elsa and Morgan gently caressed her.

Back at the farm, Cooper finally claimed his dues. She spread herself across the bonnet of the car, parting her legs with exhausted enthusiasm. She was ready for another truly vigorous fuck, and she had no qualms now about taking his huge erection into her well-honed pussy. His penis thrust swiftly back and forth inside her, raising her steadily to yet another dazzling climax, after which she slumped over the car, embracing it dreamily.

'That was priceless,' Cooper commented, as he straightened his clothing.

Elsa helped Ruth up. 'Well done,' she said. 'That's the first time I've ever heard Cooper offer any sort of praise. Now it's bed for you. Have a shower, then sleep tight and don't get up until you're ready.'

'So, how did you enjoy being a sex slave, Ruth?' Judy asked. They were eating brunch on Elsa's patio. Ruth had not risen until midday, shortly before Nick and Judy arrived. After the previous hectic evening, they all felt comfortably lazy.

'It was good,' Ruth replied demurely, a bit embarrassed by her behaviour in the light of day. 'I really liked it.'

'Enough to do it again?' Judy demanded gently.

'Oh yes, although I'm not sure I'd want to go as far as Zelda did. Can you tell me more about Conrad?'

'You'll meet him later,' Elsa announced. 'He's invited to dinner this evening.'

'He's one of our colourful local characters,' Nick elaborated. 'He has numerous business interests, all very profitable. His full name is Conrad Hesseltine, but he likes to be known as Conrad Stein, or simply Conrad. It's pure affectation, really.'

'Zelda seems devoted to him,' Ruth observed with that curious touch of envy she experienced the previous night watching the master and his slave together.

'*Devoted* is an understatement,' Judy commented wryly. 'Zelda is a fanatic submissive. She uses Conrad just as surely as he uses her. We've known her for years. In fact, Ruth, you remind me so much of Zelda when she was still discovering her preferences.'

Ruth struggled to mask her feelings, not wanting to confirm Judy's suspicions until she was certain of them herself. Observing Zelda had affected her deeply, and the current conversation was striking vibrant chords inside her.

'Hey, that reminds me, we haven't seen the result this morning,' Judy declared. 'Come on, Ruth, show us.'

Ruth rose shyly from her seat and turned, lifting her shift. She knew from inspecting herself in the bathroom mirror that there was a residual pinkness across her bottom. More directly, she could feel it each time she sat down. It made her feel quite proud.

'It suits you,' Judy said. 'You have such a pretty bottom. It just cries out for decoration.'

Ruth cautiously resumed her seat. 'The first smack was hell. The second wasn't much better, but after a few more the pain diminished, and I actually began wanting to be spanked and hurt.' She looked at Elsa. 'You set that little scene up, didn't you? I had expected it would be you or Morgan who spanked me the first time.'

'We thought it would add a little extra spice if you were humiliated by a stranger,' Elsa explained.

'Sometimes I think you are simply evil, Elsa Fredericks. That girl was terrifying, and as for her brother…'

'Karly is only a Thorpe by adoption,' Elsa disclosed. 'Actually, she's Conrad's daughter.'

Ruth gasped. 'Now *that* I can believe, and more. She's malevolent.'

'There was a student took a summer job in Conrad's shop eighteen summers ago. They had an affair, and the naïve girl thought it was sissy to take precautions. Conrad arranged for the baby to be adopted by his elder sister, Jack Thorpe's mother. It was all very amicable. Conrad and the mother really care for each other, although Conrad would never marry. Karly lives with her mother for half the year in Martinique. She's rather spoiled. And if you've any more questions about Conrad, you can ask him yourself over dinner.'

Ruth shivered in anticipation.

'But now we've the whole afternoon ahead of us.' Elsa changed the subject. 'Do you want to have some time alone, or would you like to play?'

'I'd like to be in role again,' Ruth said at once.

Judy reflected. 'I've always thought a naked girl getting dirty while doing heavy manual work is a real turn-on.

And if she has to stop to be fucked once in a while, it makes for really earthy eroticism.'

Elsa looked enquiringly at Morgan.

'The load of logs that was delivered last week needs to be stacked for the winter,' he said. 'That should keep her busy for a couple of hours.'

Judy clapped her hands. 'Excellent!' she squealed excitedly. 'I shall enjoy this immensely.'

Ruth felt her heart leap as the now familiar knotting took hold of her belly.

'So strip,' Elsa snapped, assuming command.

Ruth had momentary misgivings. Entrenched inhibitions had first to be quelled, but the moment she felt the air on her naked skin, all her doubt vanished. The lure of pleasure was, as usual, defeating her reserve, and she was coming to accept her natural wantonness as a mysterious form of innocence.

Elsa sent her indoors to put on some shoes, and upon her return provided her with working gloves. She then led her across the yard to where a heap of logs had been tipped. The pile was at least three metres across and half as high. She was given a wheelbarrow, and shown where to stack the wood against the house. Before she could begin, however, she had to move chairs out into the yard so Judy, Nick, Morgan and Elsa could all watch her in comfort.

She was soon perspiring under the hot sun and drinking freely of the iced water provided. The outer logs were dry and dusty, while those within the pile were damp and covered with lichen. The dust clung to her moist body, and the damp greenery smeared her skin. In no time at all she was filthy, and growing increasingly randy. Piling logs on the barrow could not be done without stooping, so there was no way to avoid an erotic display. Therefore, she was not surprised when, after delivering the third load, she returned to find Nick waiting beside the heap.

'Bend over and touch your toes,' he commanded.

She obeyed instantly, parting her legs to present her pussy to the seated trio.

'Isn't she delightful?' Judy crooned. 'That lovely spanked bottom, and the prettiest labia I've seen in years, not to mention that perfect little bottom hole. Which will you choose, Nick?'

Ruth gave a delighted little wiggle of her hips, all modesty abandoned.

Nick did not reply immediately, taking his time to examine her closely. 'I think I'll use the moist one first and reserve her bottom for later.' He discarded his cotton shorts and presented his stiff cock at Ruth's wet threshold. She wriggled back upon him to be rewarded by the wonderful feeling of his hot weapon sliding smoothly into her vagina. She shuffled her feet, adjusting her posture to secure maximum penetration as he took hold of her waist, and began squeezing and milking his thickness as he eased in and out with a slow, smooth rhythm.

She sighed. This was wonderful! Being firmly shagged in the open air as a respite from work was one of the nicest scenarios she had ever experienced.

Nick began building his rhythm, moving faster and harder until she thought she must faint from the pure pleasure of his throbbing erection sliding smoothly in and out of her eager slot. Being vigorously fucked was the best thing a girl could experience and her mind began to drift, slipping into a hazy dream state where all consciousness was centred between her legs. Then the dream climaxed and she floated from peak to peak as a succession of minor orgasms possessed her.

Nick slowed down, and then stopped. Very deliberately

he disengaged his erection from her clinging pussy, and as the rim of his knob popped free, Ruth experienced yet again the forlorn emptiness. He smacked her bottom. 'If you want some more,' he said sharply, 'go earn it.'

Ruth thought there had never been a more pleasant way of doing work. Neither Nick nor Morgan allowed themselves to ejaculate, and she suspected a purpose lay behind this control, but it was not revealed until the stack was removed. The logs had been tipped on bare earth, and now all that remained was a lake of glutinous mud covered by broken bark and twigs. She was set to clear the biggest pieces of debris and the mud got everywhere, covering her hands and feet and splattering into her hair.

'You look like a scarecrow,' Elsa commented. 'But you've earned your reward, so lie down and see what Santa brings.'

Ruth spread herself on the ground, laughing as she rolled in the soft, sticky ooze. Then a shadow fell across her; it was Nick coming to kneel between her legs. She opened to him, and directly above her face she saw Elsa crouching and extended her tongue, instinctively searching for the juicy bloom being offered to her mouth as Nick's erection speared her. He began thrusting as she hooked her legs around him, and heedless of the rough ground beneath her, she rode him energetically while her tongue lapped and licked at Elsa's fragrant feast. Her dominant friend began playing with her nipples, and by raising her arms she was able to reciprocate. Ruth was blissfully lost in a perfect, all-consuming world of pure delight, taking and giving intense stimulation with wholehearted passion and generosity.

If she was dirty before, then Ruth was decidedly filthy after Elsa and Nick's tandem shagging.

'You dirty little slut,' Elsa teased. 'Wash yourself off before you go into my house.'

Ruth obediently started to cast around for the nearest tap, when the jet of water hit her with surprising force, drenching her as Morgan, holding the hose, shouted with laughter. He walked around her, making her take the full force on her belly and breasts. The water played over her body, sluicing away the mud and dirt as she turned around and presented her bottom to the jetting stream, revelling in the hard feel of it between her thighs. Then she sank down onto her hands and knees and bared her sex to the scourging torrent. It hit her fair and square and its operator, rising to the invitation, throttled the flow to its sharpest. Ruth felt herself forced open as the cold torrent drilled her. 'Oh yes! Oh yes!' she cried in shameless ecstasy.

The hosing continued for some time, after which Elsa ran forward carrying a towel to swathe her in. Securely wrapped, she was then led to a proper, warm shower.

A short while later, naked and glowing with good health, Ruth was once more seated on the patio sipping a drink.

'Did our party come up to your expectations, Ruth?' Judy picked up the conversation they had been enjoying before.

'It exceeded all my expectations, although, honestly, I didn't know *what* to expect. It was much more than I imagined, though. I was a strictly once-a-night girl until Elsa revived my appetite, but even my recent excesses were nothing compared to last night. I'm amazed at my own capacity.'

'It was more than just the number of blokes you took though, wasn't it?' Elsa contributed to the pleasant interrogation with an astute observation.

'Why, yes…' Ruth admitted, thinking about it. 'I get a

real buzz out of being restrained. The spanking was fantastic too. I was scared stiff, but afterwards I felt so good, and so strangely pure. And the humiliation seemed to sharpen the experience. This weekend has opened up whole new doors for me. I think... I think I'd really like to discover what it's like to be a proper sex slave like Zelda.'

'You really mean that?' Nick asked with quiet intensity.

Ruth nodded. 'Last night was a revelation. If I could afford it, I'd stop working and find someone to take me on as his fulltime slave.'

'Being a fulltime slave doesn't necessarily involve that kind of commitment,' Judy pointed out. 'Zelda has a career as well as a husband and two children.'

'But I thought you said Conrad had never married?'

'Nor did he. Zelda is Conrad's slave, not his partner. I admit, it's not a conventional arrangement, but Zelda's husband fully approves of his wife's status. He even encourages it.'

'That's amazing... I was thinking, it would be much easier if I lived up here,' Ruth mused out loud. 'If only there was some way to preserve my career and be close to the action at the same time.'

Morgan's face lit up. 'I know of a smart little business in York,' he said. 'There's a gallery and an associated shop that sells fine art prints. Both properties are just yards apart on the main tourist trail. The owners are looking for a long-term partner who would develop the gallery side and eventually buy the controlling share. It would be just the thing for you, and right on our doorstep, so to speak.'

'How much would they want?' Ruth asked eagerly. The proposition was seriously tempting.

Morgan mentioned a figure, and her excitement died reluctantly. 'No way, I can't afford that,' she said, feeling instantly deflated. 'Even if I sold everything I own, I couldn't come anywhere near that amount. Thanks for the suggestion, but I guess I'll just have to keep commuting.'

'Gracious, look at the time,' Elsa started. 'I must attend to dinner, and we'd better get our glad rags on. You'll find something in the wardrobe, Ruth.'

Appetising aromas were floating from the kitchen by the time Conrad arrived. Casually dressed in a blue corduroy jacket with black trousers he seemed much less intimidating this evening, until Ruth looked up into his eyes. Gazing into those intense black pupils surrounded by dark chocolate-coloured irises was like gazing into infinity itself, and she instinctively averted her gaze. Seated as she was on Elsa's sofa, the action brought her eyes level with his groin, and she found herself admiring the healthy bulge in his trousers.

Conrad took her hand, and kissed it gallantry. 'Delighted to meet you, Ruth,' he said. 'It is a privilege to formally make your acquaintance.' He spoke smoothly, in a cultured voice with only faint, lingering traces of his origins.

She lifted her eyes to his again, but was careful to avoid direct contact with them. Then her heart jumped in her breast as over his shoulder she saw Jack Thorpe enter the room.

'I think you've already met my nephew.' Conrad's statement was devoid of any overtones, but Ruth felt herself burning with shame as Jack took her hand. It was hard to square this excessive formality with the events of the previous night, when his cock had been buried in her bottom. Jack responded politely to the introduction, only a mere spark of interest in his eyes denoting any recollection of their intimate encounter.

The normality of the scene was oddly disturbing to Ruth. Elsa and Morgan handed round aperitifs as Jack made conversation about her Beetle while the whole time she relived the intense emotions aroused by being spanked and buggered in public. Her mouth grew dry despite the wine she was sipping as she tried to get a handle on the base and perverse desires possessing her.

At dinner, Conrad was seated at the head of the table with Ruth on his left. Jack sat opposite her, and meeting his gaze was disconcerting as she toyed with her food. Her hunger lay deeper than her tummy; it was smouldering between her thighs and she was ready to advertise it. She felt no shame, only astonishment at her own increasingly brazen appetites.

Conrad was an accomplished listener. Ruth found herself readily opening up to him, and in a very short time he had extracted a concise life history from her. He proved to be very knowledgeable about painting and knew of Lewis by reputation.

'So you and he will be officiating at the Quincy sale on Friday? That's very interesting.'

'We start preparing Broughton tomorrow,' she heard herself say eagerly. 'It should take most of Tuesday as well.'

'Will you be staying in the district until the sale?' Conrad enquired.

'Unfortunately no, we both have to be in London on Wednesday.'

'That is unfortunate, as I would very much like to show you around Highmoor House. It has some special features that will certainly appeal to you, and I would value your opinion on my modest collection of landscapes. I suppose there is no possibility of you joining me for dinner tomorrow evening?'

Ruth hesitated. The prospect of being alone with this man was immensely appealing. She was increasingly drawn to him despite how nervous he made her feel. 'It would be very difficult,' she replied reluctantly. 'Mr Stone has already made arrangements for us.'

'What a pity. It wouldn't be possible for Lewis to alter these arrangements, I suppose? I'm certain he'd find my collection of great interest.'

She grasped at the suggestion. 'I could always ask him,' she offered.

'Excellent. Please do, and ring me tomorrow with his response. I'll leave my private mobile number with you. Tuesday evening would be ideal.'

Ruth spent the rest of the meal tingling with anticipation; torn between the excitement of visiting Conrad's home and the possibility that Lewis might demure. She decided she would employ her most potent female wiles to persuade her boss to accept the dinner invitation.

After the meal the party retired to the lounge for coffee and drinks. From the easy conversation that flowed it was obvious Conrad, Elsa and Judy frequently visited each other's homes.

'I so enjoy your weekends, Conrad,' Judy commented. 'Are you planning another one soon?'

'Yes, next month,' he informed them. 'I've just finalised the participants, and the invitations are going out this week. You will come, I hope.'

'I wouldn't miss it for the world,' Elsa assured him.

'And you, Ruth? Will you be able to come, too?'

She looked inquisitively at Elsa. 'What's involved?' she asked, a slight tremor in her voice.

'It's not unlike the affair you attended last night,' Conrad answered her, 'but on a larger scale. It usually runs for two days and nights and people come from all over the country.'

She experienced another shiver of anxious anticipation. 'I'd be honoured to attend,' she said quietly.

'How about this evening?' Morgan asked. 'Have you some small diversion planned for us, perhaps?'

Conrad smiled. 'You know I never travel unprepared, Morgan. In fact, I've a prototype that requires testing. Jack, bring the box from the car, please.' He tossed his nephew a key.

Jack caught it and left the room, returning a few minutes later with a plastic box in his hands. He set it on the table in front of his uncle, and resumed his seat, his expression unreadable.

Conrad opened the box and extracted a bundle of straps. 'I'm calling this the *Janus Harness*.' He unravelled the tangled nylon. 'The webbing is made in my own mill. It's a simple matter to sew it together, and my present interest is the sensations its wearers will experience. The main shortcoming is that it requires two people of similar heights, such as Ruth and Elsa. Will you lovely girls be my guinea pigs?'

'Of course,' Ruth replied at once, in her eagerness forgetting she was not authorised to respond for Elsa. 'What would you have us do?'

'I want you to undress,' he answered, as casually as he might order a drink at a bar. Ruth stood up and reached for the zip of her dress, but he checked her. 'If you please, I'd prefer to do that for you. Jack, perhaps you will assist Elsa?'

Once naked, Ruth and Elsa were positioned back-to-back and the harness was lowered over their heads. The shoulder straps each parted to form an inverted Y-shape that framed their breasts before joining a horizontal band across their chests. At each side were adjusters, and once

Conrad was satisfied with the fit, they were locked into place by plastic fasteners.

Elsa giggled. 'It's like sharing a bra.'

They were indeed joined as one; Ruth could feel Elsa's shoulder blades against her own, and their buttocks were pressed together, which was a very pleasant sensation. She clenched her cheeks, and caused Elsa to make appreciative sounds in response. They held hands, their fingers curling around each other's, intensifying the feeling of being one.

Ruth was anticipating the next stage. It required little imagination, and she parted her thighs in preparation. She felt Elsa follow suit, being obliged to do so by the restriction of the harness, and her libido began to soar. The tight restraint of the strapping was stirring that delectable excitement in the pit of her stomach, a feeling amplified by contact with another woman experiencing the same thing. Then Conrad fastened their wrists together with more straps, before asking with wonderful aplomb, 'Whose penis would you prefer, Ruth?'

She glanced around the room, slightly taken aback by the directness of the question, although the prospect of being taken while standing up and bound to her friend appealed to her. 'I... I'd like it to be yours,' she whispered shyly.

'And you, Elsa, whose penis would you like?'

'I think Nick's would work best,' Judy suggested. 'Don't you agree, Morgan?'

Morgan nodded sagely.

Ruth had to bend and stretch a little to obtain the right position, which required Elsa to cooperate, and moving in harmony was a very sensuous experience. Unable to assist with Conrad's penetration, she had to depend on him to prepare her. He stroked her labia and teased it open with one hand while unzipping his trousers with the other, and she thought again how wonderful it was to be held immobile while a man used her.

She accepted him by rising on tiptoe and lowering herself slowly over his stiff penis. She sighed contentedly as his girth stretched her open, and once he was fully engaged she had to lean back, which required Elsa to adopt a similar stance. Cooperation felt amazingly good. He pushed into her, pressing her close so her breasts were crushed against his chest, and then she felt him reaching around her for Elsa's nipples. She knew when he found them from the sudden stiffening of her friend's body against hers even as she moved to accept Nick's erection. They were so close she could sense every one of Nick's thrusts behind her through the pressure of Elsa's back and buttocks, and she was almost able to predict the precise moment when his hands would come around in search of her breasts.

The two men and the two girls remained locked in a quadruple embrace for a long time. Sensing each other's needs with finesse, they slipped into a smooth rhythm, the men thrusting and the girls riding. Ruth was moving towards that heavenly state when her whole being felt centred in her pussy and clitoris, and through the haze of pleasure she could feel Elsa's fingers gripping her own with increasing fervour. Riding the swift penetrations alternately pressed their bodies together and dragged against the harness. They were truly sharing each other's experience, and it was wonderful. Ruth closed her mind to external distractions, focusing wholly on this glorious act of communal sex. The power, the movement, the tightness of the restraints, all built her climax with breathtaking speed. She held herself in check, however, striving to match Elsa's rhythm, until her excitement grew too strong to control and she surrendered to it, her mind exploding as her body flooded with perfect bliss.

Chapter Ten

Lewis Stone surveyed the room with satisfaction. 'I think we've covered everything in here, Ruth,' he decided. 'We'll do the pictures next. You and Oona move on to the banqueting hall while I collect the small pictures from the library.'

'Of course,' Ruth agreed with brisk efficiency. 'If you will take the catalogue and clipboard, please Oona, I'll carry the rest.' She set off for the dining room with mixed feelings. After the weekend she was unsettled and trying to cover up how she felt with a cool, professional attitude. She missed the potent stimulus of role-playing, yet she was also pleased to be with Lewis again. Oona was an added dilemma. It was good to have her helping, but her presence hampered Ruth's ability to get really close to Lewis, especially as Oona sported a wedding ring, making Ruth instinctively wary of her; not every woman was as freethinking as Janet Dobson.

Oona walked ahead of her as they traversed the ground floor corridor. Ruth surveyed the girl's back critically. Oona was a solicitor's clerk who had been delegated to unlock the house and keep an eye on their work, and neither she nor Lewis had been inclined to reject her offer to help. After all, more hands made everything move more quickly, which ultimately meant more time to themselves later. Oona was a pretty girl. The close-fitting black trousers and sheer white blouse she was wearing showed off her well-rounded figure. She had a beautifully prominent bottom that flexed delightfully as she walked, and her little lace bra was more decorous than supportive.

They entered the banqueting hall, a typical piece of Quincy ostentation. It was really only a large dining room, and the two Parry landscapes rather overwhelmed the space. This was where the auction would be conducted on Friday. Tomorrow, the porters would arrive to create more room, erect a rostrum and install seating. The sooner that was done the longer she would have Lewis to herself until they drove to Conrad's, though as yet she had been unable to extend the master's invitation to her boss.

Oona stood gazing around the room, absentmindedly fanning herself with the catalogue. 'God, it's hot!' she exclaimed.

Ruth agreed.

Oona tilted her head towards the corridor whilst eyeing Ruth. 'Your boss is a bit tasty, and so easygoing,' she said cautiously. 'Mine would go spare if I showed up to work like that.'

Ruth was suddenly aware of the way her unfettered breasts were attracting Oona's attention. 'I wouldn't ordinarily dress like this in the office,' she said defensively.

'But you've got lovely breasts,' Oona said openly, taking Ruth by complete surprise, then before she knew what was happening the pretty girl set her burdens down on the table beside them, pulled up Ruth's tight T-shirt, and her mouth closed over Ruth's left breast, sucking it while her tongue laved greedily at her hardening nipple.

Ruth sighed with astonished delight and stroked Oona's long brown hair with one hand while holding her shirt up with the other. Then Oona paused, lifting her face to smile up at her. 'This is lovely,' she cooed sweetly. 'It's been so long since I tasted another girl. Thank you so much.'

Ruth made no answer except to twist her torso and present Oona's mouth with her other breast. She then pulled her T-shirt over her head and cast it aside. Freed of the need to hold it up she could give her full attention to the lovely girl, so continuing to stroke Oona's silky hair with one hand, she opened her blouse. Oona offered no resistance, and the loose silk slipped easily off her shoulders. Ruth then pulled the skimpy bra upward, and let Oona's firm orbs bounce free. Greedily, she cupped their weight in her hands, strumming the hard teats with her thumbs as the other girl moaned with pleasure.

Ruth felt Oona's hands on her thighs, moving upwards and teasing the valley of her buttocks. A delicious hunger boiled up inside her, and she ached for those expressive fingers to explore further, to slip beneath the tight waist of her jeans and tear her flimsy panties away. Her pussy was positively begging for attention, and moistened eagerly when Oona's firm fingers did just that and burrowed inside and into her panties.

'Oh yes… oh please…' Ruth's voice was an ardent whisper. She rolled Oona's nipples between her thumb and forefinger and felt the girl stiffen in response, which encouraged her to pinch harder.

Oona gave a little cry and pulled away, and alarm was etched on her face as she tugged her bra back into place. 'Oh, I'm so sorry!' she gasped. 'I'm so sorry!'

Utterly confused for a moment, Ruth then noticed movement over her shoulder, and saw Lewis framed in the doorway. His eyes sparkled and she smiled at him knowingly.

'Please, don't apologise for such a pleasant display, my dear,' he said. 'Believe me, I fully appreciate the nature of young ladies' needs.'

'Then you know what *I* need, sir,' Ruth said flirtatiously.

Oona stopped in the act of retrieving her blouse.

'If you will be so good as to properly prepare yourself,'

Lewis spoke coolly, 'I will endeavour to oblige you.'

'Really, Lewis.' Ruth assumed a scandalised tone as she unzipped her jeans. 'Think of Oona. Surely a gentleman would not embarrass a lady by excluding her?'

He rose to the occasion. Turning to Oona with mock gravity, he said civilly, 'My dear lady, I beg you to accept my most sincere apologies. I cannot imagine what I was thinking by suggesting I should make love to Ruth whilst leaving you out. I am, of course, more than willing to offer you the same service if you desire it.'

Oona backed away coquettishly. 'Sir, how could you think that a respectable married lady would harbour such base desires?' she asked.

Ruth was already naked. 'He knows you're gasping for it,' she said frankly. 'Now let's have some fun.'

Lewis laughed, and pure wickedness flashed across Oona's lovely countenance as she dropped her blouse again and reached for her bra clip.

'Be fair, Lewis,' Ruth urged. 'Make both of us come, and then we'll give you your relief together. Come here, Oona, and lay beside me on the table... that's right, head to toe, bottoms on the edge. Lewis will have to move back and forth, but the exercise will be good for him.'

While Lewis was discarding his trousers Ruth settled herself as comfortably as possible on the large dining room table. It felt good being snuggled up next to another girl again.

'Who'll be first?' Lewis enquired diplomatically.

'Surely guests take precedence,' Ruth replied, squeezing Oona's nipple and caressing the other girl's breasts so she could feel her back arching as she accepted Lewis's impressive length. There was a lovely wet sucking sound as he eased out of her pussy, and back in again as Ruth sought her own clitoris, and fingered herself in preparation

134

for the greater pleasure to come.

She could sense the moment Lewis withdrew; Oona's sense of loss was almost palpable. Compassionately, her fingers sought Oona's clitoris. It was easy to find as she was fully aroused, her labia blossoming, her bud full and proud. She touched it and Oona cried out, her back arching with pleasure again at the very moment that Lewis's silky, lubricated fullness drove firmly into Ruth's willing sheath.

She felt herself soaring towards her peak as his length and girth repeatedly drove her open around it. The wonderful feeling of fullness seemed to spread throughout her entire being while her mind grew comfortable with the knowledge that her life was complete. She abandoned herself to the pleasure, drinking deeply of contentment as ecstasy wove itself through her nerve-endings.

The prelude to orgasm washed over her, that dreamy, trancelike state when reality fades away and all her senses are concentrated in the vortex of her loins. But in the midst of it Lewis pulled out of her abruptly, and for a fraction of infinity she remained suspended on the crest of her rising climax, and before her joy could ebb, Oona's fingers fastened on her throbbing clitoris and she soared higher into the warm, rose-coloured world of pure pleasure. As Oona's fingers played with her clit, Ruth played with hers, and the bud under her fingers grew and stiffened as she felt Lewis's penis slide in beneath it again. She rubbed it, circling the little stem, forcing it into greater prominence. Oona was wailing now, unable to contain the sensations being wrenched from her body as Lewis thrust vigorously. At the crucial moment he began pulling out, and Ruth played on the hard nubbin between her fingers, assuring Oona's satisfaction. In the instant Oona's orgasm burst Lewis pulled out of her completely, and fed his rampant erection back into Ruth, driving deep, slamming his balls against her quim. She gasped, shockwaves of joy surging through her body as his pendulous sac swung against her labia. Then she was lost, once again freefalling through the most amazing experience life has to offer – a mind-blowing orgasm.

Both girls got up unsteadily while at the head of the table Lewis slumped in a big chair, his hard-working erection still proud. Ruth went to him, and kneeling between his legs kissed his glistening tip while lovingly cupping his balls. He smiled down at her as Oona leaned over the back of the chair to kiss his head, stroking his face with her sensitive fingers.

'What can I do?' the girl asked Ruth.

'Change places with me and bring Lewis off with your breasts,' she told her. 'But we both get a fair share, okay?'

Oona came around quickly, fell to her knees and leaned forward to take Lewis's cock between her ample breasts. She pressed her fleshy mounds together to firmly enclose his shaft, and took to her task with relish, swaying energetically back and forth.

Ruth leaned across Lewis's chair, offering her hard nipples to his lips. He sucked and licked them with delight, and she felt her contentment returning, flooding her mind as her love flowed forth. With her fingers she began to tease his nipples in return. They were small by comparison but equally sensitive, for she felt them growing pert beneath her fingertips. He whispered something. His words were too soft to discern, but she felt them on her flesh and knew they were words of love.

Then Lewis let her nipple slip from between his lips as his body went taut and his breathing quickened. 'I'm coming!' he gasped. Suddenly his back arched, and Oona threw her head back as the first thick string of semen spouted from between her cleavage, spattering her throat. Ruth lunged in, licking the salty cream from her flesh as the second jet burst upon the other girl's face. Oona ran her tongue around her lips as the viscous fluid trickled warmly down over her chin, and she twisted to take the next gush on her breasts. Ruth massaged the cream into her skin as Lewis kept coming like a fountain in full flow, until both girls were coated with his cream.

Ruth reached for his subsiding member, enclosing it lovingly in her hand, savouring its heat and softness. Her other hand insinuated itself between Oona's thighs, pushing until she was cupping the gloriously puffy lips that seeped a fluid onto her palm. She kissed Oona and then Lewis, gently and lovingly.

'Are you and he an item?' Oona asked, as she and Ruth were cleaning up in the cloakroom.

Ruth gave her a sideways glance before answering cautiously, 'We have a relationship, but nothing involving a firm commitment, as yet.'

Oona smiled knowingly. 'That's not how it seems from here. It's in your eyes – yours and his both. With your kind of open relationship, what's holding you back?'

'We just haven't gotten around to it, I suppose. Anyway, you must have a very understanding husband yourself.'

Oona grimaced. 'No, quite the opposite, actually. Andrew is so possessive it's almost stifling. I hardly dare look at another man.'

'But what about today? Will you tell him?'

'Certainly not. I don't make a habit of it, so he's no reason to know, or to ask. Actually, it's the first time I've been with another man or woman since we were first engaged, six years ago. I don't miss the men so much as the girls. It was really nice being with you.'

'Thank you,' Ruth said quietly. 'It was really nice being with you, too.'

'I've been thinking quite a bit about that recently. I suppose being predisposed made today happen more easily. I wish I could persuade Andrew to be more adventurous. I think he would be less possessive if he could share experiences with me like you and Lewis do with each other.'

'Maybe,' Ruth said thoughtfully. 'It doesn't always work out that way, though. I know.' She was thinking of Stanford.

'What I'd really like is a female lover,' Oona confided. 'I'd be more than willing to share her with Andrew. Someone like you would be ideal.'

Ruth looked at her. They were still naked and her figure was tantalising. As she moved about her full breasts swayed invitingly. She felt a renewed urge to suck them and to slip her fingers in the juicy pussy peeping between Oona's slender thighs. She breathed deeply, keeping herself in check. 'I'm flattered,' she said at last. 'If I lived nearer to you I'd be willing to explore. As it is, I can't offer you much.'

'That's a pity. Don't misunderstand me, Andrew and I have a pretty varied sex life. It's not more variety I need so much as a different perspective. No matter how good Andrew is in bed, he can't be a woman, and I have more than one facet to my sexuality.'

'You need to explore yourself,' Ruth agreed.

'Exactly. How refreshing of you to understand. Couldn't we work something out?'

Ruth shook her head doubtfully. 'I have a pretty crowded schedule,' she said. 'Look, I can give you a number. Ring my friend, Elsa. She lives nearby and has lots of contacts.'

'Thanks, you're a breath of fresh air.' Oona stepped

forward, embraced and then kissed her passionately.

Ruth luxuriated in the touch of feminine flesh and felt herself heating up as her pussy began to moisten again.

'I suppose you should be working,' Oona murmured between kisses. 'We'd better get dressed.' But her lips locked over Ruth's, her tongue forcing its way between her teeth.

The two girls walked back to the banqueting hall where Lewis was already dressed and busy with the task in hand. He looked up appreciatively as they entered the room, still naked.

'I wish I'd chosen to wear a skirt today,' Oona reflected. 'Trousers seemed appropriate for the job, but they're uncomfortable in this heat.' She picked up her panties while wrinkling her nose. 'And I have an aversion to putting on previously worn underwear.'

'No problem,' Ruth said. 'I've several skirts in my bag. I could easily lend you one, along with some clean panties, too. Mine will fit you. Or you could just go without. It will certainly help keep you cool.'

Oona made a face of uncertainty.

'Perhaps not,' Ruth agreed, smiling. 'Mind you, I'm not putting any on yet myself.' It took her only a few seconds to slip on her skirt and top and trip away. She returned a moment later carrying a skirt and a clean pair of panties.

'I was just complimenting Oona on her sexual skills,' Lewis remarked.

'Fidelity doesn't necessarily imply a dull sex life,' Oona said defensively.

Once the girls were dressed, they returned to checking the lots and attaching labels, a long and tedious task. After a while Lewis suggested they break for lunch and went to collect a pre-packed hamper from his car. They ate their picnic around the big table while Ruth mused over the fact that only a short while before she had been sprawled on its surface while being very competently fucked. It was a satisfying thought, and one guaranteed to awaken all her appetites. Looking across the table, she caught Oona's eye and knew similar thoughts were in her head.

As if to control her internal waywardness, Oona stood up and walked around to gaze intently at one of the Parry paintings. She inspected the title plate. 'So, this is the cause of that endless searching through the old accounts.'

'Oh, so *you* had that job,' Ruth commiserated. 'Did you have any luck?'

'I found two entries, two years apart, that both read, *Paid to J. Parry, Esq. the sum of forty pounds for painting the factory*. Or something like that.'

'Excellent!' Lewis beamed and turned to Ruth. 'You see how such an entry could be overlooked, as indeed it was. At least we can be certain of the location of two Parry's. Now you can arrange to view them properly and begin your monograph.'

'Do you really think I should?' she asked.

'Most certainly. It was your specialist knowledge that identified these two. Yes, Oona, you can blame Ruth here for your ponderous chore.'

Oona returned to the table. 'You're going to write a book?' she said. 'How exciting.'

'Lewis thinks I should publish an in-depth study of Parry's work, a sort of technical biography,' Ruth explained.

'Oh, you must, yes,' Oona encouraged.

'It's a big job,' Ruth pointed out. 'The paintings are scattered and the location of many of them is unknown. I don't think I'd be able to find the time, do my work, and have a private life if I undertook such a project.'

'It doesn't have to meet a deadline,' Lewis said firmly. 'Take as long as you like, but start it before someone else does.'

Ruth thought it was time to change the subject. Her primary objective was finding a way to continue exploring her submissive nature. Researching a book, no matter how absorbing its contents, did not sit comfortably alongside this burning ambition. 'I promise I'll think about it,' she lied. 'Tell me, Oona, what will happen to this house?'

'It's already been sold,' Oona informed them. 'The sale can't close until the contents have been cleared, but then it will be converted into a luxury hotel with a championship golf course in the park.'

'And whose money is behind that?' Lewis asked.

'The purchaser is a local company, *Holstein Holdings*.'

Ruth's ears pricked up. 'And would one Conrad Hesseltine be involved in the transaction?' she asked.

'Yes, I believe he's the chairman of the company,' Oona confirmed.

'Do you know of this man, Ruth?' Lewis sounded intrigued.

'I've met him,' she confessed. 'In fact, we've been invited to dinner with him tomorrow evening. I was intending to tell you later. I told him you might not be able to accept.'

'What else do you know about him?' Lewis directed his question to Oona.

'He's very successful, and I believe he has a reputation as an art collector.'

'Has he indeed…?' Lewis said pensively. 'Ruth, I think we should accept his invitation.'

'I'm afraid this hotel is not what I'm accustomed to, but I'm assured it offers an excellent ambience,' Lewis apologised as they got out of the car.

'I'm sure it will be perfect,' Ruth assured him, appraising it. The building had a solid, important air where it stood at the head of the town square. The porch was supported by two stone columns and was reached by way of a flight of granite steps. As before, the reservations had been made in their real names.

They had worked as late as possible at the house, only leaving when Oona declared she simply had to get home. Very little remained to be done on the following day, and they had agreed to meet Oona at ten o'clock the next morning in time for the carriers.

'I've booked dinner for eight in a highly recommended restaurant just outside town,' Lewis informed Ruth as they entered their suite. 'Would you like to have tea now?'

'If we can have it served in the room,' she said. 'I'd like to relax for a little while.'

He agreed, and she retired to the bathroom where she luxuriated in a warm shower, letting her mind wander while the soft water cascaded over her body. Oona figured prominently in her thoughts and she fantasised about things she might do with the girl's voluptuous body. She was not sure whether she was more surprised by Oona's forthright advances or by her own brazen response to them. Where once she would have debated her actions, this morning she had plunged in and taken the lead. She knew she had changed a great deal in only a few days, and she hugged herself in celebration. Life had suddenly become a great exciting adventure.

Turning off the shower, she slipped a silk robe on over her wet skin and padded out to join Lewis in the bedroom. He was standing by the window enjoying the view. She crossed over to him and began opening his shirt. 'You should relax, too,' she urged softly.

He turned, and placing his hands on her waist held her lovingly as she worked on his buttons. 'You're a truly beautiful girl, Ruth,' he said, slowly exploring her body through the smooth material of her robe.

'Beauty is in the eye of the beholder,' she teased.

'The exquisite evokes universal admiration,' he insisted.

She slid her hands inside his open shirt, running her fingers over his skin, combing the sparse curls on his chest, brushing his nipples, and relishing the firmness of his pectorals. She felt his hands pressing her lumbar dimples, pulling her against his firming manhood, and a powerful feeling of security and contentment filled her, which rapidly transformed into a healthy lust.

A knock at the door announced the arrival of tea. Resisting the instinctive urge to break off contact, she called, 'Come in!' and pulled Lewis closer, pressing him against the rigid points of her breasts.

The door opened to admit a waitress who glanced rather enviously at the embracing couple as she set down the tray. 'Will that be all?' she enquired, preparing to withdraw.

'For the moment,' Lewis replied. 'Tell me, what's your name?'

'Dawn, sir,' she answered politely.

'Thank you, Dawn.'

'She's very pretty,' Ruth observed as the door closed behind the maid. 'I almost wish we could invite her to stay for a while.'

Lewis chuckled and kissed the tip of her nose. 'Your affinity with other girls surprises me,' he said.

'Does it shock you?'

'Quite the contrary, it is refreshingly pleasant, and I don't intend to dissuade you from your Sapphic pleasures.

This morning, for example, was thoroughly enjoyable. I've never known a girl who swings both ways so easily. It adds to your allure.'

'I think I've always had the inclination,' she said openly. 'It took me a long time to admit it to myself, but I'm glad I did, finally. I wouldn't want to change who I really am deep inside.'

'Nor should you. I thoroughly approve of who you are… Some tea?'

'Yes, please. Would you prefer me to remove my robe?'

'As you please.'

'Then I think I'll keep it on for the moment.'

Freed from his embrace, Ruth sat and let the robe fall away from her legs.

'Will you pour?' Lewis asked, she nodded, and while she attended to the teapot he undressed and donned his own bathrobe. 'There are many aspects of your personality that are equally surprising to me,' he went on as he sat, 'and they are all intensely engaging.'

'I'm continually surprising myself,' she admitted. 'I've never been a shrinking violet, as you must have realised, but until quite recently I was very conventional, an easygoing girl as long as we used the missionary position.'

'And now?'

She passed him a china cup filled with rich tea. 'I suppose I've experienced a revelation. The best way I can describe it is like having a box of delicious chocolates and finishing the first layer only to discover the second layer contains lots of new flavours, with more layers beneath it containing even more new flavours. I don't want to close the box.'

He smiled. 'I can see that.'

She studied him while she drank her tea. Then she placed the empty cup carefully on the tray and moved around the table to perch on his knee. She took his cup and saucer and placed it beside her own before putting her arm around his neck and snuggling closer. His hand rested on her naked thigh, and she immediately parted her legs in invitation.

'And how do you cast me?' he asked. 'Am I a soft centre, a hard centre, or a fellow connoisseur?'

She wriggled herself into a more comfortable position. 'Let's have a tasting session,' she murmured, biting her lip and moaning as his fingers parted her labia.

Ruth relaxed back, enjoying the caress of balmy summer air on her bare shoulders as the Mercedes purred down the country lane. She had her window open, as did Lewis, and she glanced across at him fondly. Between her thighs her pussy was still throbbing, fretting at being confined. His skill in bed was improving by leaps and bounds, not that he had been lacking at any stage in their relationship. But this evening he had fucked her to orgasm four times in one hour. He had left her deeply satisfied, but not yet satiated. The night was still young.

Lewis was a fine man to know. The feelings she had for him were probably as close to love than she had ever been before, but a nagging doubt restrained her, holding her back from making a final commitment to him. Could he alone satisfy the myriad sexual flavours she was beginning to realise existed in the world?

The restaurant was set amongst the trees on the edge of a small village. The low building bore the stamp of calculating understated quality, and they entered through a small foyer to be greeted by a concierge wearing an immaculate tuxedo. His eyes lit up appreciatively when he saw Ruth as well they might, for she looked stunning in a formfitting crimson dress. He led them to a table set in an intimate alcove. The ambience of the establishment was one of restrained dignity, the furnishings discrete, with light music being played by an unobtrusive trio. She settled back into the well-upholstered chair and let herself be guided through the comprehensive menu by a man of experience.

After the superb meal Lewis ordered brandy, to be followed by coffee. As she held the balloon glass, the rich aroma of the spirit stirred her responses. She sipped the warming, sharp liquid feeling extremely relaxed and pampered.

Lewis watched her carefully. 'Tell me Ruth,' he said, 'what do you want out of life?'

Something in his face told her the question was vitally important to him, and that she had best answer carefully. 'Obviously, I want to have a successful career,' she began, 'either with the firm, or independently. I want financial security, and probably children when the time is right, but above all, I want to be happy.'

'And what will bring you happiness?'

'Who can tell? That's why I want to explore myself. As I said this afternoon, there's a whole spectrum of experiences out there I've not yet tapped. At the moment I know I find the deepest satisfaction in situations where someone takes control of my sexuality. I like to be tied up, chastised and used. I want to thoroughly explore every aspect of my submissive nature.'

'I think I understand,' he said, nodding pensively. 'Tell me, what do you know of Juliette?'

'Enough,' she said. 'You don't have to explain, I'm not jealous.'

'You misunderstand me, Ruth. My purpose is to make matters clear, to secure an unambiguous understanding. Juliet was not the first woman in my life, but she was the most influential. We never married. It seemed neither necessary nor appropriate to our relationship. She had total freedom of action, and it was her choice, respected by me, to take up an opportunity in the States. We both had regrets, but one of the promises we made to each other before she departed was that our pasts would not stand in the way of new relationships. Even so, parting was very hard, and I never expected to find anyone who could match Juliette's affinity with me. Until now, that is.' He paused to sip his brandy, and then said earnestly, 'Ruth, you must understand that you are not a substitute for Juliette. My feelings for you lie much deeper... they are far stronger.'

She gazed at him steadily, struggling to anticipate where this was leading. She was aware her feelings for him were being reciprocated, that their relationship was more than a transient affair, but she had not resolved the conflict between this satisfying state and her need for freedom to explore all the intriguing corridors of her sexuality, which kept branching out around her. 'What are you saying, Lewis?' she asked cautiously.

'Well, will you marry me, Ruth?' he asked bluntly.

The question hit her like an emotional tornado, shattering her serenity and nearly stopping her heart. She stared foolishly over her glass at him, her thoughts in utter turmoil. 'Oh, Lewis!' she whispered, and in the farthest chambers of her mind the exclamation sounded frivolous even to her.

'Obviously, my proposal was more unexpected than I had believed it would be,' he said, a bit stiffly.

'Well, yes... oh, I'm flattered, certainly... honoured, actually, but I shall have to think things through before I can give you an answer. There's so much I want to do before I'm ready to settle down, Lewis.'

'Believe me, Ruth, I'm not contemplating domesticity.

I hear what you're saying. Why else would I have asked you about your desires? Knowing you is tremendously exciting to me. I suppose I want to share your world, and explore it with you, not keep you from it.'

'Does that include sharing lovers?' she asked frankly. 'Would you have been so cool about Oona if we had been married?'

'I love you, Ruth,' he said simply. 'It's not a condition I've just selected off a menu. I've felt that way for days now. I believe that exclusivity in marriage is an outdated concept. Fidelity, constancy, call it what you will, includes much more than sex. Monogamous sex is almost a contradiction in terms if you are truly being faithful to each other's happiness, and truly seeking to fulfil each other's needs and desires.'

She regarded him with great respect. 'One of the people I met this weekend is sexually enslaved to one man and married to another,' she informed him. 'She lives a perfectly conventional family life, except she has her husband's consent to have a master who has been granted total control of her sexual being. Could you go that far, Lewis?'

He pondered the implications before he answered. 'It would all hinge on trust, I believe. The master and the husband could not be rivals. Of course, to be both master and husband would be ideal, but if your happiness depended on such an arrangement, I think I would be able to accept it. So, will you marry me?'

Her mind was calm now; she was sure of his sincerity. 'It's going to be interesting working out the details,' she mused. 'I quite like the idea of being your sex slave,' she added, and seeing the light in his eyes, knew she had made a sound choice.

He reached across the table, took her glass from her

and set it down. Then he grasped both her hands tightly in his as he gazed into her eyes. 'Ruth, you have made me the happiest man in the world, and I promise I will strive to make you the happiest woman in the world.' He raised a hand and clicked his fingers imperiously.

A waiter appeared instantly, and was sent off for a bottle of champagne. When it arrived, and Lewis had poured them both a glass, he raised his. 'A toast! To the perpetual happiness and total sexual satisfaction of Ruth Stone.'

Chapter Eleven

Ruth rode back to the hotel in a rose-coloured haze, pleasantly surprised by the turn of events. Following her acceptance of his proposal, Lewis fired off questions about her time at Elsa's, and grew visibly aroused by her graphic descriptions of the things she had been made to do. As they climbed the hotel staircase a potent excitement gripped her, setting her pulse racing and making her mouth dry.

Inside their room the tension between them soared. She stood perfectly still, gazing at him in feverish anticipation.

He said nothing for a long moment, merely studied her as he might study a painting, absorbing its character. 'You're a brazen wench,' he commented at last. 'The way you seduced Oona was quite shameless.'

She averted her eyes. Being confronted by her own naughtiness exposed her thinly buried sense of guilt.

He pulled the solitary chair from beneath the room's writing table, and sat down. 'Come here,' he commanded in a quiet voice.

A fierce tremor shot through her body, causing her to shiver in anticipation as she stepped towards him. She knew what to expect, and made no protest as he took her arm and pulled her facedown across his lap. She felt his fingers on the smooth skin of her thighs, and shivered again as his hand slid up beneath her skirt. With a decisive gesture he flipped it back, exposing her bottom, and she bit her lip to contain a moan of excited fear. He caressed her buttocks, smoothing the silk seat of her panties over her soft round orbs. She squirmed.

'And so you might, you little minx,' he whispered. Again he smoothed the fabric, this time lingering on the tight elastic waist, fingering the prominent dimple in her back. Then he lifted the elastic, and let it snap back into place. She started, and felt a telltale tingle in her pussy. Very slowly he lifted the elastic and began to peel the tiny garment off her. She squirmed again, her face burning with embarrassment. To be so blatantly exposed by a man was as shameful as it was erotic. Any moment now he would see the damp spot within her gusset and know her for the randy tart she truly was.

He drew the brief panties down to her knees, and then returned to caressing the exposed mounds of her bottom. He eased her legs apart until the elastic, tightly stretched around her knees, threatened to snap. The improved access allowed him to stroke her sex, and the moment his fingers touched her vulva she almost wet herself with pleasure.

He caught one of her arms, bending it across her back to contain her and hold her still. Then suddenly, without warning, he spanked her. He gave her one hard smack with his open palm directly on the fullness of her right cheek.

She cried out.

He smacked her again, provoking a second cry from her, and continued to spank her, raining blows down across her writhing bottom. Again and again, without mercy, he hit her bouncing flesh with his hard hand. 'You have earned this by your shameless wanton behaviour,' he told her. 'Every time you seduce some poor unsuspecting girl into your lascivious games, you must expect a punishment like this.'

The burning, stinging sensation soaked deep into her

flesh, spreading all through her body, but especially targeting her juicing pussy. The whole of her vulva, labia and clitoris together, throbbed and ached with longing. When at last he stopped spanking her to press a finger into her soft, moist folds, she climaxed around his digit, squealing in ecstasy and nearly falling off his lap.

'You are incorrigible!' he said severely. 'You're a sex obsessed little minx, nothing but a bitch in heat.'

'Yes, master,' she sighed.

He hauled her to her feet.

Instinctively, she clasped her hands to her burning bottom.

'This "master" business sounds so contrived, but then this is all a contrivance, I suppose. Let me think.'

'*Master* is traditional, sir. It falls naturally from the tongue.'

'*Sir* I like better. It sounds good. Yes, you will address me as "sir" until I think of something better.'

'Yes, sir.' She gazed at him hopefully. Already the peaceful satisfaction of her orgasm was ebbing and her appetite was reviving.

'I cannot think how I shall ever contain you,' he murmured, as if reading her mind. He took off his robe and unthreaded its silken cord. Making it into a lasso, he dropped it over her head and drew it tight around her waist, settling the knot in the small of her back. The long end he threaded through her legs, pulling the cord up into her crotch before threading the spare end under the waist loop.

Ruth wriggled. The sash was lying firmly in her cleft, and its touch was sexy, arousing.

He smiled, and tugged sharply on the cord, causing it to slice into her pussy. Her labia parted to accommodate it and her clitoral hood was pulled back. The super-sensitive bud burned as the material dug into it, and she gasped from the excruciating pleasure. His smile deepened and he pulled on the cord again, drawing it hard against her bud. She was in his thrall unable to resist anything he did, even had she wanted to. At this moment all she desired was contact with her lover, and another massive, mind-blowing orgasm. He slid a finger inside her, stroking and teasing her sensitised inner flesh, and she moaned in frustration, twisting her hips to try and force his digit in deeper. A second finger joined the first, pushing up on the other side of the cord, and he took one of her nipples between his teeth, nipping it gently while his embedded fingers probed her. At the same time he tugged on the cord, hauling it against her clitoris, and a shaft of burning pleasure pierced her. Her head swam, her vision blurred, and she was sure she must faint with delight as he massaged her vagina. The sweet fire in her pelvis flared, overwhelming all her other senses. She flung her arms around his neck and leaned against him as his fingers stirred heaven up in her womb. With a wail of ecstasy she yielded to another climax, writhing and bucking on his fingers while wave upon wave of pleasure swamped her, blotting out the whole world, its enchanted horizons the glorious spasms in her sheath.

By small degrees Ruth regained some semblance of composure. Lewis guided her onto the bed and she lay there conscious of his finger still inside her and the cord continuing to exert its irresistible pressure against her pussy. She imagined her body was a parcel, her skin the wrapping, the contents pure lechery, all tied up with a magic string. She knew her lucidity was transient. Unless he released her, in a few moments she would once again be submerged in orgasmic paroxysms, and she had no desire to escape.

She shifted her position, brazenly thrusting her pelvis forward, generating a sudden and obvious pressure on her clitoris that surged through her like an electric shock.

'You are as horny as a sow,' Lewis said, withdrawing his fingers.

The words sank into her brain like poetry; even insults felt wonderful. But her empty pussy protested, the absence of pleasure the only true pain. She felt abandoned, empty... then she experienced a thrill of joy as warm, living flesh nudged her opening. He eased the cord aside while his swollen organ forced its way into her open, eager entrance. He settled the cord alongside her clit as he filled her body with heat and life, and she seemed to be bursting with him, as though he was stuffing the whole of her belly with his erection. She focused all her feelings in her vagina, using that miraculous organ to convey her love as she clung to him with her inner muscles. She closed her mind to all distractions, striving to turn the wonderful sensations flooding her body into expressions of regard, respect and worship. And as she tightened around him her own pleasure became amplified. With each thrust the cord was dragged back and forth by his cock so it roughly caressed her clit, stirring sensations within her she had only dreamed possible. Even the most careful masturbation had never taken her this far. Her body was being lifted by his power to new heights of joy. A breathtaking spasm clenched her sex around his marvellous shaft as it filled her completely, displacing all her thoughts, and another wail rising from deep in her chest marked her surrender as he drove in hard, gripping her to him as he spurted his seed into her belly.

Lewis took her lovingly in his arms as their carnal passion subsided, and then he made as if to remove the cord.

'No, please don't,' she murmured. 'You must understand

154

that, for me, being restrained and controlled is the most wonderful thing on earth. Trust me. Make me your slave. Use me. Hurt me. It's what I desire more than anything.'

'But I can't lavish you with tenderness unless we're equals,' he protested quietly, staring soberly down into her eyes.

'No debate, please, sir.'

'I admit, having you in my power is the most exhilarating experience. When you respond, and I see that you're happy, it fills me with an amazing contentment. And, paradoxically, my respect for you grows fantastically, so much so that I want to take you to even greater heights. Forgive me, but I'm still defining parameters. I'm still not certain what is proper and what isn't.'

'You see me enjoying pain and want to hurt me more,' she clarified simply. 'What's wrong with that? I'm not forced to accept. There's no coercion. I can always call a stop. So long as I accept your actions, you're pleasing me, and yourself. We share, and sharing is the foundation of love. So let me stay in my role as your slave, please.'

He hugged her tightly for a long time before pulling her across his lap to examine the lingering blush of his spanking. When her pulled her buttocks apart to view her anus, she gasped, 'Oh yes, please, sir.'

'Minx!' He spanked her firmly.

She kicked and cried out, struggling under his firm grip, but she made no real determined effort to escape. She knew by instinct that her writhing bottom spurred him on. The increased frequency and intensity of his smacks confirmed it. Her cheeks burned, passing beyond pain into a fiery feeling of lust.

Despite the active night, Ruth woke refreshed and eager for the day. After breakfast, which they had delivered up to the room, she dressed according to Lewis's instructions. He chose a white cotton skirt for her, the lightest, briefest panties she possessed, and a scoop-necked red shirt that displayed her cleavage nicely.

He insisted they go shopping, and walking beside him in the town square made her feel immensely proud, especially when heads turned to watch them. She was certain everyone could sense how closely she was controlled, and the thought made her pussy juice and hardened her nipples. Their destination was a small jeweller's shop where Lewis purchased a simple diamond ring for her. Ruth was acutely conscious of it as she left the shop, the unaccustomed presence of it on her finger awakening memories of Judy's slave ring and renewing her awareness of her gold ankle bracelet, her own voluntary slave adornment.

'You learn quickly,' she remarked, as the car sped up the dale. 'Last night was wonderful. Using the cord was inspired.'

He smiled. 'Inexperience does not equate with ignorance. Much has been written about domination and submission. One would have to be stupid not to have picked up some basic principles on the subject. You see, I can carry the tune, but I must rely on you to teach me the more refined harmonies.'

'I'm a mere novice myself.'

'Then learning together will be fun,' he concluded.

Oona had opted for a skirt, too. It was short, showing off her shapely legs and flattering her tight bottom. Ruth thought she looked stunning. 'So, Andrew's jealousy doesn't extend to your dress code?' she commented, as together they moved some of the smaller lots into the salesroom.

'He likes me to dress provocatively as long as he's with me. If I go out alone, he expects me to be ultra-conservative. He gets a kick out of seeing men ogle me while he preens. You know the sort of message men can project, "yes, she's a cracker, mate, and she's mine, so keep off". And he knows how that frustrates me. By the way, I rang your friend, Elsa, and she invited Andrew and me to a party on Saturday. I've told Andrew they're people I met through work, so I'm hoping he'll go with an open mind.'

'It sounds to me as though he's got a definite sadistic streak. You'll have to find out how to play on it.'

'I intend to. Yesterday was an eye-opener for me. God, your boss was something else!'

Ruth waved her ring ostentatiously.

Oona clasped her chest in envy. 'You lucky cow!' she blurted. 'I hope you'll be very happy together, I really do.'

'I'm sure we will. We're very clear about the sort of relationship we want.'

The morning was busy and passed quickly. Ruth felt an affinity with Oona, and it was good to confirm the fact that she could share Lewis in a very intimate way without feeling jealous. The carriers arrived and quickly set up the rostra and the seating. The telephone men installed temporary lines, and by lunchtime the empty van was being loaded with unimportant books to be sold off through an associated dealer. Finally, the three of them did a final check of the upper floors.

'What will happen to the furniture up here?' Oona wondered out loud.

'It goes with the house,' Lewis told her. 'The few important pieces have been removed downstairs for the sale. Practically all the valuable items were displayed on the ground floor. The Quincy family were extraordinarily mundane when it came to their sleeping quarters.'

'Sleeping or breeding quarters?' Ruth asked playfully.

'I should think sleeping since the line seems to have petered out after a mere three generations.'

'A great shame,' Oona said, opening some French windows that led out onto a balcony. 'My word, look at this view.'

The balcony overlooked the park at the rear of the house. Beyond it lay the full vista of the dale, with the distant town nestled in a fold of the valley. The landscape Parry had seen was discernible, although the dominating feature of the mill and its chimneys had been erased, restoring a more pastoral aura to the scene. Ruth felt transported back in time as she looked out over the rolling hills, seeing the dale very much as the artist had seen it. Parry had captured the essential rural spirit blanketed by industry, and her admiration for his work increased, which brought with it a nagging desire to follow Lewis's advice and do the research for a book.

'That would be a lovely place to picnic,' Oona observed.

Ruth followed her gaze to where a natural pool had been incorporated into the park's landscaping, a screen of trees creating a quiet haven of privacy.

'An excellent idea,' Lewis agreed. 'It's a pity to waste this fine weather.'

Completing their checks, they returned to the car, where Lewis extracted the hamper and carried it to the little copse they had spied from the balcony, where they set out their impromptu picnic.

Ruth sank down onto the grass, lifting her skirt to expose her legs to the sun.

Lewis's eyes sparkled. 'What would be truly idyllic,'

he remarked, 'would be *Dejeuner sur l'Herbe*.'

Oona looked to Ruth for enlightenment.

'The painting by Manet of two couples picnicking in a forest glade, the men formally dressed, the women wrapped in diaphanous veils, except that one woman has lost hers and is quite naked.'

Oona's face lit up. 'I'm game if you are.'

'She won't need persuading,' Lewis assured her.

'Lewis, you'll have people thinking I'm a girl of easy virtue,' Ruth protested.

'Not at all, you're very virtuous, in a strictly unconventional manner.'

She was already busy with buttons and clips. In moments, she was completely naked. 'You know, I think I spend more time naked than dressed these days.'

'I wish I could,' Oona declared wistfully as she too stripped off her clothes, leaving on only her high-heeled sandals.

Ruth shifted her position, wanting to have a more equally balanced view of her companions. As she rose to her knees, she heard Oona squeal with surprise.

'What happened to your bottom, Ruth?'

'She got a little above herself,' Lewis replied. 'Sometimes she has to be brought to her senses.'

'You enjoyed it just as much as I did, sir.'

'You *spanked* her?' Oona shivered expressively.

'He's a real beast,' Ruth teased.

'Careful,' Lewis warned. 'This particular beast lurks very close to the surface. Too many quips like that might unleash him.'

'You see?' Ruth appealed to Oona. 'What can I do with a man who lacks basic self-control?'

Lewis made as if to rise. As he did so Ruth jumped away, putting a tree between her and her fiancé, ducking this way and that, provoking him with laughing eyes. 'Help me, Oona! Save me from this primitive beast!'

Lewis lunged.

Ruth ducked sideways, feinted, and hopped the opposite way as he grasped at empty air. She skipped behind another tree, replaying the scene. Then a pair of naked arms closed around her, capturing her firmly. She struggled, but the other girl held her tightly.

'Here Lewis,' Oona called. 'I've caught the little tease for you. Give her what she deserves.'

'Traitor!' Ruth cried, struggling to free herself. 'How could you betray the female cause?'

'Because I want to see you spanked!' Oona gasped with suppressed laughter. 'So don't spoil my fun.'

'If it turns you on that much, *you* get spanked instead,' Ruth challenged.

'You don't mean that, do you?'

'Of course she doesn't mean it. Protesting is all part of the game, isn't it slave?' Lewis seized hold of Ruth's arms.

At his touch Ruth fell quiet and let him pull her over to an old tree stump that provided a natural seat for him. He lowered himself onto it and pulled her down across his lap. She began a half-hearted struggle. 'Be still,' he commanded, and spanked her hard.

Oona saw Ruth's firm cheeks wobble, and a patch in the shape of a hand colour the residual pinkness to an angry scarlet. She gave a little cry of emotion. 'Oh, I'm so sorry!'

Lewis smacked Ruth again. The sound echoed oddly off the trees, followed instantly by her cry of pain. 'Don't be sorry,' Lewis said. 'She really does enjoy it. She'll keep shouting, but in a few moments she'll feel no real hurt. Watch…' He smacked her six times in quick succession.

Oona watched Ruth's firm flesh quiver and bounce beneath the assault. She saw the other girl's skin lighten momentarily before a furious redness infused it, and the lovely rounded bottom seemed to glow. Ruth was kicking and twisting, pushing her bottom up, inviting more smacks while showing the lovely, juicy bulge of her labia. The cleft between her buttocks widened, revealing her dark anal rose as Lewis's hand rose and fell steadily, until the whole of her bottom and her upper thighs was an even shade of painful red. She was still reacting to each smack, but her struggles were minimal and her cries muted to a low mewling that was part sob, part purr.

Lewis delivered two final blows, one to the crown of each buttock, and then released his hold on her. She lay limply across his lap for a full minute, crooning softly to herself, flexing her cheeks as she wallowed in the afterglow of a delicious torment. Then she stood up slowly, regaining her feet with disciplined determination and ruefully clasping her burning buttocks in her hands. Her face was flushed, but in her eyes triumph burned.

Oona had been unable to resist the temptation to touch herself as she watched another girl getting spanked, and her fingers were still probing the warm moisture of her cleft.

'You dirty beast, you're turned on,' Ruth accused her.

'I confess,' Oona gasped. 'Please, one of you spank *me*.'

Ruth flaunted her flaming bottom. 'You want your bottom to look like this? What will Andrew say when he sees it?'

'Can't you do it gently, so it doesn't show afterwards?'

'Not if you really want to feel it. Even a light spanking will leave a lingering blush for a while.'

'Oh dear, if only I could be spanked where it won't show…'

Lewis and Ruth exchanged a glance, momentarily at a loss, then Oona's face lit up suddenly. 'I *know*, you could spank my pussy. *That* won't show. If it does, I can just pretend I'm really turned on. Anyway, Andrew never looks at my cunt, so he'll not notice.'

'It will hurt a lot more,' Ruth warned.

'I don't care,' Oona declared passionately. 'I want it to hurt. I want to be hurt more than you were.'

'I think you'd better do it,' Lewis suggested pragmatically. 'Your hands are smaller than mine, better suited to tight spaces.'

'She can spread her legs quite wide enough for you,' Ruth countered.

'No, you do it, Ruth,' Oona said. 'I shall enjoy being spanked by a girl, but Lewis must hold me down.'

'Okay, but pinch her nipples at the same time,' Ruth insisted.

Oona lay on her back across Lewis's knees, her feet placed squarely on the ground and her knees spread wide apart. She let her head fall back, exposing the lovely creamy smoothness of her throat. She was totally vulnerable, and Ruth felt her stomach tighten at the sight of Oona's breasts flattened against her ribs making her nipples protrude. She positioned herself carefully, running her hands sensuously over Oona's thick labia, feeling how the cushion of fat protected the sensitive interior. Oona moaned, clenching her abdomen. Again Ruth stroked her, and elicited another moan from the girl. A tiny pink ridge was visible between the dark outer flesh, and after another caress the delicate frills of her inner lips came into view. Ruth continued giving her long, encouraging strokes, until the whole of Oona's sex was spread open before her eyes with the inner lips framing the dark eye that was the entrance to her inner self. After a few more caresses

Oona's clitoris was pouting proudly as Lewis worked on her stiff nipples with his fingertips. Ruth flicked the proud clit with her fingernail and Oona moaned, closing her eyes, but then she opened them again to gaze at Ruth's hand poised above her body.

Ruth smacked the other girl's exposed pussy with her open palm. Oona's reflexes brought her thighs together, but not quickly enough. Ruth's hand landed firmly on her soft, moist target. Oona was hot. She squealed beneath the impact and clamped Ruth's hand with her legs, grinding herself against the heel of her palm.

'Hold her thigh, Lewis,' Ruth ordered. 'And you, my lady, keep those legs spread or I shall have to tie you up to make sure you do.' She raised her hand and saw Oona tense up. She paused, letting anticipation work its magic. Oona began to make soft little sobbing sounds, begging to be hurt and spared all in the same breath. Ruth understood. She smiled at her victim, and struck again. Her hand landed squarely on the exposed vulva with a sharp smacking sound. Oona cried out shrilly, her body jerking on Lewis's lap as she tried in vain to clamp her legs together. Ruth nodded at her fiancé, who released his grip on the girl's thigh, and Oona promptly squeezed them closed and rubbed them together to provoke her orgasm.

After a moment Ruth forcibly parted the gorgeous thighs, and while Lewis held them open, she delivered four more firm smacks in quick succession to the succulent quim at her disposal.

'Oh, my God, I want to come!' Oona gasped. 'Please make me come!' Her labia was fully engorged, the dark void of her vagina pulsating at its centre. And at the crest of her rosy vulva, her clitoris jutted out hard and pink. Ruth teased it, flicking its tip and circling its base with

163

one of her fingernails. Oona squirmed, voicing her passion as Lewis pinched and rolled her nipple between his fingertips. Ruth could see and feel the tension in her victim and she once more teased the ripe clitoris before smacking her pussy mercilessly, inflicting severe distress on the tender flesh.

Oona's back arched, thrusting her belly upward as a climax rent her. And before her legs closed, Ruth eased her thumb into the dark opening of the girl's tormented sex, letting her grind against her wrist while her vagina sucked and dragged at her relentless digit.

'Lewis, are you erect?' Ruth asked breathlessly.

'Naturally.' He laughed at the absurdity of the question.

'Then do it for her,' she urged.

Oona offered no resistance as Ruth extracted her thumb and helped her sit up. Still deep in the throes of ecstasy, Oona instinctively opened her legs to straddle Lewis, and Ruth eased her down over his rigid penis. A new wave of convulsions swept through her writhing form as his cock slid into her hungry body, and he went to work at once, thrusting upward, lifting her as he fucked her mightily. Oona flung her arms around his neck and rode him with shameless fervour, her cries soaring into the trees as peak after peak of pleasure possessed her.

Chapter Twelve

Conrad's house stood below the shoulder of the moor, a Georgian gentleman farmer's house built for comfort and located at a discrete distance from the more functional buildings. There were several cars parked on the gravel drive. Ruth recognised Elsa's, and the pick-up truck surely belonged to Jack Thorpe.

She climbed out of the Mercedes feeling supremely confident in her green tulle-and-silk outfit with a brilliant in her navel and her erect nipples thrusting at the delicate fabric. Her natural modesty was dying; it was becoming second nature to her to proudly display her body. As she stepped towards the house, she recalled reading somewhere that Georgian women of high birth often wore dresses cut low enough to expose their nipples, and she wondered whether this decadent London fashion had ever spread this far north. During Queen Victoria's outwardly prim but secretly debauched reign, had this house possibly been dedicated to wild carnal pleasures?

Lewis pulled the antique bell, and it jangled distantly within. Ruth felt a flutter of apprehension, and then the door swung open.

'Good evening, Mr Lewis Stone and Ms Ruth Parrish, I presume?'

Ruth caught her breath in admiration. The girl was beautiful, petite and perfectly formed. She had a gentle face and large, gorgeous grey eyes. She was also totally naked.

'I'm Aisha.' The exquisite creature smiled as she

identified herself. 'Welcome to Highmoor House. The master and his guests are gathered in the library. Please follow me.' Her speech was musical, English perfectly enunciated in a delightful accent with distinct Latin overtones that did not match her obvious Asian ancestry. She walked ahead of them, leading the way with an easy swing of her narrow hips that was relaxed and earthy, evocative of sunlit islands. Ruth licked her lips, aroused by the girl's overt sexuality and beguiled by her flawless skin, which was the colour of creamy coffee. Her beauty was crowned by exquisite chocolate-drop nipples and enhanced by rich, dark shadows around her crotch.

'Isn't she gorgeous?' she whispered to Lewis.

'You're incredible,' Lewis whispered back. 'Every other woman I've known would have turned green with envy and put my eyes out so I couldn't enjoy the sight of her. I guess I've still got some major adjustments to make.'

'Perhaps I feel more secure than most women.' She squeezed his hand as Aisha swung open a door and stepped inside to introduce them.

Ruth's eyes swept the room. She saw Jack, Elsa and Morgan. Also present were Nick and Judy and a slightly older couple she thought she remembered from Judy's party. And finally, sitting by herself, was the domineering Karly.

'Welcome.' Conrad's voice preceded him across the large room as he came forward to receive them. He subjected Ruth to a penetrating inspection, fleetingly eyeing the engagement ring on her finger, and then smiled. 'I think everyone knows Ruth, so let me introduce her fiancé, Lewis Stone.' He went around the room making the introductions, which identified the unknown couple as Wendy and Tom.

Aisha reappeared silently carrying a tray of drinks. Lewis

took a glass of sherry for himself and Ruth chose some white wine.

'Do you require anything else, master?' Aisha asked in her lovely musical voice.

'Dinner as I ordered in thirty minutes,' Conrad replied without looking at her. 'Nothing more until then.'

'Very good, master.' She bobbed a little curtsey and left the room, her breasts swaying gently and her luscious buttocks flexing as she walked.

'What a beautiful creature,' Lewis declared, expressing everyone's admiration.

'She *is* quite special, isn't she?' Conrad was clearly flattered by the compliment. 'A remarkable jewel.' Then, as if deliberately changing the subject, he asked Lewis about the Quincy sale, and the two men were soon immersed in conversation.

Denied Lewis's attention for the time being, Ruth cast an eye around the room again. She was surprised to find it was a real library. Hundreds of books were stacked ceiling high, and she felt sure they had not been bought for their visual effect. She noted a large and comprehensive art section, a few other shelves devoted to history, and a massive collection of erotica. This was a room she could drown in. Then Elsa asked her about Oona, and she described the girl and the fun they had shared. Naturally, Elsa spotted the ring on her finger, and congratulated her effusively.

Lewis detached himself from Conrad, and headed their way.

Elsa grinned at him. 'I demand the return of my runaway slave!'

'For me to agree to your demands, I would first need some reassurance that she will be appropriately treated.' He played along with her sportingly.

'Sir, you know the penalty for absconding as well as I do. It calls for a severe penalty.'

'What are you proposing?'

'I suggest she be sentenced to marriage. She must become your obedient wife and slave for life.'

Lewis sighed. 'Have you no pity?'

'None, sir, and there will be a charge, too.'

'A charge, on me?'

'Naturally, sir,' Elsa raised an eyebrow, 'since you incited her to this act of betrayal.'

'Name your price, woman, though I warn you, I shall dispute it.'

'The price is the return of this slave for one whole day three times each year to be my plaything.'

'The price is too high,' Lewis said firmly, still playing along but also in deadly earnest. 'I will offer her to you five times each year.'

'You drive a hard bargain, sir.' Elsa smiled. 'Very well, on one condition, that she wears the ankle bracelet permanently.'

'I was planning to anyway,' Ruth commented.

'Silence, slave,' Elsa commanded. 'She has become very insolent, don't you think? It seems to me she deserves a sound spanking.'

'I agree, both to your terms and with your judgement,' Lewis decreed. 'You may spank her yourself before we leave.'

A gong sounded, filling the house with its vibrant tones.

'Dinner is served,' Conrad announced, rising to lead his guests to the dining room.

An impressive table ran along the centre of the room flanked by two enormous antique sideboards set against the panelled walls. Shields and weapons alternated with grand formal portraits, adding to the classical ambience.

Ruth cast a professional eye over the paintings, speculating as to whether they were genuine ancestors or merely purchased decoration.

Aisha received the party, directing each guest to his or her place. She was still naked, but so at ease with her body that she blended in quite naturally with the dinner suits and formal evening gowns. Ruth was not surprised when the girl took the last place at the foot of the table opposite Conrad. When the ladies were seated, their host indicated the men should sit, too, and settled himself in his chair last of all. 'We are ready, Aisha,' he said.

The girl rang a little hand bell, a section of panelling swung open, and two young women entered the dining room carrying soup tureens. The first girl was blonde, her platinum hair falling straight down to her shoulders. She was naked except for a wicked looking chastity belt clamped tightly around her vulva, and two bulbous weights suspended from rings in her pierced nipples. The second girl was tall and almost painfully slender, her angular body framed in a black leather harness that concealed nothing. Small, firm breasts with bright red nipples jutted prettily from between the straps and her pelvis was broad, accentuating her hips and her lovely plump pudenda, framed and enhanced by narrow leather straps passing on either side of it. A tiny bell hung from her labia that tinkled as she walked, and seemed to be connected to something inserted in her vagina. It was the only sound she could produce, for a grotesque ball gag, the strap of which held her dark hair tightly against her head, filled her mouth.

Ruth stared at the gagged girl trying to understand why she seemed so familiar. Perhaps she had seen her at Judy's party as one of the slaves, or maybe as a guest. She searched her memory, until suddenly recognition dawned and she was transported back to that fateful day when she parked in the market square and ran into Elsa. This was the girl who had walked away from an adjacent car, the prim and proper ice maiden herself. Ruth stared at her as she ladled soup into Lewis's bowl, scarcely able to believe her eyes.

Something brushed her arm, and she turned her head sharply to find the girl wearing the chastity belt leaning over her. It was one of the weights hanging from her breasts that had touched her arm.

'Soup, madam?' the serving slave enquired with a pleasantly lilted Scandinavian accent. One of her breasts had been decorated with words tattooed around her aureole, *Lisette, property of Conrad*.

'The girls expect to be touched,' their host announced. 'Lisette has been confined for misbehaviour, and she will appreciate her wickedness all the more when her weights are pulled. Corinne suffers from too free a tongue, and a thoughtless display earlier today has won her the gag. But she can still communicate through her bell, which I request no one remove, please.'

Ruth glanced across the table at Lewis, who had been seated opposite her. He caught her eye, and framed the word 'wow' with his lips. She responded by running the tip of her tongue along her upper lip, and smiling at him lasciviously.

'Uncle always provides good entertainment over dinner,' Jack Thorpe commented from where he sat on Ruth's left.

She turned to him, and saw that he was feeling Lisette's bottom, running his palm over the delicate curve of her buttocks where it was spread by the thick strap of the chastity belt.

'Pity about this, though,' he added, tapping the casing

enveloping Lisette's sex.

'I'm very sorry, sir,' the slave murmured. 'I humbly apologise for spoiling your pleasure.'

'Too late now, but I expect I shall enjoy seeing you properly punished later.'

'I'm certain of it, sir. I hope you find my chastisement entertaining.'

'That's what I like to see.' He gave her buttock a sharp smack. 'A girl who really knows her place.'

After they had served the guests, Corinne and Lisette placed the tureens on the sideboard and stood quietly by, waiting. Their stance was studied – hands clasped behind their backs and their feet placed well apart, their shoulders straight and their chests thrust forward. They gazed straight ahead, avoiding any eye contact.

When all the diners had finished their soup, the girls retrieved the tureens. Corinne took a position at the head of the table, and even though she stood perfectly still, her bell tinkled.

'She's enquiring whether you would like more,' Aisha interpreted for everyone's benefit even while addressing Lewis directly.

Ruth gazed at Corinne in amazement, and felt the bitter taste of envy for the first time. The beautiful slave must have rung the bell by flexing her vagina. She would have to learn how to control her inner muscles that well.

The dinner progressed smoothly. A light poached fish course was followed by roast lamb and grilled vegetables. Dessert was a selection of mouth-watering confections along with a sumptuous cheese board, and a carefully selected wine complemented each course.

The two slave girls collected a lot of attention as they served and cleared, alternating sides so they were both equally available to all the guests. Ruth found Lisette's weights irresistible, and took great pleasure in lifting each bauble to tease the nipple supporting it. Lisette stood perfectly still while she was touched, totally in control of herself, perfectly concealing her responses and thus frustrating Ruth's burning curiosity as to how much hurt or pleasure her actions were generating in the other girl.

Corinne was more accessible. Ruth discovered how pleasant it was to caress and finger a very moist pussy while being served exquisite food. Afterwards, the scent of feminine juices lingered on her fingers and seemed to enhance the flavour of each dish. If Corinne recognised or remembered Ruth from that afternoon in the square, she did not reveal it, and took all the attention she received with commendable equanimity. Ruth noticed that Corinne bore no tattoo, but on the outer part of one thigh, between her knee and her hip, was a distinct mark in the shape of a decorative letter *K*. The scar had the texture of a burn, and she realised with a shock that Corinne had been branded.

Ruth enjoyed herself with the two serving slaves while conversing with Conrad on her right and Jack on her left. Jack continued to exercise the same fascination that had first gripped her in the garage office, but it was to Conrad she was powerfully drawn, and it was to him she talked about her life and her ambitions. Her attraction to her enigmatic host grew more powerful by the minute, and each time she looked towards Lewis the table seemed to have grown wider between them.

When Conrad suggested the party retire to the drawing room she quickly sought her partner, slipping her hand into his to feel the security the contact filled her with. They were last in line, except for Conrad and Aisha, who were also holding hands.

Ruth let out an involuntary gasp of delight when she

entered the drawing room. 'Oh look!' she cried, sounding like a child who has just won a gift certificate to a toyshop. 'It's a Parry!'

The landscape hung above the fireplace. Like the paintings at Broughton, it was one of a series Ruth had not yet seen, and yet she knew instantly that it was a Parry from its style and composition.

'Excellent,' Conrad said from behind her. 'Of course, neither you nor Lewis has seen my house. Allow me to offer you a guided tour.'

'That would be a privilege,' Lewis accepted the offer with alacrity.

Conrad smiled. 'There is much that you will find interesting, I'm sure.'

Leaving Aisha to serve as hostess in his absence, Conrad led Ruth and Lewis out into the hall. Turning towards the rear of the house, they passed a door identified as leading into the kitchen by the sounds and aromas escaping from within. Ahead of them, a pair of swinging double doors took them from the house proper into a large vaulted extension. Ruth stared around her in amazement, sensing Lewis's excitement through the tightening of his fingers around her own. Both sides of the gallery were hung with pictures. On the left were nudes, many overtly erotic. And on the right hung the most comprehensive collection of Parry paintings she had ever beheld. She felt overwhelmed by the sight.

'So *you're* the collector responsible for the escalation of Parry's value,' Lewis mused.

'Regrettably,' Conrad admitted. 'When I bought my first Parry he was virtually an unwanted Victorian curiosity. Of course, now that his prices have soared, I shall never be able to acquire the whole of his work. However, I think I now own the best representative collection of Parry

173

'anywhere in the world.'

'You must accept the honour of having restored the artist's reputation,' Lewis said soberly. 'He's finally recognised for the truly great painter he is. Students now seriously study him, as Ruth did.'

'And she became one of the leading authorities, I hear. It is partially her fault that I shall have to offer an exorbitant bid for Quincy's pair.'

'She would be the foremost authority on Parry if only she would publish,' her fiancé and employer said proudly.

Conrad turned to her. 'Tell me, Ruth, how do you rate my collection?'

'I'm overcome! It's truly magnificent. I could spend hours in here.'

'As I do myself. I would be delighted to enable you to study them in depth, if you wish.'

'Thank you! Of course, there would be distractions… so many of these other works are equally arresting.' She indicated the nudes.

'I buy what I like where erotica is concerned, though a few are commissioned. This one, for example.' He indicated a large full-length portrait occupying a central spot on the far wall.

The painting was hard to miss and Ruth had already registered the subject. The beautiful slave, Zelda, was depicted chained naked to a rock and threatened by a fiery dragon hovering menacingly on her right.

'One of Zelda's favourite fantasies,' Conrad said, reading Ruth's mind. 'The dragon rapes her.'

'Zelda is your slave.'

'Put crudely, yes. We have a complex relationship that satisfies both our needs. Our association is rooted in a mutual respect and trust some people might describe as a form of love.'

Ruth studied the framed photographs hung adjacent to the painting. Some were posed, while others were clearly *camera verité*, telling evidence of the absolute trust Zelda possessed in her master. She felt her belly tighten, and the gusset of her tiny panties clung damply to her vulva. 'Do you photograph all your slaves?' she asked, the catch in her voice betraying her emotions.

'Of course, it's a testimony to their fidelity.'

'How many slaves do you have?' Lewis asked curiously. 'Recruitment must be rather difficult.'

'In all, I probably have ten slaves who are still active. As to recruitment, it just happens. Zelda was my first success after a long, hard search. After her, the others came easily and voluntarily. The foremost rule is that there must be no coercion involved. The submission I demand is based on consent. Nothing happens without consent.'

'Even branding?' Ruth asked softly.

'Even branding. You've noticed Corinne's mark, I see. All my slaves, as you call them, carry my mark. Each chooses the mode of marking that suits them best. The only rule that applies is that the mark must not be concealed when they are with me. Hence Lisette's breasts can never be covered in my presence, that is her little conceit, and Zelda must discard the wig she wears in public.'

Ruth looked confused.

Conrad smiled. 'Of course, you could not see it the other evening due to your own involvement in the scene. Zelda carries a tattoo on the crown of her head.'

'And Aisha? I couldn't see Aisha's mark.'

'Aisha is not a slave. Aisha is an employee. She is my housekeeper, and Tali, her twin, is my cook.'

'But she goes naked and calls you master.' Ruth's confusion deepened.

'It is her choice to do so. Aisha and Tali grew up in a

commune on a privately owned island in the Caribbean. They went naked from birth. When they were in their teens the authorities decreed the environment to be depraved. The leaders were arrested and everyone younger than eighteen was taken to what they termed "a place of safety". Aisha and Tali were sent to an institution in the States, their parents were imprisoned. At eighteen they were thrown out on the streets. I found them in New York. They were homeless, hooked on drugs and prostituting themselves to survive. I brought them home with me and allowed them to live the life they desired. It was their choice to work for me, and their choice to call me master. Aisha said it came naturally to her. Now they live as my wives. Tell me, how old would you say Aisha is?'

'No more than twenty,' Lewis guessed.

'She's thirty-years-old. If that isn't a testimony to the benefits of nudity and liberated sexuality, tell me what is. Now, enough of this, and let's continue our tour. There is so much more that might interest you both.'

Beyond the vaulted hallway they entered what Ruth supposed must have been the farm range. Although extensively modified and carpeted, clues remained in the brickwork and the low ceiling. A corridor led to a much loftier area, and her stomach knotted again at what she beheld. In addition to a comprehensive collection of familiar exercise machines were all kinds of frames, stools, boxes, poles, bars, pillories and cages. The walls were festooned with chains, dark leather harnesses, collars, whips, canes and paddles. Finally, a large glass case held row upon row of dildos of every imaginable size and configuration.

'This is our training suite,' Conrad explained. 'Postulants have to be fit, but most importantly they are taught to trust and assisted in exploring the limits of their sexuality. I'm sure Ruth has already learnt how pain and sexual pleasure are interwoven. For some people there is no distinction whatsoever. For them, extreme suffering can bring exquisite experiences that surpass the most intense sexual orgasm. But not all who have the inclination can reach that pinnacle of perfection. Here they learn to discover and accept their limits.'

Lewis looked around him, taking stock of the bewildering array of devices. 'Amazing... I recognise many of these pieces as adjuncts to corporal punishment. What of the others?'

'Spanking, whipping, caning, these are the most common forms of punishment that complement sexuality, and we can take subjects to the highest level in these areas. Others find that being restrained heightens sexual arousal – Ruth, for instance. Am I right?'

'Yes,' she admitted. 'Being tied up is a very potent aphrodisiac for me.'

'Exactly, and an extension of that is sensory deprivation. See here?' Their host slid open the door of a closet. On hangers were dozens of rubber suits, and on a shelf above them dummy heads displayed rubber and leather masks and bridles. Ruth was immediately fascinated by a tight rubber mask that sported a solid penis where the mouth should be, and she knew instinctively the base extended inward to form a gag. The thought of wearing it to fuck Elsa or Oona made her feel hot all over.

'For example,' Conrad went on complacently, 'we can fit a subject with one of these masks to cut out all sensory inputs except touch. She is then securely fastened and a vaginal dildo inserted. This becomes her sole source of sensation. As time passes she begins to please herself until she achieves orgasm. Unlike normal sex the arousal

177

does not fade, so she begins another cycle. In this way she learns to focus all her attention in her vagina and develops the facility to seek continuous stimulation. The same techniques can be adapted to all forms of sexual activity. I fancy Ruth would like to test some of these herself.'

'Oh yes,' she whispered, glancing at her partner. 'I could spend days in here.' Her heart was pounding and her body was aflame with need. Lewis took hold of her hand, and his touch sent a tingling current of sensation directly to her nipples and her pussy. She instinctively cupped herself through the filmy silk of her skirt, and felt that the fabric was wet.

'What is your estimate of your capabilities, Ruth?' Conrad asked her abruptly.

'Properly inspired, I don't think I'd have many limits at all,' she replied fervently.

'Well spoken. Now come, there is more to see.'

From the barn they moved into another wing. Conrad swung open a door, and Ruth found herself looking into a stable. It was clean, with freshly whitewashed walls and hay spread out as a bed. Along the front edge of the space the brick flooring was depressed to form a drain, and in a near corner there was a tray of sawdust. Ruth wondered at its purpose. She sniffed the air seeking the smell of horses, but the scent that greeted her was more domestic, and the truth dawned slowly through her stunned mind – this was not the home of a horse.

Conrad nodded. 'You're right. This is Corinne's stable. She would not clear her tray, hence the gag. We have four boxes such as this, and in the next bay there are six stalls. When we run our festival they will all be occupied, either by my own girls or by visiting competitors.' He led his awed guests out into the open air and a quadrangle hemmed in by the farm buildings. 'Another training area.' The yard floor was bricked over, and there were several walls and a variety of wooden constructions. In the centre stood a thick pole with a crosspiece from which dangled a variety of pulley blocks. 'The far side of the range is given over to garages and workshops, not part of the training facility, which continues in our indoor school. For practical purposes we are listed as an equestrian school. It will ease the sale should I ever decide to retire from my hobby.'

Ruth and Lewis followed their host into a large, modern space. Low barriers created narrow spaces with bench seating, while the main part of the vast floor was given over to an arena covered in gymnastic matting. Here and there were stacked pieces of equipment, and Conrad stood by with an expression of proprietary pride as his guests drank in the details. 'A very useful place in the winter,' he pointed out. 'Of course, the best place for any sexual contest is out of doors, but this makes it possible at any time of the year. I shall send you invitations to the next meeting. I'm sure Ruth will enjoy competing.'

She gazed at him in awe. In a matter of minutes her horizons had expanded beyond her wildest imaginings. Work, career, marriage and a family were all suddenly unimportant. She was ready to commit every moment of her life to achieving her new ambition. She looked at Lewis, trying to gauge how far he had been swayed and how much latitude he would allow her.

'What do you think?' Conrad's question was addressed to both of them.

'Impressive,' Lewis replied. 'There is much more to this persuasion than I had ever imagined. I must get you to explain things to me in more detail sometime.'

'The only boundary is your imagination,' Conrad stated

emphatically.

'Or the subject's physical limits,' Ruth added.

'Which are in part determined by her own imagination,' Conrad argued pleasantly. 'All limits are capable of being exceeded, Ruth, as experience will teach you. Now I think we should return to the others. It is not good for either Corinne or Lisette to enjoy too long a reprieve.' He shepherd them across the yard and through a door adjacent to the training room, which brought them to a smaller room fitted out in a similar style. 'Our playroom.'

Ruth noted that the playroom contained a shaggy horse, a whipping stool and an arrangement like a short set of asymmetric bars. There were more paintings, of naked girls again. She recognised Lisette and Corinne, and the others she guessed were the rest of Conrad's slaves. Each portrait was surrounded by photographs in the same way Zelda's had been, and the range of activities the girls had been caught in seemed endless. Lewis and Conrad were talking, so she edged closer to examine the nearest of the photographs. Despite her apparent desperate circumstances, the girl in the pictures looked happy, even in the shot where she was suspended by the ankles whilst subject to the attentions of a wicked looking whip. The gleam in her eyes was one of passion rather than distress.

Suddenly Conrad pressed a switch and a section of wall rolled back to reveal the drawing room. Ruth had not absorbed details of the room previously, her attention having been riveted on the Parry, but now she noted how the fireplace was situated on the outside wall and flanked by two tall windows. Opposite them was the door connecting with the rest of the house, and the panelling Conrad had just withdrawn formed the third wall while a fourth wall was concealed by full-length drapes.

She whispered to Lewis, 'I wonder what surprises are

hidden behind there.'

'I'll ask when the opportunity arises,' he promised. 'Hey, see the girls?'

Lisette and Corinne had been secured to the wall with wrist chains, one on either side of the door, and Karly was playing with Lisette's nipple weights.

As Conrad entered the room, Corinne's bell tinkled.

'What is she saying?' Elsa asked.

'She needs to relieve herself,' Conrad translated dismissively. 'She must wait. She knows better than to do it in here.'

'Time they were punished,' Jack declared.

'I agree. Lewis and Ruth, please take a seat. Aisha, drinks for our guests, please. Tell me, Ruth, what sanction is appropriate for a disobedient slave who is bursting for a pee?'

Ruth started, caught off guard by the question. Recently her fantasies had extended to include the idea of punishments, often extreme, but each fantasy had cast *her* as the recipient, never as the perpetrator. Her mind whirled helplessly as she struggled to embrace the concept of determining the nature of someone else's suffering. 'Remind me, please, what exactly were their faults?'

'Corinne's you know, defiance aggravated by impertinence. Lisette was discovered playing with herself after being told to avoid stimulation and orgasm.'

Ruth recalled the pleasure of spanking Oona and the feel of her plump pussy beneath her hand. She remembered Oona's feigned protests, and the obvious ecstasy underlying her struggles. 'I suggest each girl is given a pussy whipping while confined in the Janus harness. And neither girl must orgasm until she has requested, and been given, permission to do so.'

Conrad's face lit up. 'Plus an inverted suspension. A

very appropriate punishment, Ruth, well done. Karly, prepare the Janus. Jack, prepare the slaves, Corinne first.'

The party crowded expectantly into the playroom. Corinne was brought in and stripped of her harness by Jack. Ankle cuffs, joined by a wooden pole, were fitted to her where she lay and a stout rope was lowered from a pulley in the ceiling. A loop at the end of the rope was linked with a carabineer to a ring on Corinne's ankle spreader, and she was quickly hauled up to hang with her fingers trailing on the floor. Ruth noticed her vulva was shaved, leaving only a small neat tuft of hair to decorate her mound. The outer lips of her labia were parted, with the bell lying mute on her ripe, pink clitoris. She imagined the scourging to come, and shivered, clenching her thighs to contain her excitement.

Lisette was fetched next, stripped, and tied down in the same fashion. When she was hauled up Conrad took great care to match their relative positions, for Lisette was a little taller than Corinne. Lisette was also shaven, in her case completely, and like Zelda she was pierced though the clitoris. Ruth thought how prettily the ring decorated her pussy and began rubbing herself again surreptitiously as the Janus harness was fitted, pulling the two girls together at the shoulders.

Wrist-to-thigh straps restrained their arms, rendering them virtually immobile, and then Jack reached between their legs and gripped Corinne's bell. He pulled, and Ruth watched open-mouthed while caressing herself frenziedly as Corinne's pussy spread open before her eyes. The fleshy inner lips blossomed, parting wider and wider as the object inside her was withdrawn. The entrance to her straining sex grew to an impossible size as the smooth ball came free, pulling out with a rushing sound, and it was so big that Ruth almost swooned with admiration.

Corinne's labia closed again slowly, sensuously, and the tension in the room was palpable as everyone marvelled at the cruel stretching the girl had just taken without making a sound. The gag had left her no choice, but now it was removed.

Ruth's empathic tension was eased somewhat when Lewis's hands suddenly cupped her breasts from behind.

'Who shall do it?'

'What shall be used?

'Which girl gets it first?'

Questions were fired out rapidly by different members of the audience.

Conrad held up his hand. 'Ruth has selected the format, let Lewis choose the means.'

Lewis looked flattered. 'Thank you, but I take it spanking is not appropriate, so I shall need some guidance.'

'Spanking, by all means, if that is what you wish, but an implement will be more efficient. They are experienced subjects who will appreciate a full, sharp impact. We have proper pussy-whips, which are quite effective, but rather tame. Plaited whips are very good, but require some practice to administer safely. Straps are easy to use and have a sharp impact. However, a tipped quirt is the obvious choice if you want them to carry marks afterwards.'

Slipping her arm in his, Ruth watched Lewis carefully as he weighed the decision. She pressed close, feeling the warmth of his body through her flimsy dress and sensing the excitement being stirred up within her lover by the situation.

'I shall nominate they be strapped,' he said at last.

Ruth kissed his cheek in approval of his choice, and suddenly became aware of Conrad studying her even more intently than normal. She felt exposed, mysteriously naked beneath his scrutiny, as though he knew exactly what she

183

was thinking. Then their host's voice filled the room as he decreed, 'Karly will administer ten strokes to Lisette, and Ruth will deliver the next ten to Corinne.'

Chapter Thirteen

Ruth's mouth went dry. She felt hot, as though everyone was staring at her, but in fact everyone, including her, was looking intently at Karly.

Karly strode across the room with the confidence of one basking in approval. She selected a short strap fixed to a stubby handle, and turned, a sardonic smile on her lips. She flicked the handle, making the strap snap against itself with a terrifying *crack*.

Lisette flinched, and Corinne jerked in sympathy.

Karly walked around the suspended girls slowly, ensuring Lisette got a clear view of the strap destined to beat her unprotected labia.

Lisette closed her eyes.

Karly took her position, raised the strap, flicked it sharply down, and then up. The leather curled in a lazy *S* and cracked against itself just millimetres above the vulnerable flesh of Lisette's quim. The crowd gasped, and Lisette jerked as the sound in her ears and the draught across her wet labia combined to fool her brain. Karly laughed, a hard, cold sound, and twice more repeated the cruel taunt. Finally she stepped back, swung the strap where Lisette could easily see it, raised it, and planted one foot forward. The strap whistled wickedly through the air and cracked again, but this time the gesture was no feint. Lisette screamed, and began sobbing in anguish.

Ruth trembled, frightened yet beguiled. She leaned hard against Lewis, calmed by his presence even as his firmness aroused her.

Karly struck again. The leather smacked sharply over the girl's delicate flesh, and Lisette's cry was one of sheer anguish. Karly smiled wickedly at her plaintive sobs, and delivered two more strokes in rapid succession. Lisette's body twisted and jerked as she fought the pain, and Corinne's fingers twitched as though she was trying to comfort her partner. Ruth empathised, aware of how much sensation was being transmitted through their closely confined bodies.

Lisette sobbed wildly. Her vulva was red and puffy, the flesh angry from the chastisement. Three more rapid blows followed, the flat *smack* of the strap echoing strangely through the silent room. Lisette's fanny glowed an angry red, yet her clitoris stood stiff, the silver ring strung through it contrasting sharply with the rosy flesh around it. Karly lifted the strap and flicked it down with gentle precision so the very tip seared across her victim's clit, making the ring dance, and Lisette howled in pain, or ecstasy, or both.

Karly laughed. 'Yes, you'd like to come, wouldn't you? But not yet, slave. Not until I tell you to.' She pinched Lisette's inner labia then resumed her stance to deliver the last two strokes with calculated ferocity. As Lisette struggled to contain herself, Karly held the strap handle over her throbbing pussy, twisting it around to tease the opening into her juicing sex. 'Not yet, slave,' she warned. 'You must wait until your partner has the same need.'

Karly continued to tease her victim for several more seconds before she pushed the blunt handle home, burying it deep in Lisette's cleft, leaving the strap trailing over her tortured labia. Then she swung around to face Ruth. 'Your pleasure,' she said, her voice heavy with sarcasm.

Ruth took the leather-bound handle presented by Conrad, trying to avoid eye contact with Karly; the girl's hardness was frightening. Instead, she looked down at Corinne's inverted eyes, reading the unspoken plea for a quick release. She then asked Lewis to hold the strap, quickly discarded her blouse and, kneeling, offered Corinne her exposed nipple. The girl took it eagerly, sucking on it greedily and sending waves of pleasure through Ruth's body. The action also calmed her somewhat, diluting a little of her trepidation. It made her feel good, as if what would follow was an exchange between lovers, for she was incapable of replicating Karly's overt domination.

Ruth pulled her nipple free of Corinne's sucking lips, straightened up and retrieved the strap. She gently stroked the plump fanny spread invitingly before her, not surprised to feel that Corinne was moist. She teased the eager bud into view, encircling it with a moist fingertip, and in the corner of her eye she saw Elsa with her skirt lifted echoing the action on her own clitoris. Tom was behind her, and from her friend's stance, Ruth deduced that his cock was embedded in her bottom. She felt a surge of envy, and the pussy before her suddenly became doubly inviting, the desire to smack it irresistible.

She took up her position, balanced the strap carefully, raised it, and brought it down. She was aiming for the plump crests of Corinne's buttocks, but her lack of expertise let her down. The strap curled viciously over the girl's open labia, which contracted beneath the impact as Corinne cried out in agony. Lisette voiced her frustration with a loud moan as Ruth struck a second time, aiming for Corinne's bottom again, but once more the strap smacked fully across her vulva, which seemed to blossom in agony, exposing its juicy pink interior. The invitation was blatant and impossible to ignore. Abandoning her earlier objective, Ruth laid into the greedy pinkness with energy, delivering two smacks directly to the full labia, and two directly over the hard nubbin. Corinne twisted and jerked beneath the attack, pushing her pelvis forward and eliciting more moans of protest from Lisette.

Quickly, Ruth planted four more sharp blows across the helpless girl's pussy. Each smack seemed to echo back through her own body, triggering a desire to share the deliciously incisive pain she was giving. And feeling suddenly guilty that she was feeding her own needs more than Corinne's, she stepped forward and pushed the end of the handle firmly into the girl's pulsating void. Corinne gasped with pleasure as she gripped the handle firmly, and began pumping it in and out of her. There was no way Corinne could hold out; she succumbed to an orgasm almost at once, and her convulsions pushed Lisette over her own edge.

Ruth pumped away as one climax after another possessed the two suspended bodies. Nothing could stop her driving them on to even greater heights, even when she felt her skirt lifted from behind and her panties pulled down. The warm stiffness that drove into her vagina was pure bliss. She pushed her bottom up and out, taking the gift with pleasure. It was not long before her mind darkened and she felt all her thoughts drowning in a pure, ultimate bliss.

The sky was tinged with dawn when the party broke up. Ruth was naked – she had been that way since Corinne's chastisement – and so were most of the other guests. Sex had been their sole occupation for several hours, yet no one seemed replete. It was the demands of the dawning day that dictated their pragmatism. As Ruth searched for her discarded clothing, she reflected on the pleasure of being in mixed company where inhibitions were unknown. The stimulation had been continuous, with orgasms following swiftly one upon another. The women in particular enjoyed themselves because in this environment they were not dependant on male recovery time. It was also good that, without exception, the men were aware of their full feminine potential, taking as much care to serve their partners as they did to satisfy their own needs.

Conrad approached her, his penis still erect, and Ruth eyed it greedily. Of all the men in the room, Conrad was the only one she had not pleasured tonight. It was as though he was avoiding her. Or saving her for later…?

'Splendid,' he said with feeling. 'I hope you and Lewis have enjoyed yourselves.'

'Immensely,' she assured him.

'Quite astonishing,' Lewis murmured beside her.

She turned naturally into his embrace. How nice it was to feel his arm around her naked shoulders. She snuggled against him. 'Do you think the hotel will admit us at this hour?' she asked.

'You needn't go back to the hotel,' Conrad said at once. 'Use one of my guest rooms. It will enable you to get a few hours of rest before breakfast.'

'Thanks, that's good of you.' Lewis's exhaustion was evident in his voice.

'Not at all, it's my pleasure. Aisha, take my friends up to the griffin room, please.'

Aisha approached them, smiling amiably and looking as fresh as ever. It was impossible to believe she had just taken part in a night of debauchery. Ruth was envious, knowing what a wreck she herself must appear.

The lovely servant led them to a large bedroom with a four-poster bed. 'The bathroom is on the right. Please make use of all the facilities. Will an eight o'clock wake-up call be all right?'

'Make it eight-thirty, please,' Lewis replied.

Aisha smiled, and withdrew.

Ruth glanced eagerly towards the bathroom. 'I shall be glad of a hot shower.'

'Amen,' he sighed wearily. 'Lead they way, my love.'

Ruth had mixed feelings about the journey to London. She wanted to be with Lewis, but there were things she had to do at the flat, and she was becoming accustomed to life in the north and was loath to leave. Their late start ate into their already tight schedule, and she was therefore surprised when Lewis took a detour into York city.

'I thought we might have a look at the gallery,' he explained.

The gallery and the shop were lovely. Ruth liked the setting and the owners, who turned out to be a pleasant couple in late middle age. The husband had retired from a series of directorships and his wife was the artistic director. Ruth took to them at once, and left feeling more enthusiastic than ever about the prospect. Apart from the intrinsic value, there was the added attraction of being close to the action.

As they walked back to the car park, Lewis asked, 'Tell me, Ruth, do you own a tennis dress?'

'No, I wear shorts and a T-shirt on the few occasions I play,' she told him. 'Why do you ask?'

He shook his head. 'The conditions set by Elsa still apply.'

She smiled. 'Of course, but I'm not intending to play tennis in the foreseeable future, so why the curiosity?'

'I think you should be equipped for all eventualities. Look, here's a sportswear shop. Let's go in.'

She followed him obediently, and allowed herself to be persuaded into choosing a brief white dress that exposed her panties. There was a certain thrill in sharing this

190

intimate purchase with her lover, and she suspected something exciting lay behind it.

It was late afternoon when they arrived back at the office. Although Ruth had been away only a few days, she found the large building rather oppressive and hectic.

Janet was in, and Ruth slipped gratefully into her office for a good gossip. The older woman wanted to know all about the days she had been away, and inspected her engagement ring with due reverence.

'You're a fortunate girl, Ruth. Mr Stone has never made such a commitment to anyone before. He must care for you very deeply.'

'I'm sure he does, Janet... oh, it sounds so smug when I say that, but I'm not being conceited. I just feel loved, truly loved, by him. Tell me, why do you always call him Mr Stone?'

'Habit, I suppose,' Janet acknowledged. 'To use his Christian name would seem unduly familiar.'

'But why, you care for him, don't you? You feel much more than just a polite respect for him, I know you do. He should be the one putting *you* on a pedestal.'

'I'm a happily married woman, Ruth.'

'Maybe, but if the offer were made, you'd jump on it. Admit it.'

'Well, I suppose you're right.' Janet sighed. 'It *would* be nice to have at least one illicit affair before old age sets in.'

'You're not old.'

'I have about five years before menopause, Ruth. What then?'

'Nonsense. A woman's sexuality lasts forever. I think you're a lovely person, and if Lewis doesn't make you an offer, I'll seduce you myself.'

'Ruth!'

'Don't be so shocked, Janet. It happens more often than you imagine, and it's perfectly healthy and enjoyable. Open your mind and let life flood in!' She smiled at her own triteness.

'Now you're embarrassing me, Ruth.' She averted her eyes. 'Um, by the way, I've booked the squash court for you at eight this evening.'

'Pardon?'

'Mr Stone… *Lewis*… rang and said you wanted a court for tonight, and that I was to book it for you.'

'That's the first I've heard about it.'

'He said he'd see you there later this evening.'

Ruth shrugged. 'A man of mystery, I like that. Thanks for the chat, Jan. I ought to be clearing my desk and getting home. Now, remember what I said, charm him and grab what you can for yourself. I could never be jealous of you.'

Ruth let herself into her flat. On the lobby floor she had found a small white envelope with her name on it. She dumped her bag and the carrier from the sports shop on the couch, and tore open the envelope. She recognised Lewis's writing, and felt a potent tingle of excitement run through her as she hastily scanned his instructions. Then she went hot with excitement and trepidation as she rushed to the phone.

'Hello, Helen? This is Ruth. What do you know about a squash court?'

'I know you and I are going to be playing on one this evening. A mutual friend of ours, Elsa, rang me yesterday with some very saucy instructions. Have you received some, too?'

'Just. You'll obey them?'

'Naturally, to the letter.' The girl giggled coquettishly. 'It sounds a hoot. Shall we meet at your place?'

'All right. Is half past seven good?'

'Yes, fine. Give me directions.'

The heavy atmosphere and black clouds towering in the west heralded the end of the heat wave. Capricious squalls tugged at the girls' short skirts and played teasingly over their bottoms. Both were wearing short white tennis dresses and nothing else underneath. They had both received identical instructions and had obeyed them to the letter. Ruth's naked pussy was moistening and she suspected her new friend's was as well. Helen was a striking blonde with enviably full breasts and legs that went on forever, and a smug awareness of her good looks glowed in her large blue eyes.

At the fitness suite the duty manager eyed them coolly, scanning their brief costumes with a critical eye. Ruth knew he could see her hard nipples pressed against the fine, close-fitting material, and it made her feel extremely sexy. Soon, very soon, she must find a good firm cock to satisfy her cravings.

As they were already dressed for the game they went directly to the court, and Ruth considered the glass screen with amusement. 'If we keep the returns high, we can preserve some of our dignity,' she observed.

Helen laughed. 'I say if we're going to give a show, let it be a good one.'

'You're right, of course. Keep 'em low; a first class show.'

'Keep 'em low!' Helen echoed enthusiastically.

The game began. Neither girl was taking the play seriously, but they quickly entered into the fun of it, moving the ball around the court to keep each other on the move while stooping to receive the low returns each was making an effort to create.

'The gallery's empty,' Ruth noticed, disappointed. 'If it fills up I shall bend really low and then you can smack me, as if by accident, of course. I want them to have a really good look at my bottom.' She slammed a ball into the lower corner. It came out high and Helen had to leap for it. The stretch pulled her dress right up, exposing her bottom completely, and Ruth was so dazzled by the beauty of it that she failed to make the return.

'Well, we've got ourselves an audience now,' Helen said as she stooped to recover the ball.

Ruth looked up at the gallery without breaking her crouch. A young man hurrying along the corridor had stopped to stare in disbelief at the unexpected sight of a pert, naked bottom. He was now also probably staring at the lingering marks left by her spankings, and if that did not completely arrest his attention, nothing on this earth would. She wiggled her bottom teasingly, and served her next shot in a stooped position, aiming for a low hit that would make Helen bend over too. She cast another quick glance over her shoulder. Sure enough, there was a second figure behind the glass now.

Helen got in a powerful shot that came back high across the court, and Ruth had to concentrate to reach it, stretching to the limit. Helen reacted quickly, keeping her on her toes. The speed of the game occupied her mind until Helen missed a return, and in the lull she checked the gallery again. A sizeable crowd was gathered now.

Helen served, and the game went on. Ruth immersed herself in the fun of it, and in the sheer sensual pleasure of flaunting her body so flagrantly. Then a rise in the background noise warned her of someone's approach as the door of the court was flung open, admitting a blast of strident protests. Distracted, she just managed to dodge the hurtling ball, but before she could recover her arm was seized by one of the grey-haired matrons in a tweed suit who stormed onto the court.

'You sluts need to be taught a lesson you won't forget!' the woman cried in a shrill voice. Ruth was competently bent over and clamped against her assailant's hip. Hoisting Ruth's tiny skirt, the woman spun her around to point her bottom at the crowd in the gallery, and began systematically spanking her exposed buttocks. Ruth swore and kicked, but the woman was an expert and her struggles were in vain. She tore at the heavy tweed, intent on ripping her attacker's skirt away, but the beastly hag only hit her harder.

'You bitch!' Ruth screamed, clawing at the thick fabric. 'Let me go!'

'Quiet down, you little whore, or it'll be the worse for you.'

Ruth felt something click in her brain. Beneath the assumed shrillness, the voice possessed a timbre that was uncannily familiar. She clawed at the hem of the skirt, crying out in protest at the heavy spanking being administered to her posterior. Desperately she hauled the thick tweed skirt up, exposing sexy lace-trimmed stockings and taut suspenders that made her gasp in surprise. 'I know those legs! You pig, Elsa Fredericks!'

Elsa smacked her even harder. 'Shut up and take your punishment, worm. I promised you a good spanking, and you're getting it. Play the part, or we'll all get arrested.'

Ruth kicked and wriggled, and from the yells nearby it was obvious Helen was reacting equally violently to her chastisement.

Elsa delivered two more sharp smacks and then pulled the red-faced Ruth erect. She slipped off her tweed jacket and wrapped it around Ruth's waist. 'Go and make yourself decent, slut.' She gave her a hearty shove towards the door.

Ruth collided heavily with the duty manager, who had just succeeded in pushing through the crowd gathering on the threshold. The jacket fell away and she bent over to retrieve it, contriving to expose her scalding bottom to his full view. She wriggled her pert mounds and parted her thighs so he could get a glimpse of her pouting pussy.

Before the man could react, Elsa rounded on him. 'You should be ashamed of yourself, allowing a disgusting spectacle like this to be perpetrated in an exclusive club! Why weren't these two trollops banned?' Then, as the manager struggled to find the right answer, Elsa gave Ruth another shove, pushing her roughly through the crowd.

Ruth felt hands groping her bare bottom. She twisted away, but a strong hand grabbed her arm. She protested, only to fall silent as Lewis's voice whispered in her ear, 'The car's outside. Get in it while I rescue Helen.'

She dashed out of the centre. It was raining hard, and even though she ran to the car she was soaked by the time she made it inside. Her nipples stood hard and erect against the translucent fabric as she dove for shelter, dropping her racquet. She was breathless, flushed and excited. She was also horny as hell and desperate for relief. She yanked off her sodden dress and plunged two fingers between her thighs, teasing her willing clit free and rubbing it with vigour. When Helen was finally bustled into the back of the car, Ruth was in the throes of her third orgasm.

A body barged against her, forcing her up against Helen, who was also struggling out of her wet dress. 'Stop indulging yourself and help me out of these soaking-wet clothes,' Judy snapped.

Ruth forced herself back to reality and groped at Judy's fastenings in the confined space. Elsa was being attended to by Helen, and by the time Lewis, in the driver's seat, had pulled out of the parking lot, Judy and Elsa were down to stockings and suspenders.

'Do your duty,' commanded Judy. 'I want a really stupendous climax.'

Ruth bent eagerly to her task, and she heard Elsa making similar demands of Helen as Lewis drove them all out of the city.

At Lewis's home, Ruth and Helen were bent over and subjected to a detailed examination.

'I thought as much,' Elsa declared as she ran her fingertips over the curves of Ruth's tingling buttocks. 'This was not a good job; it was too rushed in there.'

'Not any more, please,' Ruth pleaded.

'What, a dedicated slave declining the pleasure of punishment?' Elsa mocked. 'I can't believe my ears.'

'I can't either,' Lewis said, and joined Elsa in caressing Ruth's bottom. 'If she wants to spank you again, then she will, and I don't want to hear one more peep out of you, young lady. In fact, another sharp spanking would put her in the right mood, Elsa. I think she would also benefit from having a butt-plug inserted while you do it. You have just enough time before Lionel arrives.'

'Who's Lionel?' Ruth demanded.

Elsa pinched her bottom sharply. 'You'll find out in good time. Now position yourself over this chair, please.'

Ruth shamefacedly moved to the required position, spreading her legs to present her bottom for another spanking. Although she was sore from the last one, she could not deny that the prospect of another beating was as exciting as it was alarming. She gripped the chair tightly, until her knuckles showed white, and waited for the butt-plug with trepidation and longing wondering who Lionel was.

Elsa was an expert spanker. She laid each blow accurately and systematically over the marks of her earlier chastisement, until Ruth was smarting over every inch of her posterior. The butt-plug was tightly lodged inside her, and each smack caused her sphincter to grip it firmly, inducing lovely feelings in her bottom that worked their way up to her sensitive clit.

Elsa paused to observe her work.

Ruth's bottom glowed and burned. She tried to keep still, but the intense sensations in her body made her want to squirm. She wondered if Elsa had finished, and closed her eyes to prevent herself breaking her role by looking around.

When Elsa finally spoke, her words were tinged with relish. 'And these are to teach a lesson to someone who took an unusual delight in hurting one very defenceless pussy last night.'

Ruth tensed. She knew what was coming, and the prospect was terrifyingly delectable.

Elsa's hand landed squarely on her open quim. The blow stung and hurt unbelievably; Ruth felt as though she had been branded. The sensation seemed to burn through her entire being and she howled in despair even as deep inside her a voice cried, 'Again!'

Elsa obliged her silent plea. Five more heavy smacks impacted on Ruth's puffy labia until it burned and stung like never before. She felt thoroughly drained, humiliated and hurt beyond her ability to express it. She wanted to drag herself away and hide in a corner where she could weep undisturbed and mentally lick her wounds. What she could not quite understand was the curious desire echoing around her brain to experience the whole agonising ordeal again.

When she was allowed to stand, she saw a man had arrived and was setting up an artist's easel. She concluded this must be the mysterious Lionel. He had a rather intense air about him, and although he studied her openly, there was no glimmer of desire in his eyes. She felt neglected. In recent days she had grown accustomed to men and women expressing desire in some form or another when they looked at her.

'You're Ruth?' he asked after he had finished his preparations.

'Yes, I'm Ruth.' She looked to Lewis for enlightenment, but received none.

Lionel came over to her, and surveyed her critically.

She was accustomed to artists, and recognised the purposeful professional eye with which he was viewing her. She moved provocatively, hoping to generate a reaction in him, but her efforts were in vain.

'Lie on the couch, please,' he instructed her. 'On your side, and bend your upper leg slightly, I want to see your crotch, but not all of it. Understand? I want to feel your sensuality, but I don't want you to come across as a prostitute selling her wares. Rest one hand on your hip and support your head with the other.'

Ruth took up the position he indicated, allowing him to move her around until he was satisfied.

'That will do,' he said at last with grudging approval. 'Now hold that pose for at least twenty minutes.'

She tried to empty her mind. She had served as a model to a life class at university, and she knew how trying it was to hold a pose for a protracted amount of time. Here it was even harder, where all around her were naked people intent on enjoying their intimacy. And worse, Helen was

199

being set up for another spanking. She had to work hard to contain her passions as the sound and sight of Helen being chastised flooded her brain. And when the beautiful blonde was subjected to the same pussy whipping she had just endured, Ruth thought she would burst with longing, but she forced herself to hold still.

At last, Lionel indicated he was finished, and Lewis helped Ruth off the couch. She was allowed to see the sketch, and viewed it critically. She had to admit it was good. It was a simple pencil drawing, but Lionel had caught her features and her aura perfectly. She could hardly believe she was capable of projecting such sensuality. The pose and expression were accurate, the background fictitious. She was depicted lying on a stone floor. Around her neck was a collar, and from it a chain extended to a ring in the stonework above her head.

'We're calling it *Ruth Restrained*,' Lewis informed her. 'But now it's time for bed. Elsa, Judy and Helen are staying the night, but I don't think they'll disturb us. Take a hot shower while I see Lionel out.'

Chapter Fourteen

The saleroom at Broughton was filled to capacity. Among the familiar dealers Ruth spotted Elsa and Morgan and other members of their group. She felt satisfied with the results of her work and happy with her commitment to Lewis. The previous evening had been devoted to wedding plans. They agreed Highmoor House would be an excellent venue, and the date would be set as soon as Conrad could accommodate them. In high spirits, she addressed the day's task.

Bidding began at ten o'clock. Ruth, demure in a formal suit, sold the minor lots while Lewis officiated over the major items. The two Parry's, now confirmed as authentic, fetched astonishing prices, both going to Conrad after he beat off a fierce competition. Ruth was pleased to learn the paintings were to remain at Broughton after its conversion, and by three o'clock there remained only some small items, which she disposed of quickly. The saleroom was almost empty when the last lot sold, so she was surprised when Lewis took the stand again.

'Ladies and gentlemen, this is a private sale open to invited bidders only. It is not connected with the main event and consists of a single lot that will be of interest to connoisseurs of erotic art. On offer is an original pencil cartoon entitled *Ruth Restrained*. It is an excellent example of the work of Lionel Fischer, who the cognoscenti among you will immediately recognise as being one of the world's rising stars in this genre.'

A porter began to parade the picture around the room,

and Ruth hid in the background, puzzled by this turn of events.

'The lot consists of the cartoon,' Lewis went on, 'plus an exclusive option on the projected full size oil painting, at no extra cost, to be completed within three months of commissioning. I have Fischer's letter of commitment, which is included in the sale, and the price should reflect this. There is no reserve on this item. Are the telephone bidders online?'

Two porters relaying phone bids indicated in the affirmative.

'Good. Who will offer me two thousand pounds?'

Ruth scanned the room trying to understand why her picture should attract such interest. Three dealers had remained behind. Two more in the act of leaving turned back, and watched keenly. Conrad, aloof and haughty, retained the centrally located seat he had occupied all day. On the far side of the room sat Elsa, Morgan, Nick and Judy.

A low bid came from one of the dealers, and Morgan immediately followed with one of his own. Then a telephone bid was entered and the price rose quickly past the two thousand pound mark.

Ruth watched in a daze, flushed and embarrassed by all the attention her portrait was getting. Being an exhibitionist amongst friends was one thing, but abstract notoriety was something else entirely. Her emotions began to boil. She could hardly believe a picture of her could be worth so much.

The phone bids were still active, as were Judy's and Elsa's, inching the price ever upward. So far, nothing from Conrad.

The action slowed. The price had already exceeded Ruth's wildest estimate, and Lewis was preparing to sell.

Then Conrad upped the bid. Judy bid against him, but was once again outbid by Conrad. Ruth buried her head in her hands to shut out this mad dream. More bids came over the phones, but Conrad topped them all. Finally, she heard the hammer fall and Lewis declared the sale. The price was beyond belief.

Ruth rushed to the rostrum. 'What does this mean?' she asked in a brittle tone, angry at Lewis for not explaining to her what was going on.

'It's my wedding present to you,' he said. 'You now have the means to buy into the York shop.'

She stared at him in disbelief. 'This was a rigged sale? That's unethical!'

'Darling, do you rate me so low? Would I risk my reputation on such a dodge, even for the person I love most? I assure you, the price resulted from a fair and open sale.'

'But who was bidding over the phone?'

'Two of America's principal dealers in erotic art. I rang them yesterday. They were buying a Fischer, not you, but had they been successful, you might have become an international celebrity.'

Ruth capitulated, secure once more in Lewis's regard. She could scarcely comprehend that another part of her future was now assured.

Conrad approached the rostrum, and said in his rich and sensuous voice, 'At last I possess the perfection that is Ruth Parrish.'

'I hope I bring you much pleasure,' she replied quietly, aware of sounding awkward.

Conrad's fingers pressed a fraction more firmly over hers. 'You will, my dear, many, many years of deep fulfilling pleasure, every moment of which is to be anticipated and savoured like a fine wine. But now you must excuse me. I must settle the bill.'

She stared after him, drawn to him by a mysterious, irresistible force. She had felt the same attraction the day she met Jack Thorpe, but this was infinitely more compelling. She fought it, concentrating her thoughts on Lewis to break its grip over her. She wanted to wrap her arms around her lover and use him as a shield against such demanding power.

With a supreme effort, she shook herself free of the invisible bonds between her and Conrad. There were things to be done; only the sale was over, not her responsibilities. As she turned away she stole one more glance at the master. Now she understood the nature of the chains that bound Zelda, Corinne and Lisette. There were no tangible links. It was something far stronger, unbreakable emotional shackles they themselves had forged.

The next morning Lewis drove them to York. They went first to the gallery to enter a formal offer in Ruth's name, and with that done, they toured agencies in search of houses. Lewis had concluded it was quite feasible for him to commute to London, since his presence in the office was not essential every day. Ruth was ecstatic about this, all her quandaries resolved. Also, Conrad would be accessible. Although yesterday's flush of passion had dissipated, she remained determined to get closer to the enigmatic man. And the best thing was, she knew Lewis understood how she felt.

At a restaurant in the centre of the city they ate a light lunch, mindful of the comprehensive menu Elsa was sure to provide that evening.

'What shall I wear tonight?' Ruth asked.

'No bra and no panties, that much is certain.'

'Oh, sir, you're so strict,' she teased happily. 'Not even

a little thong to preserve a girl's dignity?'

'Slaves have no right to dignity,' he replied soberly, enjoying his meal. 'I've a good mind to send you to the affair stark naked. That would tell everyone what a little tart you really are.'

'And will you send me as a common whore ready to serve all and sundry?' She tried to suppress her eagerness at the prospect.

'No, tonight you must seduce Andrew, for Oona's sake. Concentrate on that.'

'But I've been on very short rations today,' she protested. 'And after last night I have an appetite for some serious confinement.'

'Slaves are not allowed requests. You must be obedient.'

'Then tell me what to wear, sir.'

'I suggest we shop for something suitable after lunch.'

•

'Not in role tonight?' Elsa asked, surveying her guest with envious approval. Ruth looked stunning in shimmering electric blue. The dress boasted a high neckline and a plunging back, and the ankle-length skirt was slit to the hip, outrageous and yet elegant.

'I'm a lady of quality with a mission,' Ruth explained.

'Oh yes? Come on, you can tell me.'

'Tonight I must liberate Oona.'

'Good for you! I like Oona, she's nice and she's more than up for it. I invited them early to ease Andrew into a party mood. I've put them in the sitting room with a porno video and some drinks. I'll send Helen in later to help widen his perceptions a little.'

'Good thinking,' Ruth said approvingly, looking around for her new blonde friend. Helen was naked except for a collar and the mandatory slave bracelet. She walked over to her. 'Hello Helen, you look gorgeous. I could eat you alive.'

'Of course, madam, whatever you desire.' Helen stuck her tongue out at her mischievously.

'Show a little more respect, girl,' Ruth retorted playfully. 'Remember your position.'

'My position is bent over with my legs spread. What's yours?'

'Mine's a bit different tonight.' Ruth turned away, a gleam in her eyes.

In the sitting room Oona and Andrew were intent on the blue movie. Ruth glanced at the screen. She knew the film, which was unusual in that it had plenty of action built around a strong plot and well-rounded characters. Andrew seemed to be engrossed, for he made only a perfunctory acknowledgement when Oona introduced them. Ruth assessed him carefully. In looks and build, he reminded her of her discarded Stanford, though his general demeanour and his taste in clothes showed him to be a bit more down-to-earth. He seemed personable and fit, but one did not have to look very far to see he was deeply involved with himself and rather conventional.

Oona looked delightful, filling her simple dress to perfection. It was the sort of dress you could buy in any chain store, but on Oona's luscious figure it looked exclusive.

Ruth seated herself on the sofa with Lewis on her right and Andrew on her left, separating herself from Oona, whom she gave an encouragingly smile as she quickly summed up the situation. Andrew was drinking freely and was absorbed in the film; he should be easy to manipulate. 'Oh, this bit's good!' she exclaimed. 'Watch the girl's face when he enters her. Is that great acting, or does it really feel that good?'

'It looks real to me,' Oona cast her fervent vote.

'Rubbish,' Andrew said sharply. 'It's all simulated. It has to be, for technical reasons.'

'I beg to differ,' Ruth argued. 'There's something really special about the moment when a really hard prick goes in, the way it stretches and fills you. It's hard to fake that reaction. Don't you agree, Oona?'

'Yes, especially if it's a really big hard prick.'

Andrew looked at her curiously.

'Like Andy's,' she added quickly. 'You'd know if you'd had him, Ruth.'

He scowled, but gave Ruth more attention than the occasion deserved before turning back to the film.

Ruth bided her time.

The film had entered its final sequence when Helen arrived. Andrew stared at her, his eyes flitting rapidly between her nipples and her crotch. She stood with her legs slightly parted as she enquired whether anyone wanted more drinks, while on the screen a group of naked bodies vigorously continued copulating. His attention was hopelessly torn between the living girl and the shagging actresses, and Helen's position was such that part of his view was framed by the twin peaks of her labia. When he took his re-filled glass from her, he was almost panting.

Helen refilled Lewis's glass standing before him in the same way.

'Quite delightful,' Lewis said as he accepted the drink with one hand and with the other reached up to stroke her pussy.

'Bloody hell!' Andrew murmured.

Helen smiled, spread her legs wider, and Lewis inserted two fingers into the beautiful blonde. She thrust her pelvis forward invitingly. 'Do you want to fuck me, sir?' she asked sweetly.

'Naturally,' Lewis replied. 'Bring me a lead.'

Helen curtsied and trotted away, returning in moments with a leash she held out in both hands.

Lewis took it from her. 'Down,' he ordered.

She dropped obediently onto all fours.

He clipped the lead to her collar. 'Walk,' he commanded, and then led her away just like an obedient pet.

'Bloody Hell!' Andrew said again, more loudly.

'Let's see the end of the film,' Oona insisted. She had put the action on *pause* while his attention was diverted.

Ruth edged closer to him, letting her skirt fall open so she could press her bare leg against his. On his other side Oona laid her hand on his thigh close to his groin, and Ruth felt him stiffen as he glanced down at the increasingly prominent bulge in his trousers. 'I love this ending,' she said, sighing. 'It's so licentious. It really turns me on. And look at that girl… have you ever seen such a gorgeous bush?'

Oona seized the cue. 'And look at *him*. God, his cock is *huge*. That would put a smile on my face for sure.'

Andrew rose predictably to the bait, breaking off from his preoccupation with the onscreen action. 'What is it about women, this obsession with size?' he demanded testily.

'Believe me, size matters,' Ruth assured him.

'You should try Andrew,' Oona repeated generously. 'He's enormous.'

Andrew turned on her again. 'Stop twittering. I'm trying to watch the movie.'

'Then watch *this* bit,' Ruth commanded.

The camera closed in on the huge prick nosing its way into a soaking quim. The stark, explicit detail drew crude comments from Andrew, which grew more animated as the action developed to a vigorous shafting. Then the angle shifted, tracking over the woman's navel, loitering suggestively on her wobbling breasts before moving quickly up to her face, just as a ripe pussy descended over her mouth. The picture flicked back and forth between the two vulvas, one full of cock the other full of tongue, faithfully recording the escalating action as the supine woman pleasured a man and a woman at the same time. The slurping, gasping, grunting soundtrack flooded the imagination as a triple orgasm built, and broke.

The credits began rolling and Ruth pressed her body against Andrew. 'I need some of that,' she whispered. 'It's hours since I had a good fuck.' Her tone challenged him.

Oona had one hand inside her panties while the other kneaded her husband's very prominent bulge, and she made no protest when Ruth's hand closed in to take over. 'And it's centuries since I felt a woman's tongue in my pussy,' she declared, tugging off her panties.

Ruth could see Andrew's internal battle reflected in his eyes. He was trying to speak, but no words issued from his lips, and he made no protest when Ruth eased down his zipper.

Oona was naked now, and she sprang forward to help her friend strip her dazed spouse. Then she knelt to take his erection in her mouth while Ruth slipped out of her dress.

Andrew stared at the blue fabric shimmering its way down to the floor. 'You're not wearing kickers!' he blurted.

She winked at him. 'There's no point when I'm partying with real men.' She lifted Oona from behind, her hands cupping her breasts. 'Come away, now, I want to lick that pretty pussy of yours.'

Oona obeyed slowly, holding Andrew tenaciously so that he slid forward off the couch and onto his knees.

The couple was still interlocked as Ruth spread herself on her back and wriggled, feet first, beneath Oona, enclosing Andrew with her legs. Then she reached up and pinched Oona's hard nipples. The girl cried out in shocked surprise, letting go of Andrew at the same moment a tongue drilled into her pussy. 'Oh, my God!' she groaned, squatting over Ruth's face.

Ruth's tongue responded urgently as she moved her hands from Oona's breasts in search of Andrew's cock, groping blindly for it until she finally closed over his warm hardness. She heard him groan, and felt his erection's powerful jerk in her grip.

'Yes, oh yes…' Oona sat bolt upright, pushing her hungry sex onto Ruth's busy tongue while cupping her own breasts to pinch her nipples sharply as she moaned, 'Oh, God, that's incredible… more, please, give me more…'

Ruth spread her legs open, urging Andrew towards her ravenous pussy. She felt his hands playing with her breasts, and then his fiery tip parted her labia and nosed at her opening. She lifted her lips, her hunger growing as he breached her opening.

Oona leaned back and supported herself with her arms to flaunt her treasures, making certain Andrew saw her open sex and Ruth's powerful tongue darting swiftly from her labia to her clitoris.

'Fucking hell,' he said, and Ruth's breath was forced from her in an explosive gasp as he rammed into her, lifting her bodily and making his balls slap against her labia. Abandoning self-control he surrendered to his lust, pounding her savagely as she wrapped her legs around him, riding his wild bucking thrusts while still managing to give Oona head. Such passion could not last long, and she vaguely wondered who would come first.

Andrew's motions grew desperate. He drove himself home with a single piercing thrust that jarred Ruth to the bone. His rigid cock jerked inside her like some great lever, and his ejaculation felt like a hose aimed straight at her cervix. Only moments later Oona threw herself sideways and fell back across the carpet, writhing and yelling as she, too, was overwhelmed by a massive orgasm.

Ruth lay still with Andrew slumped against her, breathing heavily. She felt content, but a long way from satisfaction. Instinctively she deployed her abdominal muscles. With so much use they were becoming stronger and more skilful, and she was rewarded by a flicker of response from the hot, thick weapon still lodged inside her. He groaned, burying his face in her breasts as she squeezed him again, milking him and feeling him rapidly regaining his stiffness.

Oona sat up, her knees bent, her ripe pussy on full view. 'That was incredible,' she said dreamily. 'And I want it all again. God, I just want to be fucked silly!'

Andrew raised his head. 'Fucking hell, you two are like bleeding rabbits.'

'Go on, Andy, give her a good shagging,' Ruth urged. 'You're stiff enough.' She bore down on his shaft, squeezing it rhythmically with her inner muscles until he groaned with pleasure. 'Look how ready she is, Andy. She's like a ripe fig just begging for your gorgeous prick to burst her open. I want to see your spunk gushing from her cunt.'

'You're a bloody witch,' he accused, pulling out of her and grabbing for his wife. She leapt away from him and crouched on her hands and knees, lifting her bottom towards him while offering him her ripe cleft. Kneeling behind her, he gripped her hips and drove into her without ceremony, ramming her deep and hard and making her

211

shout with surprise and pleasure.

As Ruth watched the couple, the heat in her sex flared up and became almost unbearable. In wild desperation she grabbed an empty mixer bottle from the drinks' table and rolled over to squat before Oona, spreading her legs wantonly.

'What are you doing?' Oona gasped.

'I need to be filled. Help me push.'

Oona tried to take the bottle. It was awkward, for Andrew was thrusting madly into her and her hands were fully occupied keeping her balance. Valiantly she made an effort to present the bottle's slim neck to Ruth's palpitating opening.

'No, the other way around, base first!' Ruth begged. 'Give it to me!' She grabbed the bottle and jammed its blunt base against her vagina.

Oona was babbling incoherently as she watched Ruth's labia stretch to engulf the trophy. Then lowering her head she pushed the bottle deeper into Ruth with her forehead, feeling the smooth, slippery insertion.

'Hold it in!' Ruth pleaded. 'Oh yes... oh yes, I'm coming... I'm coming... oh, God, I'm coming!'

Andrew, committed to his own conclusion, drove relentlessly into his wife, who also wailed her ecstasy as the three of them emulated the blue movie and came together.

Oona was the first to regain control of herself. Andrew was lying on his back in a trancelike state, breathing heavily. Ruth was lying with her knees drawn up, her eyes fixed on the ceiling as though mesmerised with it. Oona crawled over and knelt between them. With one hand she played with Ruth's nipples, taking Andrew's flaccid cock in the other.

They stayed like that for some time, until Andrew regained some degree of lucidity. He sat up and gazed at Ruth, who was still cruising in her private world, her eyes closed as she fingered herself.

'Should we wake her up?' he asked.

'No, she's really happy.' Oona planted a kiss on his knob, and took it into her mouth.

He moaned with pleasure. 'If you'd told me it would be like this, I wouldn't have agreed to come.'

'I hope that wasn't a pun,' she mumbled, her mouth full of his cock. Then she suddenly stopped sucking and looked sharply up at him. 'You're not taking me home.' It was a challenge, not a question.

'I ought to, but you seem to be enjoying yourself.'

'I am. And I want to enjoy myself some more. You've had Ruth, so I want to have someone else, too. Fair's fair.'

'What's happening here?' he demanded uncertainly. 'No one's been to see us since that girl went off with Lewis. Should we mingle, or what?'

'I'll mingle if I can have my share,' she insisted.

'What's got into you, Oona?' He sounded strangely vulnerable.

'It's what *hasn't* gotten into me. I want to feel another big prick in my fanny. Come on admit it, you've loved every minute of this.'

'Well, I can't deny that.' He nodded at Ruth. 'Will she show us where the action is?'

Oona patted his rising cock. 'Down boy, wait your turn.'

Ruth gradually recovered her senses, and after a few minutes was ready to show them round.

'Aren't you going to dress?' Oona asked her.

'I don't feel like it,' she said. 'I imagine most everyone else is naked by now, but please yourselves.'

'Is it okay to go around like this?' Andrew indicated his revitalised erection.

'Perfectly. But beware, it's an invitation that will be snapped up in a flash.'

Oona decided to remain naked. She had a lovely body and Ruth licked her lips as the soft evening light outside bathed Oona's delicious curves. The sound of voices drifting from the barn gave them their direction.

There were about twenty people inside the barn, all of them engaged in some sort of erotic activity. Nearest the door, Judy was perched on a stool and drinking lazily from a tall glass while a kneeling girl lapped at her pussy. She was obviously enjoying the attention without struggling to achieve orgasm, but now she stared admiringly at Andrew. 'Hmm, you look delicious, young man. Debbie, leave be and bring these people something to drink. Then you may please the lady.'

The girl sprang to her feet, politely enquired their preferences, and trotted away to the bar. She was attractively plump and very sexy. The slave bracelet denoted her status.

Judy pulled up a stool for Oona, and took Andrew's erection in her hand. 'So, these are our new friends.'

Ruth completed the introductions as Debbie returned with a laden tray. Having served the drinks, she then sank obediently to her knees and her tongue began servicing Oona.

'Is she performing satisfactorily?' Judy asked, as though Debbie was a pet she was still in the process of training.

'Perfectly,' Oona replied breathlessly. 'She has exactly the right touch, just enough to keep me simmering without boiling over.'

'Would you prefer a cock?' Judy asked graciously. 'There are plenty of willing ones around.'

'Oh yes!'

'I'll call Nick. And don't worry, I'll keep your husband well in hand… well, I'll keep him in somewhere.' She laughed at her own little joke. 'Debbie, go find Nick. Tell him to stop shagging whoever he's shagging and come serve a lady who needs him more.'

Debbie trotted prettily away again, and Ruth moved around to stand beside Oona so she could play with her nipples.

'This is wonderful,' Oona sighed.

Nick arrived, and immediately took Oona's hand. 'Come,' he said. 'There are plenty of bales free.'

In the centre of the barn, straw bales had been placed to enclose a square space. Other bales covered by blankets had been drawn up to provide impromptu seats.

Ruth found Helen, and dragged her over to an empty bale. 'Now, do your duty,' she commanded, desperate to feel Helen's tongue on her pussy. After the fullness of the bottle, her cleft felt uncomfortably empty. She sat with her legs apart, enjoying Helen's skilful attention while other couples made themselves comfortable. Then Jack entered the makeshift arena, which she noticed was carpeted with canvas sheets.

'Friends, this is a freestyle contest of unlimited length,' Jack announced. 'Standard wrestling rules apply, with the addition that no direct clitoral stimulation is permitted. The contest will be decided when one contender is shafted to a climax. Your referee for this bout will be Mr Tom White.'

Two girls climbed over the barrier as Jack stepped out. Apart from masks over their eyes, they were both naked. Their hair was tied back and they were clean-shaven, their bodies shiny with oil. Ruth recognised Lisette at once by her nipple rings and her tattoo, but the other girl, a brunette, was a stranger to her. They met in the centre of the square, where Tom subjected them to a thorough manual inspection. He then carefully fitted each contestant with a strap-on dildo and made them shake hands.

'Wrestle on!' he declared, and stood back.

Ruth watched, getting powerfully excited, as the wrestlers circled each other warily while Helen's tongue circled her clitoris and probed her pussy. With their skin gleaming under the strong lights both young women looked magnificent, and almost grossly erotic with big dildos jutting from their neat, smooth mounds.

The contest was as exciting as it was arousing. Both contestants were highly skilled as well as being strong and supple. It took some minutes of grasping and throwing for Lisette to gain an advantage and penetrate her rival. Her dominance was not destined to last, however, for the brunette soon twisted free, and the bobbing, ducking and groping began anew.

This time it was Lisette who was penetrated. The unknown girl took her in the missionary position, pinning her to the canvas as she vigorously humped her. At first Lisette fought the intrusion, but very soon the effect began to tell on her and she surrendered to the obvious pleasure of a thick dildo surging in and out of her. She hooked her legs around her opponent and threw her arms around her neck, graciously and elegantly submitting to a most pleasant defeat.

Ruth, enraptured by the scene, pressed Helen closer, twisting her hand in the lovely blonde hair to ensure compliance. Helen responded willingly, lifting her rapidly to a luscious climax. 'Mm, that was lovely,' Ruth murmured. 'Thank you.'

Helen looked up. 'Thank *you*. Wouldn't you love to learn to wrestle like that?'

'Yes, I would. Perhaps our chance will come.'
'I hope so.'

Satisfied that Oona and Andrew were converts, Ruth reckoned her mission was complete. Being a free agent was all very well, but her task had restricted her availability. True, she had been competently filled by Andrew, but what she craved was some serious restraint. Right now a good spanking would be just the thing. Feeling truly randy, her eyes swept around the barn looking for an opportunity to behave badly.

Elsa was laid out on some bales against the wall being purposefully shagged by John, and an evil thought crossed Ruth's increasingly naughty mind. She headed purposefully across the barn, and hopped lightly up on a bale to kneel over her friend's face.

Elsa looked up, smiling through her pleasure. 'Oh yes, give it to me Ruth,' she begged, extending her tongue invitingly.

Ruth smiled, and eased her pussy down over the lovely face.

Chapter Fifteen

The next month passed in a whirl as Ruth adjusted her life. She disposed of the lease on her flat, sent her furniture into storage, and cleared her desk at the office. She and Lewis chose their new home – a country house of great character close to Richmond – and forced themselves to be patient for a while as the legalities ground slowly towards completion.

Ruth informed her family of everything during a lengthy telephone call. Her father, who doted on his daughters, was initially concerned about the age difference between her and Lewis but seemed reassured when Ruth told him how happy she was.

At the office word spread quickly. Janet was effusive with her good wishes, and took maternal control of the wedding preparations. Ruth grew ever more fond of her, and began to feel slightly guilty when she saw how much extra work her happiness would mean for the older woman.

'When you're away from home and you need the comfort of another woman,' Ruth told Lewis one evening, 'promise me you'll remember Janet.'

'I couldn't even consider it,' he protested. 'She'd be shocked.'

'Oh Lewis, how can you be so blind? Janet worships you. She's aching for you to make an indecent suggestion to her. Believe me, you have a thoroughly satisfying relationship just waiting on your word.'

'Good God, who'd have thought it! Ruth, I make a

solemn promise to you that I will indeed make a dishonest woman of Janet at the earliest opportunity.'

Ruth's personal effects fitted easily into the Beetle. Lewis came to see her off. It was a fond farewell, and then she headed north.

As the miles rolled by her spirits soared. The life she was leaving behind had always been good, and in the last few weeks it had become exhilarating, but ahead of her lay a lifestyle that promised to transcend the very best she had known. All her inhibitions were dead and her wildest dreams were coming true.

Elsa came running out to greet her. 'I've decided you should be in role from now until the ceremony,' she announced.

Ruth spent the afternoon being gently and continuously stimulated by direct physical contact and through a cunningly contrived ambience. The experience was delicious, keeping her desires bubbling without lifting her to the point of frustration.

Early in the evening Morgan departed to Lewis's stag night at Highmoor House. Ruth wondered if Lewis would be celibate, and guessed not, since he was in no way a slave. She pictured him gloriously embedded in Lisette or Corinne, and felt pangs of jealousy she quickly suppressed.

Soon after Morgan's departure, Oona arrived bubbling with enthusiasm for the forthcoming hen night. Helen had arrived earlier, and she and Ruth were directed to strip Oona and bring her off repeatedly until she declared satisfaction.

They were all four stark naked when Cooper appeared to collect them, and he sat patiently in his taxi while Ruth was prepared for the journey to Judy's house. A love egg was inserted into her vagina and a slim vibrating dildo slipped up into her bottom. Then she was marched out to the car and installed on the milking machine. The suction cups were brought to her nipples, and surged into life. Being handcuffed denied her any control; she was a slave to the machine. Her three naked attendants sat behind her and played with her exposed pussy while the vibrators and suckers filled her with pleasure. Then someone began to smack her bottom and her thighs, and the combined onslaught of sensation drove her close to the edge.

Elsa spotted how close Ruth was to climaxing. 'Oh no you don't.' There was a series of clicks, and the cups over her breasts ceased their delicious suction.

Ruth swayed back and forth as the taxi turned left and then right, quivering with need, teetering on the verge of an orgasm.

Cooper drew to a halt outside Judy's house. The other three girls got out, leaving Ruth attached to the machine as Judy emerged from the house.

'Cooper lets our group use his car,' Elsa explained to Oona. 'Anyone who uses his service must offer intercourse or some equal favour in return as payment. We call it *Cooper's fare.*'

Cooper climbed from his seat, hovering expectantly and studying Ruth through the window.

'Not Ruth, I'm afraid,' Elsa told him. She's being saved for the wedding. You won't forget to fetch her tomorrow, will you?'

'Of course not,' he replied gruffly. 'And I can wait for my fare.'

'You may have to wait a long time. Ruth's next orgasm must be from her husband. But there'll be plenty of other young women for you to choose from, I can assure you. As for now, you have your pick of Helen and Oona.'

'You're new,' Cooper said bluntly, looking intently at Oona.

'It would be my pleasure to pay your fare,' she said shyly. 'How would you like me?'

'On the machine.'

Ruth was released and Oona took her place. When the cups were offered to her breasts, she crooned with pleasure beneath their deep vibrant sucking while Cooper pulled down his trousers and knelt behind her, offering his thick cock to her ready pussy.

With her dildos still buzzing delicately inside her, Ruth watched with jealous pleasure as Cooper's thick length slid sensuously from sight. Oona pushed back against him, and he groaned. He appeared rough and uncouth, but Ruth knew him to be an accomplished and considerate lover. The lusty sliding thrusts of his prick would feel wonderful to Oona, and her clitoris was sure to be generously worked by his fulsome presence. She longed for the freedom to rub her own clitoris, and struggled against her restraints. The action only served to increase her needs, however. She was condemned to simply watch Oona steadily rising to her climax as Cooper thrust purposefully. Then his whole body went rigid and he ejaculated as Oona whimpered her triumph and forced herself back on his pulsing cock.

'Oh, that's good, that's so good...' Oona cried as she ground herself back against him.

Ruth felt a tiny orgasm bloom inside her. It was lovely, and she concentrated hard to conceal it from the others.

The evening passed in a haze of pure hedonistic indulgence. Ruth was subjected to every conceivable delight except the ultimate one of penetration, but otherwise she shared fully in the glorious pleasures of the others. In the small hours of the morning Cooper returned and drove them home, with Oona going last. She remained naked, riding the milking machine, as he drove away with her. 'I'll see to his fare!' she called out.

Elsa came quietly into the room and gently shook Ruth awake. 'It's ten o'clock,' she said gently. 'Cooper will be here in ninety minutes.'

Ruth rolled over, rubbing her eyes, then smiling she threw back the duvet and swung her feet to the floor. 'This is it, then,' she said. 'How strange life is. If we'd not met outside that pub, this would probably not be happening to me. I have so much to thank you for.'

Elsa smiled. 'I'm certain you'd have found your way without me. I'll send Helen to help you.'

After her shower, Ruth sat quietly while Helen attended to her hair. She was not allowed to dress, and contrary to her expectations, familiarity did not rob nudity of its sensuality. Being naked always made her feel vulnerable, and the touch of air on her skin was wonderfully erotic.

When Helen had finished doing her hair, they strolled down to the kitchen for coffee and croissants. While Elsa was serving, Judy appeared with a small box she set down on the counter.

Ruth stared at the box. 'Is that it?'

'Yes,' Elsa replied, 'that's your bridal outfit. You're sure you want to do it this way?'

Ruth nodded emphatically. 'Dead certain.'

Elsa lifted the lid. 'You've decided to open another box.'

Ruth felt a fluttering in her stomach.

'There's not much,' Elsa warned.

'Quite right, too. What does she expect?' Judy tried to sound harsh. 'She's only a slave. Clothing is hardly appropriate to her status.'

'Wow!' Ruth's mouth went dry with excitement.

'Locks all around,' Judy sounded proud of the design. 'I wonder when Lewis will use his key?'

Elsa lifted a white leather collar from the box. Ruth took it with trembling fingers, which fumbled slightly as she fastened its buckle. The tongue had a small hole in the end through which she threaded the tiny padlock. Helen looked envious, and Ruth smiled at her. The touch of leather made her feel deliciously naughty. She still marvelled at the amazing effect wrought on her by any form of restraint, even the simply symbolic.

'Let's go next door,' Elsa suggested. 'You'll see the effect better in the mirror.' She picked up the box and the others followed her.

There were anklets joined by a chain and fashioned from polished stainless steel. Ruth slipped them on, securing them with more padlocks, and her arousal notched up. Trembling, she took the matching wrist cuffs and fastened them in the same way. She glanced at the other women, and blushed. Trussed and under control her libido was soaring, and it was obvious.

Helen pinned a light headdress on her from which flowed a short veil. 'Good luck,' she said, planting a kiss on Ruth's cheek. 'I must get ready now.'

Elsa abruptly slipped two fingers into Ruth's pussy, and the invasion was so wonderfully unexpected that she nearly climaxed.

Elsa pulled her fingers free, and wagged them at Ruth. 'Bad girl, and with so long to wait. You must control yourself. It won't be easy, especially with these inside you.' She pushed a pair of balls into Ruth's open cleft and gave her a sharp slap on the bottom. The balls instantly made themselves felt and Ruth's head swam with pleasure. Then Judy hooked her wrist chain onto a ring above the doorframe and they left her there while they went to dress.

Once restrained Ruth was simply a sex object, devoted to giving and receiving unlimited pleasure. There were no conflicts, only a sense of perfect fulfilment and contentment. Being physically restrained liberated Ruth in a mysterious way.

She heard the front door close, and a car drive away. Moments later she heard the clatter of Cooper's taxi pulling up and her stomach gave a lurch. The longed for moment had arrived.

Elsa returned. 'Time to go,' she said, and unhooked Ruth's chain.

Outside Cooper was holding the taxi's door open, and his eyes brightened when he saw Ruth's chains.

Elsa gave her a farewell hug. 'Love you!' she whispered. 'Be happy, and enjoy it.'

'I will. Thank you for everything, Elsa.' Ruth ducked inside the cab. The door closed and she settled back, the leather seat cool and sensuous against her nakedness. She spread her thighs, mindful of her status, allowing cool air to flow up into her hot pussy.

The taxi traversed the woods surrounding Highmoor House, emerged from the trees, and came to a stop. Cooper made no move to alight, nor did he speak. Ruth let herself out with some effort, and walked towards the main door, stepping gingerly over the sharp gravel. She was intensely aware of her nakedness and of the way her breasts quivered when she walked. In her vagina, the love balls were rippling.

She rapped the knocker and a flutter of trepidation caused her to tremble, a natural reaction, she supposed. This was the biggest moment of her life. Standing on the threshold she saw herself as if the oak door was a mirror. She was naked except for the collar around her neck, and the silver cuffs and chains on her wrists and ankles, all secured by padlocks she had willingly fitted herself. She was restrained, a captive, a willing captive, but a captive nonetheless. Just weeks ago she had been free and single. One chance encounter had changed all that. Now the keys to her chains and the shape of her future lay beyond this door. She must enter to obtain release, but in so doing she would chain herself forever. The paradox was exquisite.

The door was finally opened by the beautiful Aisha. She ushered Ruth through to the library, where Helen was waiting. Helen looked superb wearing nothing but a tiny white thong set off with tiny brilliants. She held two small bouquets of red roses, one of which she handed to Ruth. 'Good luck!' she said, smiling happily.

'The ceremony begins!' Aisha announced in a loud, formal voice, and the duo followed her lead.

As Ruth entered the drawing room, the strains of the bridal march struck up and a sea of faces turned towards her with a collective hum of admiration. She felt radiant, her beauty springing from a sense of inner power and a profound certainty about Lewis and the rightness of her choices.

The biggest smile of all came from Lewis, standing at the front of the room. Next to him stood Conrad.

Ruth walked between the seats. She was tingling all over, and the balls inside were filling her with a subtle delight. Filled with joy she reached Lewis, who took her hand tightly in his and kissed her on the cheek.

The furniture had been pushed aside except for a table draped in white linen, and beside this stood the parson, Simon Parkes, an acquaintance of Conrad's. The rules had been explained to him and he was bright and energetic, a realist who held that the promises couples make to each other are of greater importance than conventional appearances.

'Friends, we are here today to solemnise the marriage of Ruth Parrish to Lewis Stone,' the parson began in his resonant voice. 'I must compliment the bride on her beauty. I believe it is perfectly acceptable, even proper, to reveal the true eloquence of God's creation. We should never be ashamed of what God has made.' He kept the ceremony brief, refraining from further embellishments. Ruth was satisfied with the arrangement, and pleased he remembered to include the unfashionable promise of obedience in her vows.

After the legalities were complete, Lewis thanked Simon profusely for his understanding attitude. 'We'd be delighted if you would stay for the reception.'

'Thank you, I shall stay a short while, but I have some pressing pastoral duties to attend to. I pray you will be very happy, Ruth. You are immensely brave. I admire your frankness and honesty. Have a long and happy life together.'

Conrad opened the partition, allowing the guests to flow into the playroom, where Aisha and Tali had set out a sumptuous buffet.

Ruth ate very little; she was too excited. She kept looking at the new gold ring on her third finger.

'Are you happy?' Lewis asked, holding her close.

'Sublimely.'

'I'm so glad… Ruth, I want to make you the world's happiest woman. If you want to change any aspect of our agreement, you have only to say so.'

'I know, but everything is perfect. We're married, and I'm your love slave. What more could I ask for?'

After the cake cutting ceremony came the speeches. Conrad spoke briefly in his role as best man, and Lewis answered with a concise and sincere speech of his own. Then Ruth took his place, standing proudly naked before the assembled guests.

'Protocol does not usually allow the bride a chance to speak, but I want to say something to you all. Four years ago I graduated with a degree in art history and took employment with a dealer in the city of Exeter. One winter's day, a distinguished client came to view a painting. I must have made the right impression, because not only did he buy the painting, he came back the next day to offer me an apprenticeship with his firm of professional valuators. I am glad to say that I accepted. Since then, Lewis Stone has been my mentor and my guide. Now he is my husband and my master. I learned my business from him. As time passed, my respect for him as a colleague turned to affection, though I did not suspect he harboured similar feelings for me until a few weeks ago. When we allowed nature to take its course, I found a truly gentle and understanding companion and lover. He quickly discovered my preferences, and went out of his way to cater to them, never displaying jealousy, impatience or disapproval. Lewis, you have given me so much. In return, I offer you all my love and absolute obedience.'

'Thank you,' he replied fervently. 'And I am honoured to accept them.'

'One more thing,' she added. 'My happiness today will only be complete if I am permitted to demonstrate my obedience to you before everyone present. Please, my love, put me into role and use me as you will.'

Elsa gripped Lewis's arm. 'This wonderful girl is my best and oldest friend. I hope you realise what a gem you have in her. Treat her well and make her happy.'

Lewis smiled as he prised his arm free. 'Conrad, my friend, the use of your facilities and your assistance, please?'

'You know what I would really like…' Ruth said, and whispered her wish in his ear.

He produced a key, and removed her fetters. Then everyone watched with hushed expectation as she was led to the centre of the room. Zelda appeared as if by magic, gloriously naked, carrying the spreader bar that had been used on Lisette. As she crouched down to fasten the ends to Ruth's ankles, Ruth saw clearly for the first time the elaborate letter *K* tattooed on the girl's bald scalp. She felt goose bumps prickle across her skin. How wonderful it would be to be marked like that…

Conrad lowered the suspension rope and Lewis attached it to the spreader. Ruth leaned back, trusting her shoulders to Zelda's supporting hands, and felt the rope tighten, tilting her backward as her feet were lifted. Lewis took the weight off her hips and she tried to relax as the room inverted around her. Up she went, until her hands were dangling on the smooth floor. All around her was a buzz of voices, and the strange vision of inverted legs.

Zelda appeared again, and Ruth's eyes were directly level with the other slave's shaved crotch. Her denuded lips were so lovely that Ruth wanted to sink her tongue in their rich beauty and gorge herself on the sweet, seeping nectar.

Zelda fastened broad straps around Ruth's thighs, and their tightness served to emphasise the vulnerability of her crotch. She clenched involuntarily; feeling her juices, and her own wantonness made her begin perspiring as Zelda quickly lifted her arms and strapped them to the thigh bands. She was then lowered until her hair brushed the floor and gazed rapidly around, looking for Lewis's feet. They stepped into her vision in their elegant black shoes, and dangling beside them she saw a six-tailed lash.

She felt her eyes fill with tears and was not sure if she was crying with fear or with joy.

She tensed, waiting for the first merciless lash across her delicate parts. She heard the whip whistle through the air, and her body jerked as it brushed across her skin, just flicking the tip of one of her nipples. Her tension escaped as a scream and her nipple burned hot.

Again the whip whistled through the air, striking her other nipple, and this time the pain was excruciating.

Again the whip fell, across both her breasts now as she screamed in agony. There was a pause, and then two lashes fell in quick succession on the inside of each of her thighs. These hurt, but less than she expected, and she waited breathlessly. The whip whistled above her again, she heard the crack, and then fire flared between her thighs.

'Oh, my poor cunt!' she cried, jerking and twisting as she vainly sought to clamp her legs together. Logic told her to demand release, but she did not, and the whip cracked again. The fire seared her flesh, but now she sensed pleasure beneath the torment knowing her labia was lusciously distended and her most secret self exposed to chastisement. Then came another searing cut, and another, and she could feel each separate lash curling around as it sliced her tender, sensitive skin. 'Please, another one!' she gasped.

Three more times the whip scourged her, until her flesh was on fire. Her body had never been so misused, and yet it craved more misery. She wanted more and more of this delicious pain filling her with a sense of fulfilment such as she had never known.

She felt fingers, firm and hard, pressing down on her burning clitoris, and swiftly lifting her to heights of pleasure well beyond her conscious mind. She opened her eyes. Lewis was standing close to her, his trousers open so she could look up and see his ripe balls crowned by a potently hard penis. 'Oh yes,' she cried. 'Yes!'

Zelda squatted behind her, pulling her shoulders back to grip her breasts and pinch her nipples. Ruth thought she would die from delight, and then the suspension rope jerked as she was lowered a little and her head cushioned by the other slave's thighs. She extended her tongue, trying to lick Zelda's soft, creamy skin as she felt herself filled by two, perhaps three, fingers. She arched her back as the pleasure spread through her body, and then the fingers pulled and the vibrating balls popped free. Her clitoris was stroked and teased and cruelly pinched and she groaned with pain – a pain so exquisite it possessed the same mysterious soul as ecstasy.

She recognised the feel of Lewis's penis and opened to it. She felt him slide in, slowly and firmly, so she could relish every second of his erection filling her. She arched her back again to absorb him, squeezing him and feeling him surge in response. When he pulled out all the way the sensation of loss was unbearable. Fortunately he drove into her again right away, and her body swallowed him hungrily, working him as she floated on a higher plane, lost in a realm of absolute delight. The orgasm that built inside her was conceived in pain and born in pleasure, the complete and total expression of her deepest feelings, and of her love for him.

The bridal suite was the griffin room in which they had stayed previously. The pillory stood as it had done before, but Lewis took her on the bed in the time-honoured fashion. Afterwards, they lay in each other's arms.

'I'm so glad you whipped and fucked me at our reception,' she said softly. 'It was indescribably beautiful. Thank you.'

'You want to be in the pillory now, don't you?' he asked, amused.

'Naturally.' She laughed, and allowed herself to be led across the room, where she bent meekly into the beam. The moment the bar dropped into place she experienced a sharp lifting of her sensual mood, as if her sex drive had been switched into overdrive. She felt Lewis's hands on her buttocks, smoothing her curvaceous mounds, his fingers dipping into her cleavage and stroking her sphincter. She moaned as he pressed his hardness into her secret valley and reached round to enclose her breasts in his hands. He played with her nipples, filling her with eddies of pleasure that struck delicious echoes in her clitoris.

She eyed the rack on the adjacent wall where whips and straps were hung, and licked her lips wondering which he would choose for her pleasure later.

His hand dropped to her belly, and combed her pubic hair before teasing her clitoris from its hood. He touched her hard nubbin, still tender from its chastisement, and lit a fire in her sex before he stepped away. She saw him by the rack, saw his hand hover and then select a flexible strap that would curl around her, affording her a delicious pain.

He whipped her lightly, a little sting on her buttocks that made her catch her breath and gasp, 'Thank you, sir!'

'We are going to spend a whole month here exploring your frontiers, my pet. I want you to be my paramount slave, my dearest and best. When you achieve perfect submission, you will be the first to carry my mark. I know you have coveted Zelda's status as I have coveted Conrad's, and with his help we shall emulate them… no, we shall surpass them.'

A rush of intense excitement flushed her whole body,

and the sharp cut of the strap felt like heaven as the future promised paradise. 'Thank you, sir, I am honoured to serve you.'

His response was another full-powered blow, and a scorching band seared across her bottom that made her gasp and clench her cheeks as her clitoris flared in exquisite sympathy.

'And tomorrow, my pet,' her husband and master said as the strap once more bit into her skin, 'you will discover what lies behind that curtain.'

More exciting titles available from Chimera

All **Chimera** titles are available from your local bookshop or newsagent, or direct from our mail order department. Please send your order with your credit card details, a cheque or postal order (made payable to *Chimera Publishing Ltd*) to: **Chimera Publishing Ltd., Readers' Services, PO Box 152, Waterlooville, Hants, PO8 9FS**. Or call our **24 hour telephone/fax credit card hotline: +44 (0)23 92 783037** (Visa, Mastercard, Switch, JCB and Solo only).

To order, send: Title, author, ISBN number and price for each book ordered, your full name and address, cheque or postal order for the total amount, and include the following for postage and packing:
UK and BFPO: £1.00 for the first book, and 50p for each additional book to a maximum of £3.50.
Overseas and Eire: £2.00 for the first book, £1.00 for the second and 50p for each additional book.

*Titles £5.99. All others £4.99

For a copy of our free catalogue please write to:

Chimera Publishing Ltd
Readers' Services
PO Box 152
Waterlooville
Hants
PO8 9FS

or email us at:
sales@chimerabooks.co.uk

or purchase from our range of superb titles at:
www.chimerabooks.co.uk

Sales and Distribution in the USA and Canada

LPC Group
Client Distribution Services
193 Edwards Drive
Jackson
TN 38301
USA

Sales and Distribution in Australia

Dennis Jones & Associates Pty Ltd
19a Michellan Ct
Bayswater
Victoria
Australia 3153

* * *